Also
by Ellie Alexander

Mocha, She Wrote

Ellie Alexander

St. Martin's Paperbacks

This is a work of fiction. All of the characters, organizations, and events portrayed in this novel are either products of the author's imagination or are used fictitiously.

First published in the United States by St. Martin's Paperbacks, an imprint of St. Martin's Publishing Group.

MOCHA, SHE WROTE

For information, address St. Martin's Publishing Group, 120 Broadway, New York, NY 10271.

www.stmartins.com

ISBN: 978-1-250-78942-6

Our books may be purchased in bulk for promotional, educational, or business use. Please contact your local bookseller or the Macmillan Corporate and Premium Sales Department at 1-800-221-7945, ext. 5442, or by email at MacmillanSpecialMarkets@macmillan.com.

Printed in the United States of America

St. Martin's Paperbacks edition published 2021

10 9 8 7 6 5 4 3 2 1

Chapter One

They say that love is the answer. After years of searching for answers about my future and where I was meant
to be, I was inclined to believe that statement. My world
had expanded dramatically since my husband Carlos
had arrived in Ashland. Following a two-year separation
we had finally reconciled, and there wasn't a day that I
woke up without a giddy feeling in my stomach. It was
almost too good to be true. The pessimist in me worried that something was going to go terribly wrong. All
of my dreams had come to fruition. Carlos was in Ashland and managing our growing boutique winery, Uva.
Things at our family bakeshop, Torte, were running
seamlessly and we had recently opened a seasonal walk-
up ice-cream shop, Scoops, where we served luscious
hand-churned concretes made with fresh local berries
and drizzled with dark chocolate and dulce de leche.
As if that wasn't enough to keep me occupied, Carlos
and I were settling into my childhood home, making it
our own by installing an outdoor oven and hummingbird
feeders in the backyard and hanging collections of photos from our travels together.

What more could I want? I asked myself as I turned onto the plaza. A lazy spring had given way to a busy summer. It was nearing the end of June, which meant that Ashland's idyllic downtown was bursting with activity. Tourists had arrived to take in shows at the Oregon Shakespeare Festival; kids lounged in Lithia Park, soaking up the warm sun and a well-deserved break from their studies; adventure lovers waited in line at the outdoor store to take advantage of the region's abundant outdoor opportunities from rafting on the Rogue River to hiking Grizzly Peak. The eager buzz of activity brought a smile to my face as I walked into Torte.

The bakeshop sat at the corner of the plaza across from the Lithia bubblers, offering my team and our loyal customers a perfect view of all the action. Our bright red and teal awning, outdoor tables, and window display complete with strings of rainbow bunting, papier-mâché Popsicles, and colorful beach balls gave the space a welcoming vibe. A symphony of delectable flavors greeted me as I stepped inside. Andy and Sequoia, our two top-notch baristas, slung shots of espresso behind the coffee counter. We had positioned our state-of-the-art shiny fire-engine red La Pavoni Italian espresso machine next to the exposed brick wall so that our baristas could chat with customers while grinding beans or frothing milk.

The long wooden bar transitioned into the pastry case where a line of people waited for one of our summer berry tarts, mango cream buns, or roasted red pepper and turkey sausage breakfast sandwiches oozing with melted manchego cheese. Rosa, who had taken on the role of a woman of many trades, punched orders into

our point-of-sale system and doled out chocolate croissants and slices of cinnamon coffee cake. She floated
between pastry counter and kitchen most days and was
willing to lend a hand wherever needed.

As was typical, the booths by the front windows were
occupied. The same was true for our patio seating—
picnic tables with matching bright teal and red sun
umbrellas. Finding a spot to linger during the busy season required having an eagle eye. Fortunately we had
expanded our seating options with comfy couches and
chairs downstairs and additional bistro tables along
Ashland Creek on the backside of the building.

I paused to hold the front door open for a woman balancing a plate of pastries and a steaming mug of coffee.
She scanned the busy dining room. I recognized the familiar look.

"I believe that table outside is just leaving." I pointed
behind us. "If you want to grab it, I'll have someone
come out and wipe it down for you."

"Thank you." She shot me a relieved smile before
hurrying outside to snag the table.

I adjusted the stack of mail beneath my arm and continued inside.

"Hey boss," Andy said with a wave as he deftly
poured two shots of espresso over a scoop of ice cream.
"Is that the mail?"

I had stopped by the post office on my way back to
the bakeshop after delivering a box of bread and cookies
to Scoops. "It is, and there just might be something in
this stack with your name on it." I grinned as I handed
him a large envelope.

"It came! It finally came?" Andy's boyish face broke

out into a wide smile that almost immediately turned into a worried scowl. "I don't know, though. I'm too nervous. I don't know if I want to look. No. No. I can't look. I can't do it." He clenched his teeth and thrust the envelope to me. "Maybe you should open it."

"No way." I pushed the envelope back across the counter.

He placed a drink order on the bar and waited for a customer to take her affagato and iced latte before picking up the envelope again. "Ahhhh. Look at my hands." He held out his trembling fingers. Andy was in his early twenties with broad, muscular shoulders, sandy hair, and height that he was finally beginning to grow into. He had taken on the role of head barista and had been invaluable in getting Scoops up and running. I wasn't used to seeing him rattled.

His fingers quaked. "I don't even know if I can open it with my hands shaking like this. I'm dying to know what's inside, but then again, what if it's bad news? It might be bad news, Jules, and I'm not sure if I can handle that right now. I've practiced for months for this. If I don't open the envelope then it's not a no, right?"

"But what if it's a yes? You would never know." I tapped the envelope. "There's one easy way to find out."

"Okay." Andy sighed, then ripped the envelope open.

Sequoia and I waited, watching his face for any indication of whether the news was good or bad while he scanned the contents.

Andy read the letter with serious intent. After a minute his smile evaporated.

A sinking sensation swirled in my stomach, and not

just because I had already consumed copious amounts of coffee.

Oh no! He worked so hard for this. I had been sure that he would be selected, I hadn't even considered the alternative. I pressed my lips together.

"Well, read it yourself, boss." He bent his head forward, hunched his shoulders, and offered me the paper. "It's not good news."

Sequoia put her hand on his forearm. "Sorry, Andy. You should have had it. You're the best barista I've ever worked with, and you know that is high praise coming from me."

"I know." He let out another heavy sigh.

I couldn't believe it. How had they not chosen Andy? Sequoia was right; he was the best barista I'd ever had the pleasure to call a colleague—and not only in Ashland and the surrounding Rogue Valley. I'd worked with many baristas in my years at sea, and no one had natural talent like Andy. He didn't have to spend hours laboring over ratios or recipes. His creative palate guided him. I knew without a doubt that one of the reasons for Torte's success was due to Andy. Locals and tourists returned again and again for his whimsical creations like his chunky monkey coffee, a banana chocolate blended coffee shake, or a simple Americano with his exquisitely blended custom roasts.

I glanced at the paper. It took less than a second to realize that Andy was messing with us. The first word on the page was "Congratulations!"

"Andy!" I swatted him with the paper.

"What?" Sequoia stared at me with wide emerald eyes.

"Look." I handed her the paper. "He's been selected! Andy's in!"

Andy gave us a sheepish grin. "Sorry, I couldn't resist. I had to mess with you, at least for a minute. Blame Carlos. He's constantly telling us to add more play into our work."

Sequoia let out a whoop and began clapping. "Barista Cup, baby!"

"Congratulations, Andy!" I seconded her applause. "This calls for a celebration. Our own little Andy is going to be competing in the West Coast Barista Cup. Now the pressure's really on. You have to win. I want a plaque right up there on the wall." I pointed to a spot on the exposed brick.

"This is awesome." Sequoia gave him a fist bump. "You've got some serious practicing to do. Isn't there a crazy time limit on how fast you need to get the judges their drinks?"

"Yeah. Fifteen minutes—exactly. You have to give the sensory judges a cappuccino, a latte, and a custom signature drink in less than fifteen minutes, all while being judged on your technical skills and explaining the origin of each coffee and your personal connection to the cup." He stuffed the papers back in the envelope.

"Sensory judges?" Sequoia asked.

Andy clutched the letter to his chest. "There are four judges who actually drink your offerings and score them, and then there are two technical judges who watch every move you make while you're pulling shots and steaming milk."

"That sounds like way too much pressure for me." Sequoia twisted a dreadlock. She was one of our newer hires and was the polar opposite of Andy in nearly every way. She was laid back and exuded a chill vibe with her flowing attire and dreadlocks. Her coffee style included alternative drinks like dirty chai lattes and matcha lavender-infused cold brew.

Andy could have been a poster boy for dairy farmers with his all-American style. Until recently he had played football at Southern Oregon University, but he decided to opt out of school to focus on his coffee knowledge, improve his latte design skills, and immerse himself in the art of roasting. He tended to push the envelope when it came to pairings but his style was more in line with modern coffee shops and traditional Italian high-end espresso drinks. When he and Sequoia had first started working together it had been a disaster. In fact, at one point I had thought that I might have to let one of them go. But they had worked things out and found common ground. Their unique approaches were actually a beautiful balance.

"I can't believe that the competition is here this year," I said to Andy. "You're going to have a massive cheer squad."

He blushed, his cheeks matching the color of the espresso machine. "Thanks, boss. Sequoia is right. I'm going to have to put some hours in behind the machine to get ready. Don't worry, I'll do it on my own time. Off the clock. I mean, in some ways I'm way behind. There are baristas who train year-round for this. I'm going to have to pull all-nighters from now until the start of the Cup, but I swear I won't let it impact my work here."

"No way. You are representing Torte. We want our star barista to shine." I adjusted the stack of mail under my arm. "Not to mention that I want to sample whatever you're making. Plus it's summer. We're open late anyway. We'll prop open the front door, and you can give away samples like we did at Scoops. Think of it as part of our summer marketing plan."

"Cool. I'm down with that."

"I'm heading downstairs. Anything I need to know?"

"Nope. We've got it under control." Andy shot me a thumbs-up. "When there's a lull, I have an idea for my signature drink. I've been playing around with some new flavors, but I didn't want to jinx anything until I heard for sure. I'll bring a sample down for you and everyone else to taste. I want honest feedback though. That's the only way I'll improve. If anyone says, 'It's great,' they don't get to taste anything else I make, got it?"

"Got it." I saluted him with two fingers and continued downstairs. The West Coast Barista Cup was a big deal. The event drew the best baristas from the region along with hundreds of coffee enthusiasts. The winner would advance to the U.S. Championships with a chance to compete in the World Barista Cup. There were cash prizes for first, second, and third place, along with bragging rights and the potential for future sponsorships. To my knowledge, no barista in the Rogue Valley had had the honor of competing in the Cup. Andy deserved to be recognized. He had put in a tremendous amount of effort at Torte and I wanted him to know we were all behind him.

This year The Hills, a swanky mid-century hotel on the east side of town, was hosting the competition. It would take place in two weeks, which meant that I intended to give Andy as much free time as our staffing schedule would allow to prep for the competition. I was thrilled for our young coffee aficionado to get to go head-to-head with some of the top baristas from up and down the West Coast. I was also excited to get to watch the action myself. It had been years since I'd attended a coffee competition. I knew that the industry was constantly evolving, and I couldn't wait to learn some new techniques and see the latest in brewing and roasting equipment.

I passed a group of teenagers drinking iced shakes and playing a trivia game in the cozy seating area in the basement next to retro atomic-style fireplace. I said hello and continued into the kitchen where there was a flurry of activity. Sterling, our sous chef, was assembling rows of sandwiches. He spread cranberry orange cream cheese on baguettes and layered them with thin-sliced turkey, tomatoes, lettuce, and Swiss. Marty, our head bread baker, kneaded a vat of dough with his muscular arms. Bethany and Steph, my two cake artists, were piping buttercream onto cookies and cupcakes.

"How's it going?" I asked, tossing the mail on the counter.

"Good. Just prepping our internal order for Scoops. We'll get these over to the shop before we open," Sterling replied. He finished assembling a turkey sandwich, then wrapped it in brown paper.

"Excellent. I stopped by earlier with the pastry order, so that's waiting for you." We had limited hours at the new walk-up ice-cream shop. I had hired four high school and college students to run the seasonal counter. Unlike Torte, we offered a small menu at Scoops. In addition to our concretes—our version of gorgeously creamy ice creams—we served cold brew and coffee shakes and pre-made sandwiches and pastries. Thus far it had been a great addition to the bakeshop. Not a day went by where there wasn't a line of customers waiting for a dish of our marionberry concrete or a peanut butter blossom shake.

"Did I hear excitement upstairs?" Marty asked. "I could have sworn I heard happy applause."

"You did." I glanced above us. "Hang on a sec. Let me get Andy. I want him to be the one to share the news."

I hurried back upstairs and yanked Andy away from the coffee bar. "You have to tell everyone."

He pretended to be embarrassed, but I could tell he was proud of his accomplishment from his wide toothy smile, as he should be.

"Andy has a big announcement, everyone," I said, dragging him into the kitchen.

"It's not *that* big, boss." Andy brushed off my compliment. "I am psyched, though, because I just learned that I'm going to be competing in the West Coast Barista Cup in a couple of weeks."

Everyone clapped and cheered.

"Congrats, man." Sterling patted him on the back.

"That *is* a big deal," Marty concurred. "I attended the competition when it was in San Fran a few years ago and the judges were cutthroat." He shivered. "They were so tough, they were scary."

Andy nodded. "I know. It's intense. I was just reading through the rules and regulations and Benson Vargas, who is *the* guy in the world of coffee, is the top judge again this year. I've heard he's super intense and he's one of the managing members of the entire competition, so there's a touch of pressure there, no problem." He stuck out his tongue and rolled his eyes.

"Ohhhh, I remember him." Marty let out a visible shudder before wiping flour from his hands on a dish towel. "He made one of the competitors cry, and I heard one of the baristas claim that she'd rather die than ever have to make a drink for him again."

"Great." Andy clutched his neck. "I'm toast."

"No, no, I don't mean to scare you." Marty sounded genuinely concerned. "You make the best coffee in the world. You'll have Benson Vargas and all of the other judges eating out of your hands like puppies."

"Hope so." Andy crossed his fingers and returned to the coffee bar.

I wondered if Marty was exaggerating. I was thrilled for Andy, but I hoped that his coffee dreams weren't about to get crushed before they'd had a chance to come true.

Chapter Two

For the next two weeks we rallied around our young barista. Andy spent nearly every waking hour at the espresso machine. My staff and I reaped the benefits of his laser-focused training. There wasn't a minute that went by when there wasn't a cappuccino, latte, or iced mocha waiting at the coffee bar. He practiced at least a dozen different combinations for the signature drink that he would present to the judges. The running favorite amongst our small but mighty team at Torte was a hot honey latte made with a touch of house-made orange syrup, spicy honey, flaked sea salt, fresh orange zest, and bitter chocolate shavings.

"I think this is the winner," I said to Andy the morning before the first day of competition. "The spicy honey paired with the orange and bitter chocolate is pure magic. I'm not kidding, I had a dream about this coffee last night. It might be my favorite of all time."

"You think? I don't know. I'm wondering if it needs a touch more salt? Maybe I should do a dark chocolate with a hint of sea salt in addition to the flaked salt?" He pounded his forehead with his palm. "No, no. I already tried that and it was too much salt. I'm losing my mind. I had been taking notes, but now I can't even read my own handwriting." He pointed to a notebook filled with milk-to-coffee ratios. It could have belonged to a mad scientist with its extensive charts, drawings, temperature markings, and milk-frothing times.

I noticed that Andy's fingers were cracked, dry, and wrapped with bandages. "What's with all the Band-Aids?" I asked.

He glanced at his battered hands. "It's nothing. My hands got dry and started bleeding in a couple of places—no biggie. I have a few steam burns too. It comes with the territory. Like I told you, the other baristas who I'll be going up against in the Cup have probably been prepping for this for at least a year, if not longer. Some of them have full-time coaches and teams."

"Steam burns?" My mouth hung open. "Andy, enough! You have to stop. As of this moment, I'm officially sending you home. You've put in months' worth of practice in less than two weeks. You're ready. Don't worry about what the other baristas are doing or are going to do. If you keep at it like this, you're going to keel over before the competition starts."

Andy protested. "You don't understand. You *have* to be obsessed to compete in the Barista Cup. I'm telling you, Jules, some of the baristas have *full-time* coaches. Full time! They'll be showing up with their own custom roasts. They'll have spent hours upon hours studying the science of milk fats and how to ensure that proteins are perfectly rationed in each drink. I guarantee most of them have been working nonstop for months. I'm way behind."

I held up my index finger. "Nope. This is not open for negotiation. You've been ready for this competition for years. You are extremely talented, Andy Howard, but you need sleep. Go home. Take a nap. Have a nice dinner, and go to bed early. I'll see you at The Hills tomorrow morning at eight a.m. sharp."

"But . . ." he stammered, fiddling with the Band-Aid wrapped around his thumb.

I pointed toward the door. "Go. Get out of here. If I see you anywhere near an espresso machine before tomorrow's competition, you're officially fired."

Andy's mouth hung open.

"It's for your own good." I softened my tone. "You need a break. Trust me, half of the competition is going to be mental. If you're wiped out, you're not going to be in good headspace."

He untied his apron and draped it over the counter. "Okay, boss. You're probably right. I just really want to do well."

"I know you do. And you have a good shot at winning, but not if you're depleted. Go get some rest, and I'll see you tomorrow."

He didn't argue. I could tell from the way he dragged himself out of the bakeshop that he was exhausted.

"Thank you." Sequoia folded her hands together in a Namaste pose, watching him cross the plaza. "I've been telling him the same thing, but he wouldn't listen. This competition sounds out of control. Like I tried to tell him, at the end of the day it's just coffee."

"I know. He's determined, which I appreciate and can relate to, but he's running on fumes. That won't do him any good tomorrow."

"Exactly." Sequoia moved Andy's apron and wiped down the shiny red espresso machine with a towel.

"Do you need extra help?" I took a quick survey of the dining area. Every table was packed. There was a small line of customers waiting to order baked goods and drinks from Rosa, who managed the cash register and pastry case, but at least for the moment there weren't crushing crowds. She was another new addition to our team who had quickly become invaluable. Her extensive experience working in hospitality before coming to Torte and her calm aura made her a favorite amongst our staff and customers. She had honed her baking skills at a bed-and-breakfast in nearby Jacksonville. Her conchas had become stuff of legend. The seashell-shaped sweet bread sprinkled with cinnamon and sugar always sold out within minutes of being placed in the pastry case.

Our chalkboard menu had a quote that read HUMANITY RUNS ON COFFEE. Typically, we rotate a Shakespearean quote, but in honor of Andy, Steph had sketched a silhouette of an espresso cup with Good Luck Andy! wafting in the steam. We had continued the coffee theme by swapping out the summer popsicle display in the front window with canisters overflowing with coffee beans at every stage of the process from dried green to our darkest roast, towering stacks of our custom teal and cherry red Torte mugs, and burlap coffee bags. Steph had drawn funny sayings in Sharpies on squares of cardboard, like Barista Cup or Bust and Boy Wonder Barista with a silhouette of Andy's head.

Sequoia made a foam peace sign on the top of a coconut milk latte before handing the drink to a customer.

"No. I've got it. I'll let you know if it gets too busy, but it's been a pretty steady flow this morning."

That was typical for mid-morning. We tended to get rushes of customers in waves. There was often a lull between breakfast and lunch. I made a mental note to check in a little before noon.

I left things in Rosa's and Sequoia's capable hands and went downstairs. The aroma of bread baking in the wood-fired oven made me pause and inhale deeply. I went straight to the sink, scrubbed my hands with lavender soap, and tied on an apron.

Mom and Marty were twisting loaves of challah. Steph piped a three-tiered wedding cake with dainty off-white buttercream stars. Bethany was mixing vats of cookie dough, and Sterling sautéed onions and garlic at the stove.

"What smells so amazing?" I asked, peeking over his shoulder.

"I'm working on a cheesy focaccia. I'm going to drizzle Marty's focaccia with a mixture of onions, garlic, celery seed, and cumin. Then we're going to bake it in the oven with a three-cheese blend and serve it with tomato basil soup. Think grown-up grilled cheese."

"You had me at cheesy focaccia." I grinned.

"That's verbatim what I said," Mom chimed in. She had tucked her shoulder-length bobbed hair behind her ears, revealing a pair of sparking amber earrings that brought out the golden flecks in her brown eyes.

"I didn't know you were coming in this morning," I said as I cleared space on the marble counter.

"Oh, I see. You're not happy to have your mom invade the kitchen, is that it?" she teased. Mom had always had a playful side. Her easy banter was one of the many reasons our staff and customers adored her.

"Don't test me. I had to kick Andy out. You should be on your best behavior, or I just might give you the boot too." I gave her a lopsided smile.

She winked and blew me a kiss. "I'd like to see you try."

"Why did you kick Andy out?" Marty sounded concerned.

"I had to force him to take a break. His fingers are literally bleeding from pulling so many espresso shots. He's nervous about tomorrow, which I understand, but I tried to explain that he needs to give his brain and his body a break."

"Smart move." Marty nodded to a magazine that sat on the counter near large canisters of flour, sugar, and cornmeal. "Speaking of that, I brought in an article you might want to take a look at. It's about the head judge for the Barista Cup—Benson Vargas. Andy is a great kid, but I sure hope that he has a thick skin. Benson Vargas has been known to ruin the careers of many a budding barista."

"Really?" I walked over to pick up the magazine.

"Yeah. Give it a read. He's equally revered and hated in the coffee community." Marty poked a row of holes into the focaccia dough.

I skimmed the article. Marty wasn't exaggerating. A number of coffee-shop owners and professional baristas had been interviewed for the piece. None of them had kind things to say about Benson, aside from the fact that he was an expert when it came to espresso drinks.

"Yikes." I set the magazine down and gathered flour,

sugar, and spices. "He sounds like he and Richard Lord might be long-lost cousins."

Richard owned the Merry Windsor Hotel on the opposite side of the plaza from Torte. He had a penchant for all things tacky, like his collection of Shakespeare bobbleheads. He also had an uncanny ability to get under my skin.

Marty brushed melted butter on the rising loaves of bread. "I didn't want to say too much around Andy when it came up, because I didn't want to scare him, but the reason these competitions keep using Benson is because he's known for ridiculous and dramatic outbursts. I'm sure that the organizers wouldn't admit it, but that adds flare to an already tense situation. When I was at the regional cup in San Francisco a few years ago, he spit a latte in one of the competitor's faces. It was horrible and completely uncalled for. That sort of unprofessional behavior should get you banned as judge, but instead it seems to heighten his mystique. And according to that article, it sounds like he's running the show now. He's a stakeholder in the Barista Cup, which seems like a conflict of interest as a judge, if you ask me."

A wave of unease washed over me. Andy was already stressed. He would be crushed if Benson spit out one of the drinks he'd been working so hard to master.

"Do you think we need to warn him?" I asked, adding butter and sugar to one of the mixers and turning it on medium speed to cream together.

"That's a tough call." Marty looked to Mom. "A little warning might be good. At least Andy would know that he's not alone, but then at the same time it might freak him out even more."

Mom frowned. "I'm with you, Marty. I'm not sure. Andy is a strong kid. He's shown great resolve and maturity over the past few years. Yet, I also know that this is really important to him. In some ways, maybe more than anything else he's done. I would hate planting a seed of doubt in his head."

"Yeah." I cracked eggs into the mixer. "I'll think on it while I make these cheesecake squares."

"Good idea." Mom's eyes sparkled. "You know what I say—when in doubt, bake it out. Baking is always the answer."

"Exactly." I turned my attention to the mixer, incorporating vanilla bean paste and room-temperature cream cheese. I intended to bake a large sheet of cheesecake that I would cut into squares and serve with a fresh strawberry reduction. Once the cheesecake mixture had blended together, I pulsed graham crackers, cinnamon, brown sugar, and melted butter until they formed a crumb-like crust. I pressed that into a baking tray and spread the cheesecake mixture over the top. It would bake for thirty minutes. I slid it into the oven and went to the walk-in for strawberries.

June in southern Oregon is strawberry season, which meant that the farmers markets and roadside stands had an abundance of the bright juicy berries. Our growing season resembled a Mediterranean climate and allowed for a bounty of fruits and vegetables to ripen long into late summer. Our philosophy at the bakeshop was to take advantage of nature's kitchen, using locally sourced fruits and vegetables in our soups, salads, and ever-changing line of baked goods.

I washed and sliced the strawberries, then sprinkled

them with sugar, added vanilla bean paste, and placed them in a saucepan. "Mind if I steal a burner?" I asked Sterling.

He had finished sautéing the onions and garlic. "Help yourself." He moved the sauté pan to the counter.

"What do you think about warning Andy versus letting it play out?" I asked as I turned a burner to medium low.

Sterling pushed a strand of dark hair from his face. "Honestly, I think it might mess him up. I'm glad you sent him home. I told him to get out of here this morning. He's obsessed and not in a good way."

I stirred the strawberries.

Sterling's ice blue eyes clouded with worry. "I think he's decided that if he doesn't win it's a sign that he's not destined to do this as a career or something. I told him not to sweat it, but he seems like he's way past that point. He's freaking out about the other competitors. I guess some of them have coaches. That's crazy, right?"

"Yeah. I agree." I wondered if there was more to Andy's obsession. Maybe the competition had become a replacement for school. Maybe Andy's decision to drop out of college was coming back to haunt him. He had recently decided to forgo his football scholarship and last few semesters at Southern Oregon University or SOU as locals referred to campus, to pursue his coffee passion. I'd had reservations about him leaving school early, but it wasn't up to me. Andy made the choice after much thought and consideration. His commitment to immersing himself in the world of coffee and learning as much as he could about everything from the organic farmers who grew the beans to the roasting process was nothing short of impressive. I had no doubt that if he continued his coffee education, he would be well on his way toward opening his own roasting company within the next few years.

"Not to mention, he's freaking awesome," Sterling continued. "What are the odds that this judge hates his coffee? Andy is *the man*. I told him that."

"Thanks for telling him that." I shot Sterling a smile. I had come to rely on his advice and insight. We had a similar view of the world, and I appreciated Sterling's vulnerability. Like Andy, Sterling was in his early twenties and still finding his way. When he had first arrived at Torte, I wasn't sure if he would last more than a few days, but he had quickly proved me wrong. In addition to becoming a skilled sous chef, Sterling had become a trusted friend.

He took his sauté to the bread station while I continued to work on my reduction. By the time my cheesecake had baked and cooled, I had a thick red strawberry sauce to serve over the top. I sliced the cheesecake into individual bars, topped them with the strawberry reduction, and finished them with a sprig of fresh mint. "Anyone want a sample?" I asked, passing around small bites of the bars.

"These make me want to plant a kiss on you, Jules," Bethany said, ogling the bar.

I tasted my creation. The silky sweet cheesecake had a lovely tang and married beautifully with the buttery crisp graham-cracker crust. The strawberries retained their fresh flavor but had almost a jam-like texture. I was pleased with how the bars had turned out.

"These will be gone in five minutes. I'm calling it

right now. Anyone want to put some money down on that?" Marty took another sample.

"No way." Mom shook her head. "You might get accosted walking up the stairs with these. They're delicious, honey."

"Thanks." I finished assembling the bars on a tray for the display case upstairs. The rest of the afternoon was a blur. I didn't have much time to worry about Andy, but I decided that Sterling's input was sage advice. Andy was one of the most skilled baristas I'd ever met. There was no way that anyone in the competition wouldn't agree, Benson Vargas included.

Chapter Three

The next morning I had the rare experience of sleeping in. Of course, sleeping in for a baker was relative. I woke with the rising sun and a symphony of birdsong a little before five, took a long hot shower, and left Carlos sleeping in bed. His black hair, which had grown longer since his move to Ashland, framed his face on the pillow. I still couldn't believe he was actually here. I kept wondering if I would wake from this dream. After one last glance at his chiseled cheekbones and muscular arms, I tiptoed downstairs to make coffee and breakfast.

I started a pot of steel-cut oats and took my coffee outside on the deck. I didn't think I would ever tire of the view. Sugar pines, Shasta firs, hemlocks, and redwoods formed a natural umbrella around the deck with peekaboo views of a radiant ridge line across the valley. Blue jays, northern flickers, and yellow finches flitted between the trees, signaling the start of the day with their happy chirping arias. The smell of pine needles and blooming wild blackberries reminded me to inhale deeply. My thoughts drifted to Andy during my morning mediation. I hoped he was taking a moment for himself as well. Over the years I had learned the importance of self-care, especially during times of stress.

Carlos wandered into the kitchen as I came back inside for a second cup of the medium roast with notes of brown sugar and peaches. His hair was disheveled from sleep. He wrapped his strong arms around my waist. I leaned against him, drinking in the scent of his earthy aftershave.

"Good morning, Julieta. It is so strange to have you in our kitchen. Usually you are long gone by now."

"I was thinking that same thing as I was sipping my coffee. I slept in until almost five."

"Who are you and what have you done with my beautiful wife?" Carlos kissed the top of my head and poured himself a cup of coffee. "And you have been cooking?" He lifted the lid on my steel-cut oatmeal.

"Since I'm going to support Andy at the Barista Cup and don't have to open Torte, I figured we could have breakfast together."

Carlos's deep dark eyes twinkled. "It's a shame it can't be breakfast in bed." He added a splash of heavy cream to his coffee.

"Alas, I promised Andy I would be there for moral support. He's a bundle of nerves. I've never seen him like this. I just hope that he can shake off the anxiety. His talent is unparalleled. If he can focus and not get distracted by the other competitors, I know that he'll finish as one of, if not *the,* top contender." I ladled bowls of the oatmeal then topped them with walnuts, wild blueberries, cinnamon, and honey. I had chopped apples, oranges, bananas, and berries and mixed them with yogurt. "Have a seat. It's not fancy."

"It smells delicious." Carlos breathed in the aromas. "Food, it should not be a competition. Tell Andy that he does not need to worry. He crafts every cup of coffee with love. This is the essential ingredient."

"True, but I don't think there's a category for love on the score sheet."

Carlos scoffed. "There should be."

I laughed. "Maybe you should come offer your services."

"Watch out, mi querida, I may do that. I do not believe that we should judge our fellow baristas and chefs—we should collaborate together. We should spread more love and joy in the form of beautiful café espressos." He ate a spoonful of the oatmeal. "Si, this is how food should be. I taste that you put your heart into this."

I didn't disagree. One of the reasons I had fallen hard for Carlos was his dedication to infusing food with life. He didn't simply slice a piece of bread for a sandwich. He caressed the bread, massaging it with olive oil, layering in slices of cheese and paper-thin ham. Everything he plated was a representation of his personality. Including his impish side.

As much as Carlos prescribed to the idea of infusing food with love, he did the same with fun. There was no debating that commercial kitchens are ripe with stress. That's why Carlos enjoyed pranking his team. He believed it helped lighten the mood and set a tone for fun. One of his favorite jokes to play was to tuck eggs into the apron of any sous or line chef who left the kitchen for a bathroom break. When they returned to put their apron back on the eggs would fly out, crack all over the floor, and *crack up* the rest of the kitchen staff. Another classic Carlos shenanigan was assigning any new staffers to pick and clean stinging nettles, with one minor detail left out—the fact that the nettles were stinging. Inevitably a young chef in training would raise their hand and say, "Um, chef are my fingers supposed to be stinging?"

His pranks were always lighthearted and meant to build rapport, not tear anyone down.

I took a sip of my coffee. "Like I told you last night, the entire team has tried to pump Andy up. I'll be there. Mom is coming by. The rest of the staff are going to rotate in and out for different phases of the competition. If nothing else, he'll have a huge cheering section."

"I will try to come by too when I'm finished at Uva. It will depend on how many people stop in for tastings. By the way, have you had any more time to think of the idea of a dinner in the vines?"

When Carlos had made the decision to stay in Ashland, he found a way (which I still didn't understand how) to buy out Richard Lord as a partner in our small vineyard—Uva. Richard was the only person in our little hamlet who managed to irk me at every turn. He was a classic bully. Thanks to Mom shunning his advancements years ago, when she was already married, he had made it his mission to make my life miserable and copy anything and everything we did at Torte. His latest attempt to steal business away from us was to set up an ice-cream cart in front of the Merry Windsor. Although, in classic Richard Lord fashion, nothing he served was handcrafted. He had opted for cheap store-bought containers of ice cream loaded with preservatives, candy, and fake whipped topping. Instead of serving his customers a premium product, he went for volume and inexpensive scoops filled with gums and resins used as a thickening substitute for real eggs and cream.

Carlos had yet to reveal how he managed to convince Richard to sell his shares in the vineyard, but quite honestly I didn't care. I was thrilled to be free of any ties to Mr. Lord, and Carlos was completely in his element at Uva. He had taken over day-to-day management of the winery, grape fields, and tasting room. His latest idea was to host twilight dinners amongst the grapevines.

"I love it. I have a feeling it will sell out quickly. We can market it to our already existing Sunday Supper list and the wine club members. Do you want to go with the color concept?"

When Carlos and I had worked together on the *Amour of the Seas*—a boutique cruise ship that catered to foodies—he had created color-themed dinners that became legendary amongst passengers and the crew. Guests would dress in the dinner's theme color, and then all of the food, from the first appetizer to dessert, was served in the same color. For our dinner in red he had prepared a magnificent feast of herbed lentil soup, bruschetta, and tomato Bolognese. We had finished the meal with individual red velvet cakes, sour cherry tarts, and blood-red port. The themed dinners were such a success that people would rebook their next trip based on when the next dinner would occur.

Carlos waffled. "I do not know. Maybe for this first one we have our guests come in white. We listen to some music. We drink in some wine, like the beautiful moonlight. A romantic evening in the vines. But, I think I would like the food to reflect what is growing in our region here. This farm-to-table movement it is so wonderful. What do you say?"

"Perfect. I agree. It's like blending our old world with this one." I smiled at him. That was what we had been doing with each other, why not do it with our food?

Carlos snapped twice. "Okay. This is the idea. A dinner in the vines. We will ask the guests to dress in white and we will make them such a wonderful feast. We should discuss a menu soon."

I glanced at my watch. "For sure, but right now I need to get to The Hills."

We finished our breakfast. Carlos dropped me off at the hotel with a lingering kiss. "Julieta, I do not like leaving you. I wish we could spend the day lying in a hammock under the sun, but the bud break has already occurred on the vine. The grapes are drinking in the fresh air and glorious warmth. I must tend to them and our guests. If I can sneak away early, I will come meet you to cheer on Andy. Wish him luck from me."

"Will do." I got my purse from the back seat and left Carlos with a wave.

The sand-colored hotel with its tangerine roof blended in with the sloping hills to the east. Lush green lawns and cotton-candy pink roses bloomed throughout the property. A row of orange and white cruising bikes with wire baskets sat ready to be taken for a spin.

Inside, the retro design continued with gleaming hardwood floors, arched ceilings with exposed white beams, glass bead chandeliers, and colorful burnt-orange couches with funky geometric pillows. The lobby was teaming with competitors and spectators checking out the vendor booths. Exhibitors included everything from Swiss water processing to Italian syrups to Chemex coffeemakers and artisan chocolatiers. It was a sensory overload of everything coffee.

I decided I could check out the vendors later, but right now my focus was on finding Andy. I left the lobby and followed the signs to the ballroom.

It was shortly before eight and the hallway was already jammed with people waiting for the doors to open. I pushed my way through the crowd and spotted Andy pacing near the side entrance down a long hallway. Sunlight streamed in through the large wall of windows. Barista Cup banners with coffee art hung from the arched ceiling and on every door.

"Andy!" I waved and squeezed past a group of women wearing matching T-shirts that read You Mocha Me Crazy.

"Hey, boss. You made it." His jaw was clenched. Huge bags had formed beneath his bloodshot eyes. I guessed that, despite me sending him home, he hadn't gotten much sleep.

"I wouldn't have missed it for the world. How are you feeling? Did you get any sleep last night?"

Andy ran his fingers through his hair. Instead of one of our Torte aprons, he wore a chocolate brown one with leather straps. West Coast Barista Cup was embroidered across the chest. "Not really. I mean I tried, and I do appreciate you telling me to take a break. My grandma said the same thing, but I couldn't sleep." He looked to his hands, which trembled. "I can't seem to get my fingers to stop shaking."

I placed a hand on his shoulder. "That's normal. It's just jitters. As soon as you get behind the machine, your training will kick in. Trust me."

"You think?" His eyes brightened.

"I'm sure of it. You're going to do great, Andy. I remember my first test in pastry school. My instructor asked a basic math question. It was something like, an eight-pound wedding cake needs to be divided into thirty-two equal slices. How much will each slice weigh? My mind went completely blank. I stood in front of my station with my pencil and calculator for what felt like an eternity. As time was running out the chef shouted, 'Capshaw, you know this. Focus!' That snapped me out of my funk and after that I was fine." I rubbed my hands together. "By the way, in case that comes up today, it's four ounces."

Andy laughed. The tension on his face faded momentarily.

"I'm so excited to watch you do your thing. You're going to be great."

"Thanks, Jules. You seriously are the best boss on the planet." His voice was thick with emotion.

The doors were about to open, and I didn't want to make his already tender emotional state more fragile, so I made a joke. "You better bet your bottom dollar on that fact, my friend. I'm basically amazing."

He chuckled. "Hey, can you do me a favor and keep an eye out for my grandma? I got her a ticket and she asked me to save her a seat, but I'm not sure what it's going to be like in there."

"Count on it. I'll save her a seat." I made a funny face.

"Of course, it will cost you. How much is the check for the winner?"

Andy laughed again.

I was glad the distraction had worked, only it was short lived because the smile faded from his face as a young woman in the same brown apron approached us.

"Oh no. That's her. She's here, she's really here," Andy muttered. "That's Sammy Pressman."

"Who's Sammy Pressman?" My focus drifted to the young woman. She was petite with short black hair, giant silver hoop earrings, and coffee tattoos on nearly every inch of exposed skin.

"She's the national reigning five-time champion." Andy gulped as Sammy approached us.

"Hey, you competing?" She pointed to his apron. "You must be a newbie."

Andy swallowed hard and nodded.

I'd never known him to be speechless.

Sammy held her pointed chin high. "Good luck out there today. It gets intense. Try not to sweat it too much. Most newbies do and that's the death of them. You can't give the judges anything. They'll dock you for the slightest slip. Stay cool, newb." With that she opened the side door and went into the ballroom.

"Did she just talk to me? Did Sammy Pressman really just talk to me?" Andy stared at the closed door in disbelief.

"She did. She wished you luck." Although from my perspective Sammy had sounded less than authentic.

"I can't believe Sammy Pressman talked to me. I've been following her YouTube for years. She's amazing.

Like a coffee goddess." Was it my imagination or had Andy's cheeks turned two shades redder?

"See, there you go. That should boost your confidence. You're competing against her today. That means you're in her same league."

"No way." Andy shook his head. "You don't understand, Jules. Sammy Pressman is a league all on her own. She does things to coffee that bend every rule in the book. She's won nationals five times and finished in the top three in worlds. She's a legend. You must have heard of Fluid, right?"

I shook my head.

"That's her coffee shop in Spokane. It's offbeat, minimalist. Not your traditional café. Fluid is known for their single-origin espressos, their pour-overs, and the fact that everything is roasted in-house. She's won, like, every coffee award possible for her custom-blending techniques."

He didn't have time to continue because an announcement came on the overhead speakers explaining that the doors were opening for round one. Baristas were to take their positions and spectators to find seats.

I squeezed his hand. "Good luck."

He bit his bottom lip. "Thanks."

Andy headed straight for his station in the center of the large ballroom. The cavernous space had been transformed for the competition. Ten bright and shiny burnt-orange espresso machines sat on six-foot tables draped in black tablecloths. Each station had been set up identically with canisters of whole beans, coffee grinders, an assortment of flavorings, and an arsenal of barista tools.

A giant screen hung behind the competitor's area to allow the audience a close-up view of the action. Just to the right of the screen was another six-foot table reserved for the judges. Rows of chairs for spectators filled the remainder of the room. A DJ was spinning tunes in the back. Techno music pulsed through the room.

I snagged seats in the front row. The scene reminded me of my days in culinary school. After I graduated from high school, I left for New York to attend one of the most prestigious pastry schools in the country. Life in the city had been a shock to my system after growing up in Ashland, but it had taught me so much, not only about the art and science of baking but also about myself. If I hadn't gone to New York, I likely never would have landed a job on the *Amour of the Seas* and had the opportunity to visit far-flung corners of the world and romantic ports of call.

Watching the judges circle the competitors, making notes on clipboards, sent my stomach swirling. I remembered all too well the attentive eye of my culinary instructor, who made it his mission to point out even the tiniest flaws in our baking. In the long run his critical lens had made me a better chef, but I certainly didn't enjoy having him breathe down my neck when I was whipping cream or folding egg whites.

The judges each wore the same apron design as the competitors, except that their aprons were white and said Judge across the front. I counted five judges. Three sat at the head table, chatting and observing the baristas prepping their stations. The other two roamed around each of the contestants, jotting down notes without saying a word or moving a muscle in their passive faces.

Andy appeared to be in the zone. He unpacked a tub of specialty syrups and his personal tools.

A film crew stopped at Andy's station. Suddenly, his face came up on the big screen. I clapped and turned to a woman sitting next to me—she was part of the group wearing matching You Mocha Me Crazy T-shirts. "That's my lead barista."

"Congratulations," she replied. "Has he competed before?"

"No, this is his first time. It's the first time anyone from our bakeshop has competed."

"It's great fun. I'm a super fan. I've been attending Barista Cup for ten years. It gets bigger and bigger. This year there are twenty contestants vying for first place." She pointed to Sammy, whose station was next to Andy's. "Sammy Pressman is the queen. She's a total superstar and a diva, but rightfully so. She's on another planet when it comes to coffee. Mark my words, she's the one to watch, but you should also keep your eye on Diaz Mendez. He's been getting a ton of buzz." Her eyes drifted to the station opposite Andy.

A young guy, who I would guess to be in his mid-to-late twenties, had a pair of headphones on and danced to a beat no one else could hear as he rearranged mini whisks and a thermometer. His dark hair was tied into a bun on the top of his head.

Her friend leaned over. "I see why he's getting such good buzz. He's so handsome." She fanned her face.

I had no idea that coffee competitions drew such faithful fans.

"The one you want to watch out for is *him*," the

woman next to me whispered. She used her left hand to conceal her right finger, which was pointing at a distinguished-looking gentleman in his fifties seated at the judges' table. He had a long, dark trimmed beard and a pair of tortoiseshell glasses. "Do you know who that is?"

I could wager a guess.

"Benson Vargas. If you haven't heard of him, you will after today. The West Coast Barista Cup is his baby and he's cutthroat when it comes to coffee. I hope he doesn't intimidate your barista. He looks young and eager. That's fresh meat for Benson."

I got my first in-person glimpse of the infamous judge. Benson was a foot taller than the two judges flanking him. He ran his fingers along his beard and glared at each contestant. At that moment, Andy accidentally knocked a canister of beans off his table. They spilled on the floor and scattered everywhere.

One of the technical judges walked over to help him.

"That's Piper Frederick," the woman next to me offered. "She's the head technical judge and co-owner of the Barista Cup with Benson. She's a stickler for procedure, but she won't bite the poor kid's head off like Benson."

I watched as Piper bent down to help Andy with the beans. She was about Benson's age with angular features, copper hair, and glasses that matched his. Piper wore a pair of slim white capris and held a clipboard in one hand.

I overheard Piper tell Andy that it was no big deal, but to be careful because once the competition officially kicked off, he would definitely get docked points for a spill.

I felt relieved for him. Only my relief didn't last long, because my eyes returned to Benson. He was shooting such a dirty look at Andy it made me lean back in my chair. Then he stood and snapped his fingers at Piper.

"That's an automatic disqualification. I want him out!"

Chapter Four

An audible gasp erupted in the ballroom. The woman sitting next to me nudged my elbow. "I told you he was a tyrant."

Andy's face went white.

Benson stood and bellowed at Piper and the other technical judge. "Disqualification! Get that contestant out."

Piper whispered something to Andy.

Benson bared his teeth and shook his fist. "You are a disgrace to coffee!" He addressed Andy with a face full of rage. "No self-respecting barista would allow his beans to fall to the floor. Unacceptable!"

Piper patted Andy's shoulder. Then she turned to address her fellow judge. "Benson, stop. You're making a scene. We're not going to start things off like this."

Her words did nothing to deter him. His head made jerking motions as he continued. "Would you stomp on the American flag? Would you desecrate a cathedral? No! That's what we've witnessed here. A total disregard for the sanctity of coffee."

Piper shook her head and approached the judges'

table. Her long red ponytail swung from side to side as she waved her finger at Benson.

"She and Benson have been judging together for years. She won't stand for him bullying anyone." My seatmate was a wealth of information. "Piper is responsible for technical judging. She observes the barista's techniques, cleanliness, and makes sure they come in under the time limit. Benson is a sensory judge, meaning his role is to taste each drink and critique it. He doesn't get a say in disqualifications at this point. That's entirely Piper's call."

"Got it." I smiled at her. "Is Andy in danger of being disqualified for spilling the beans?"

"No. Not at all. That's Benson trying to stir up drama. It's what he does. That's one of the reasons he draws such a big crowd." She looked around us. Nearly every seat had filled in. "Judging doesn't start until the bell goes off. Even then, if a contestant makes a mistake they aren't disqualified. They just might get a lower score on the technical section."

Tension built in the ballroom as Benson spat out insults to Piper. "Stop coddling the contestants! They don't need your protection. They're adults. If they can't take the pressure, they can find the door. We've gone over this dozens of times. I'm done with you! You're done with the Cup!"

Piper slipped her hands into her capris pockets. "Benson, this isn't the time or place."

Benson changed his stance, making himself even taller. "You're done, Piper! I don't care who hears it! Your days are numbered. This competition is going to the next level and I'm not going to stand for amateurs who spill beans everywhere." He scowled at Andy.

Piper shot a sideways glance to the other technical judge, who also approached the table. They consulted their clipboards then pointed out something on the judges' score sheets that caused Benson to groan loudly for the benefit of the crowd, but then sit down.

"See. I wasn't kidding," the mocha lover next to me said.

"Obviously." I couldn't imagine what Carlos would say if he were here.

Piper finished scolding Benson. Then she returned to Andy's station. She said something to him a low voice that I couldn't hear with the chatter of the crowd. After she finished talking to him, he shot me a thumbs-up and returned to his prep.

"Is this seat taken?" a familiar voice asked.

I turned to see Mom standing next me. She had arrived with Andy's grandmother, June, a round-faced woman in her early seventies with bright, intelligent eyes and a kind smile that matched her grandson's.

"June, you made it." I stood to greet both of them. "I saved seats." I moved my purse and sweater from the chairs to my left.

Mom sat down. "Did we miss anything?"

June sat next to her. Andy's grandmother was a frequent visitor to Torte. He had lived with her through his first few years of college, and I knew that she had been equally worried about his decision to leave school. However, like Mom and me, she had his best interest at heart. He had told me that she had been up until long past midnight with him helping him prepare for the competition.

"Well, nothing has started yet, but there's already been quite a bit of drama." I filled them in on Andy's flub.

"He'll be fine," June said with confidence. She had a brought a bundle of knitting to keep her hands busy during the competition.

"I agree. It's good that he's getting his nerves out now." Mom took off a thin wrap and hung it from the back of her chair. The wrap was pale blue and dotted with colorful chickens. Mom's signature style matched Ashland—simple, flowing, and elegant. She wore a pair of navy clog sandals and a linen dress.

"Hey, we match today." I pointed to my light blue skirt and strappy sandals. Working in the bakeshop meant that most days I donned tennis shoes and jeans. For today's occasion I had opted for a skirt, tank top, and cardigan. Plus, I wore my favorite pair of dangling earrings—another no-no in a busy kitchen.

"Great minds think alike." Mom scooted her chair closer. "Andy looks like he's in good spirits given that he got off to a rocky start."

He spotted her and June, and waved.

A man wearing skinny purple jeans and a V-neck black tee approached the competitors. He clicked on a microphone and addressed the audience. "Welcome, welcome to the West Coast Barista Cup!"

Everyone applauded.

"I'm James, the food and bar manager here at The Hills, and everyone here at the hotel along with the amazing team at the West Coast Barista Cup want to welcome you to our gorgeous Rogue Valley. I'm so thrilled to be your MC and host for this year's competition. We have such a talented crew of baristas who are going to dazzle you with their skills. Each of them is already a winner. They've had to compete in a variety of regional contests, send in video footage of their superior espresso prowess, and pass an exam that tests their coffee culture knowledge. Little-known fact: I myself, competed many, many years ago in the Barista Cup, so this is particularly exciting to me on both a professional and personal level."

I noticed Benson roll his eyes.

James continued. "Okay, so before we get started let's go over a few things. Cheering is absolutely recommended, but we ask that you remain in your seats while each of the baristas are doing their thing. We've set up the big screen, and our video crew will be giving you up-close shots so you can see these talented baristas' fingers flying. We don't want anyone raging against the espresso machine." He laughed at his own joke as the DJ played a clip of "Freedom" by Rage Against the Machine.

James gestured his approval of the song choice, then continued. "For this first round, our baristas are being tasked with creating a latte, a cappuccino, and a mocha. They'll be judged on their technique, their time, their coffee knowledge, and their ability to educate and serve, as well as the most important component—taste! Who will be the lord of the beans? That's up to our esteemed panel of judges. A total of seventy-five points is awarded for the technical portion of the competition and one hundred points for taste and flavor profile, as well as the barista's knowledge base and their connection to the cup. That gives one hundred seventy-five points in total. Any competitor who goes over the fifteen-minute time limit gets docked the number of seconds they go over. At the end of round one, the bottom two contestants will be eliminated. Then we'll have a short break. Plenty of time for you to go mingle in our café and bar. We have created some delicious coffee-themed specials for you this weekend. Don't forget to visit the lobby, where vendors will be showcasing some of the latest and greatest coffee tools and gadgets."

He paused and turned around to address the baristas. "Are you ready for a brewing battle?"

Diaz pumped his fist in the air. Sammy pressed her hands together and nodded. Andy shot his signature thumbs-up. One contestant proceeded to launch into jumping jacks. Another looked like she might throw up. The atmosphere was electric.

"Okay!" James tried to energize the crowd. "Let's count them down. The West Coast Barista Battle begins in three . . . two . . . one!"

Cheers reverberated through the ballroom. The baristas went straight to work. It was a whirlwind of activity and sound as beans pulsed in grinders and steam whistled. Andy had a singular focus. He tamped down finely ground beans with a severe look in his eyes, like he wanted to murder the machine.

"I've never seen Andy look so serious," Mom noted.

"Neither have I."

"He's been like this at home," June said, watching him with pride. "I told him that regardless of the outcome, this experience, the training, the preparation, are going to make him that much stronger—win or lose."

"Well said." Mom shared a smile with June.

We sat in awe as Andy measured exact amounts of milk and dark chocolate syrup for the mocha. He hand-whipped cream like he was giving it a beating. Then he finished the drink with a generous shaving of dark chocolate.

According to the program, competitors couldn't stray from the approved list of ingredients in this round. Their drinks would be judged on consistency, balancing the coffee-to-milk ratio, and temperature. If Andy made it on to later rounds, he would be able to showcase his unique flavor profiles.

Piper and the other technical judge analyzed the baristas every move. I felt nervous for Andy as she approached his station. A pair of reading glasses were pushed to the bridge of her nose.

"What do you think she's writing?" Mom asked.

"No idea. All of the competitors look like they know exactly what they're doing."

I watched Diaz, who appeared to be playing to the crowd, particularly the super fans sitting next to us. He flexed as he placed his latte and then cappuccino on the tray.

The woman next to me fanned her face again. "He's such a hunk."

Sammy Pressman ignored his antics. She was all business and exuded confidence. She reminded me of actors with the Oregon Shakespeare Festival with the way she added little flourishes with her hands as she swirled whipping cream on the top of her mocha.

A digital clock counted down the time as the DJ turned the music up louder.

"Five minutes," announced James. "Competitors you have five minutes! Get those drinks done and on your tasting trays."

Five minutes felt like thirty seconds. Before I knew it, an alarm sounded and the first round was finished.

"Wasn't that something?" The woman next to me bounced up and down in her chair.

"That was a total blur." I blinked twice, trying to get a handle on the speed at which the first round had gone down.

The competitors threw their hands in the air and stepped away from their stations as volunteers came to pick up their tasting trays and deliver them to the judges.

Andy dabbed his brow with a towel. Diaz flexed again. Sammy folded her arms across her chest in a show of confidence.

James motioned for the DJ to cut the music.

The room went still.

"All right competitors, when I call your name, I want you to step forward and share your coffee story with the judges." James tapped one foot. "Are you nervous? I know I'm feeling the tension. This is where it gets real. The judges want to taste your amazing drinks, but they also want to know what they're about to taste, so show them what you got!"

Sammy was up first. She took the mic from James and held the room captivated with her origin story of coffee cherries handpicked by women farmers in Guatemala. "I'm here to show you that the future of coffee is now. With everything you taste, I'll prove that. My coffees are in the genetic stage—these are rare new species, like nothing you've ever experienced." She traced the coffee's roots and informed the judges that they should taste notes of black tea, pomegranate, and cocoa. "Every step in the process was done to give you the best expression of my coffee," she said in closing.

"I feel like we've just attended a master class in coffee culture," I whispered to Mom and June.

The crowd applauded as the judges tasted her drinks, made notes, and then cleansed their palates with water before moving on to the next contestant.

"Each barista has to tell the judges what they should expect to taste," our mocha-loving seatmate explained to us. "And the judges had better taste exactly that. Otherwise they get docked points."

Diaz was up next. He had the DJ play the chorus to "Pour Some Sugar on Me" before launching into a very different presentation then Sammy's. "As a barista, I'm a student, I'm an educator, and most importantly I'm a mixologist. You're about to taste a revolution in a cup. Coffee should be fierce and angry. It should be ready to rise up and challenge your preconceived notions. This is not your grandmother's coffee. Get ready to taste smoke, ash, anise, burnt coconut, and whiskey."

I wasn't sure that his assault of flavors sounded pleasing, but the judges appeared to disagree as they gave Diaz plenty of nods and smiles while tasting his drinks. There didn't seem to be a consistent trend or flavor that the judges were drawn to. Some of the espressos that sounded delightful the judges panned, while others that sounded less than appealing, like an espresso the barista described as "carbon filled with notes of dried pea pods" received rave reviews. Most of the contestants appeared as wide eyed as Andy. Only Sammy and Diaz seemed unfazed by the pressure.

By the time it was Andy's turn, I couldn't stop bouncing my foot. His hands shook as he took the mic. "Thanks for having me. It's a pleasure to serve you. That's what I love about this industry. Yes, coffee is art and science, but it's also community. I've learned that nothing connects people like coffee. It's so much more than what we see in the cup. It's the coming together around the table. It's the farmer who planted the seeds and the guest who experiences every note."

"That's our boy." Mom squeezed my knee.

I was impressed with Andy's poise as he shared how his time at Torte had changed his understanding and directed the judges to expect to taste apricots, melons, grapes, and a touch of fermentation in his cup.

As the judges tasted each of his drinks and made more notes, Benson sighed and scowled after nearly every sip. The man was either playing into the persona of nightmare judge, or he was impossible to please.

"We'll take a fifteen-minute break to tally the results," James said. "Feel free to get up and stretch or wander into the lounge for complimentary coffee and snacks."

June stood and stretched her neck. She set her knitting on her chair. "I think I'll take a little walk. Sitting for too long is no good for my creaky knees."

"We'll save your seat." Mom said, twisting her wrap around her shoulders. Then she turned to me. "Do you want a coffee?"

"Do I want a coffee? Is that a rhetorical question?" I stood and cracked my knuckles. "Let's check in with Andy first."

We went to see how he felt about the first round.

"Hey, you looked great. How do you feel?" I asked.

Andy's checks glowed red. Sweat dripped from his forehead. "I feel like it's five hundred degrees in here. That went by so fast. I have no idea what I did, but I guess it's good that I got three drinks on my tray if nothing else."

"You were amazing. I can't even begin to tell you how proud of you we are," Mom gushed, fighting back tears.

"Thanks, Mrs. The Professor." Andy used his special nickname he had given to Mom when she and the Professor, aka Doug, Ashland's lead detective had married last summer.

"It was good to have you guys and my grandma in the front row," he continued. "Seeing you gave me a needed boost. I got off my game at the start when I knocked over those beans, but I think I pulled it together."

"What did Piper say to you? I saw her reading Benson the riot act."

"Yeah. She's cool. She told me to chill and not let him get in my head. I guess that's what he does. He tries to get a reaction out of the competitors. She said he plays to the crowd. You saw him go after her too. He's a real jerk."

"Obviously."

Sammy interrupted our conversation, peering at Andy's station with mock interest. "How was it, newbie? I told you it's intense." She held her hands loosely behind her back. "Good save at the start. I thought Benson was going to boot you. He's done it before. You dodged a bullet."

Andy tossed the dish towel over his shoulder. He looked flustered. "Yeah, that was totally crazy. I had no idea it was going to be like that."

"We'll leave you two to chat and go grab some coffee," Mom said, excusing us.

We made our way to the lobby and joined the queue for coffee. The Hills was offering the same lineup of drinks as the competitors—classic cappuccino, latte, and mocha.

"I hope he makes it through the first round," I said to Mom.

"He will. I don't have any doubt." She sounded confident. "His coffee speaks for itself, and his story was sweet and tender, just like him. But I didn't realize that the competition was quite as cutting. I was picturing more like the *Great British Baking Show*."

"This is definitely not that." I placed an order for two cappuccinos. "Think *Chopped* or *Cutthroat Kitchen*."

We returned to our seats just in time for the announcement. June was waiting for us with her knitting needles in her hands and her eyes on Andy.

James took the microphone again. "Okay, coffee junkies. Who's ready to hear the results from round one?" He paused to heighten the drama. "I have to tell you that this is some of the tightest voting there's ever been. Only three points separate first and third place. This battle is going to get wicked as the brewing heats up this afternoon."

I took a sip of my foamy cappuccino.

James started with last place and worked his way up. I held my breath as he read off the names of the baristas who would not be advancing to the next round.

When Andy's name wasn't read, Mom, June, and I let out a collective sigh of relief.

"In fourth place, a new contestant from right here in the Rogue Valley. Andy with Ashland's beloved bake-shop, Torte!"

We jumped to our feet and cheered. Andy's cheeks flamed.

James waited for the applause to die down. "Now folks, hold onto your hats because we have a bit of a shocker here. In third place, the current reigning na-tional barista champion, Sammy Pressman."

Murmurs broke out around us.

Sammy shot her head from side to side as if trying to comprehend the news. "Third? Third place?" She turned to the judges' table and threw her hands up in disgust.

Benson leaned back in his chair and snarled at her.

The second-place finisher was a barista from Idaho.

"That means in first place we have newcomer Diaz Mendez!" James went up to Diaz and raised his arm in the air. "Congratulations, man."

Diaz flexed for the crowd. Everyone went wild.

"That is crap!" Sammy shouted. She looked to Ben-son again. "You did this. You freaking creep. I hope you die!"

Chapter Five

Mom clutched her cappuccino as James had to hold Sammy back. Piper stepped in to console her. I watched in disbelief. The crowd noise came to an awkward screeching silence.

James tried to recover. "Hey, folks, this is coffee. This is what I love about our culture. We are so passionate about this work. Did you know that nearly eight hundred flavor compounds are possible when it comes to pulling a shot of espresso? And, if you think *that's* something, try to imagine this—there are over a million different roast variations and unlimited possibilities on how our competitors bring those together." He paused and bowed to the contestants. "It's a pressure cooker in here. I know. I've been there. There's nothing like seeing that timer start. It gets the blood pumping for sure. Now, like I told our baristas, this is only round one. The day is young. There are still two rounds to go, so things can and likely will change. If we have this level of competition in the first round, I can't wait to see what happens next!"

"I think bloodshed might happen next," Mom said under her breath.

James adjusted his lanyard. "We'll take a thirty-minute break to get set up. Wander the grounds, enjoy our complimentary pastries, and see you back here for espresso shots, straight up."

Piper had gathered the eight remaining contestants. I could hear her gentle voice trying to soothe nerves. Sammy wasn't having any of it. She glared at Piper and kept shooting her eyes toward Benson. He seemed to be enjoying her irritation.

Every time she looked at him, he would salute her with one finger and a smirk.

"That is the shocker of the century," the woman sitting next to me said. "Sammy has never finished in third place. Never."

"She doesn't look happy about it," I noted.

Sammy wasn't listening to Piper. Her hands were on her hips her as she stared Benson down. The caustic judge didn't flinch. He glowered right back at her. The camera zoomed in on Sammy's face. Her cold, hard eyes bared into Benson's face. If she noticed the camera, she wasn't deterred. A deep blue vein pulsed in her forehead as they continued to stare each other down.

"No. If I were Benson, I would be worried about her spiking my next drink. Do you see the nasty looks she's giving him? I wouldn't want to be in that line of fire." Mom cringed.

While Sammy fumed, Diaz bounced around his station like the disc jockey spinning tunes. Andy kept his head down. He didn't make eye contact with his fellow baristas or anyone in the audience.

Mom and I sipped our cappuccinos. June went for another walk to get a cup of coffee. She returned shortly before round two was due to start. Sterling and Bethany showed up at the same time.

"Hey! How's our guy doing?" Sterling asked. He wore a pair of black jeans and a thin gray hoodie with the sleeves rolled up.

Bethany pointed to her T-shirt. "What do you think? I wore it for Andy." The red tee had white lettering and a silhouette of a coffee cup that read I Like You a Latte.

Mom laughed. "It's perfect."

The women next to us had moved to chairs on the other side of the room so they could get a better view of Diaz. "Are those seats free?" Bethany asked.

"Yep." I waited for them to sit.

"Don't keep us in suspense, Jules, how did Andy do? He's still up there, so he must have done okay, right?" Sterling rubbed his hands on his jeans.

"He finished in fourth place, which is good for the first round." I told them about the surprise third-place finish for Sammy and that Diaz was currently in the lead.

"That guy is super cocky." Bethany stuck her tongue out. "I don't like his energy."

"You should have seen the women sitting next to us earlier," I said, nodding to the group in their matching shirts. "They are his super fans."

"They can have him." Bethany made a gagging motion. "He's gross."

I didn't disagree with her assessment. There was something off-putting about Diaz. Maybe it was that my style tended to be more inward. For me, baking was therapy. It was about getting in touch with my innermost thoughts and immersing myself in the sensory experience. Over the years, I had known chefs who saw their role as performer. Diaz fell into that category.

"How are things at Torte?" I asked.

"Good. Uneventful," Sterling replied. "We prepped everything for Scoops. The freezer is stocked with new concretes. Bread deliveries are out. Marty and Rosa have things running smoothly."

"Excellent." Not that I expected anything different, but I was glad to hear it.

A few minutes later, James returned with the mic to kick off the next round. "Are you all feeling caffeinated? If not, you're going to be by the end of this round. Our talented baristas have been tasked with delivering three unique espressos to our panel of judges—they'll be looking for baristas to put a whole latte of love into their full-flavored, concentrated espresso shots with a lovely crema on top."

Most customers who walked into the bakeshop had no idea what went into pulling a perfect espresso shot. It was so much more than simply grinding beans and turning on a machine. Andy's technique involved measuring the beans down to the gram before adding them to the grinder. He ground them until they resembled the texture of granulated sugar. Grinding the beans too fine would make the shot taste bitter and burnt. Whereas a coarse grind would mean the shot wouldn't extract properly, causing it to be watery and weak.

The way a shot was tamped into the portafilter could also greatly affect its flavor. Proper tamping ensured uniformity and consistency when water was forced through the shot. The next step was to warm the shot glasses and start the brew. Andy, like the rest of the competitors, held a timer in his hand. He would meticulously watch the time, shooting for an extraction time of between twenty and thirty seconds.

From our vantage point we could see the brown foam beginning to pour in a single line. The goal was to create a golden crema floating on the top of a dark rich shot.

"It smells amazing in here," Bethany commented as she took dozens of pictures on her phone. "I'm going to be livestreaming later. I told our followers I would give them an up-close look at all the action."

Bethany had taken over management of our social media accounts. I readily admitted that technology wasn't my strong suit. Having spent over a decade at sea, I had missed the trend—and that was fine with me. Fortunately, Bethany had an eye for design. She had quickly amassed a nice local and even regional following with her drool-worthy pictures of our pastries and specialty cakes.

For this round, competitors had fifteen minutes to pull shots for each of the judges while again telling a complete story and keeping watch over the time.

"On deck first, we have our local boy Andy." James shot his finger at Andy. "Are you ready?"

"Yep. Can you start the time?" Andy asked. He flew through the task as the large red digital clock counted down.

"I've stored my beans in an air-tight container and will pull the shots immediately after grinding," he spoke, addressing the judges in a quick, almost breathless tones. "I'm using a scale to achieve the perfect ratio of eighteen grams for each extraction."

I wondered if he was talking fast because of nerves or if he'd already sampled too many shots. Coffee novices would probably be overwhelmed by Andy's tech speak, but Piper took furious notes, and nodded her head with approval.

As with the first round, once he finished pulling shots his story shifted and became more personal. "Why does this matter? Could I simply hit an automatic button on the espresso machine? Sure, but that's not what coffee is to me. Think of the word we use to describe the process. 'Extraction.' We're extracting a piece of ourselves. The time, consideration, and thought I put into the process is revealed in the tasting experience. It's humbling to be able to serve our customers something so intimate and interconnected."

June dabbed her eyes with a paper napkin.

Watching him pour his heart into each step touched me. I studied the judges to see if they were moved by his words. Benson's permanent scowl appeared to be frozen on his lips, but Piper gave Andy an encouraging smile and jotted down more notes.

We cheered as he placed his last shot on the tasting tray and wiped his hands on his apron.

Piper examined Andy's final product, kneeling and bending over the table to study his espresso shots from every angle. She made a few final notes then moved on to Diaz's table.

His style was polar opposite from Andy's. "Hey, DJ, can you crank my tunes? Vibe check. Yeah, we be vibin' now!" He pumped his fists in the air as dance music blasted. His approach seemed to be to infuse as much high energy into the process as possible. He swayed to the beat as he adjusted the machine and flirted with the crowd and Piper.

Last up was Sammy. She reminded me of a ballet dancer as she stretched her arms and stood on her tiptoes to remove her coffee beans from a cooler of dry ice. She was putting on a performance for sure. The smoky steam from the dry ice wafted over the espresso machine while she crafted a pristine shot.

When Piper made her way to Sammy's table, Diaz huddled together with Andy. I wished the music wasn't so loud. They talked in hushed tones. I wondered what Diaz was saying. He pointed to Andy's supply station. Andy shot him a thumbs-up and scurried to scoop some of his materials—spoons, dish towels, and frothing pitchers beneath his table.

As with the first round, as soon as the final buzzer sounded, volunteers took the shots to the judges' table. The results didn't take as long to tally, since each judge only had one drink to sample.

"Okay coffee connoisseurs, how's everyone doing?" James jumped from side to side as he prepared to deliver the judges' results. I wondered how many shots of espresso he had sampled.

He waved a sealed envelope in his hand. "I have the names of the contestants moving on to round three right here, but you all don't want me to read them, do you?"

The group of super fans fawning over Diaz booed.

James ripped open the envelope. After eliminating two more contestants he read the top six names. "Keeping her spot in third place, we have Sammy Pressman!"

Sammy slammed a portafilter on the table. "No way! This competition is rigged."

Benson didn't shift a muscle. He kept the same evil sneer on his face.

James cleared his throat and tried to move on. "In second place we have our boy wonder from Ashland—the one and only Andy!"

Sterling, Mom, Bethany, June, and I jumped up and cheered.

Andy beamed.

"That's right, folks, that means holding strong in the number-one spot is Diaz Mendez!"

Diaz gave the crowd his signature flex.

"I want a revote," Sammy said, holding her hand in the air. "Someone is cheating." She glared at Andy and stood on her tiptoes to peer at his station as if expecting to see evidence of dishonest coffee practices.

That was quite an accusation. Where was that was coming from?

"Why would she say such a thing?" June sounded dismayed.

James let out an uncomfortable chuckle. "Folks, I warned you things might get heated. They always do when coffee is involved."

Sammy pounded the heavy metal tool on the table. "This is totally rigged. Everyone knows that Benson has it out for me! Someone is cheating! I want a re-do!"

Piper stepped up to the microphone. She whispered something in James's ear.

James nodded. "Alright folks, I've just gotten word that lunch is ready. Please make your way to the east ballroom for a wonderful lunch spread, and we'll see you back here at one o'clock for today's final round."

No one moved. I had a feeling that everyone was as stunned as we were with Sammy's reaction.

"Seriously, folks, you don't want to miss what my culinary team has put together. Remember, lunch is complimentary with your ticket, so go load up your plates."

People began to shuffle out of the ballroom.

We waited for the line to thin.

I watched as Sammy waved her arms, frantically pointing from Andy to Benson. Did she think that Andy was cheating?

Piper tried to calm her down.

Benson continued to lean back in his chair with the same unnerving smile.

"No!" Sammy shouted. "I know what's going on here and I'm not going to take it. As far as I'm concerned, Benson can go jump off a cliff and die." She stormed out of the ballroom.

"Whoa. Someone needs to lay off the caffeine," Sterling commented.

"Yeah," I agreed as we headed out for lunch. Internally I was rattled. Was Sammy accusing Andy of cheating? And what was the deal with Benson? Putting on a steel exterior was one thing, but he seemed like he had a personal vendetta against Sammy. I had a bad feeling about how the afternoon was going to play out.

Chapter Six

Lunch was delicious. The Hills kitchen staff had marinated tender pork with cilantro, onions, garlic, peppers, and pineapple juice. The pork had been grilled and served in corn tortillas with pinto beans, cilantro lime rice, farmer's cheese, and fresh pineapple slices.

"I'm going to run and check in with Andy," I said to Mom, Sterling, June, and Bethany after polishing off two tacos. "Unless he's had a complete shift from yesterday, I bet he hasn't eaten anything."

"I'm sure he hasn't," June agreed. "I had to force a piece of toast on him on his way out the door this morning."

"Good idea," Mom said. "If he hasn't, we can fix him a plate."

"I'll be back in a few," I said and headed for the ballroom. On my way, I noticed James having what appeared to be a fierce conversation with someone in the alcove. James had his back to me and his body blocked my view of whoever he was speaking to. What was apparent, however, was that the conversation wasn't going well.

"You're not going to get away with this!" James threatened. He was naturally thin, but he made his stance wide to take up space.

I froze.

"You have ruined one too many lives. I'm not letting you do it again." James lunged forward.

"Nothing has changed, has it?" Benson stepped to the side. "You're the same whiny complainer you've always been."

I tried not to gasp.

James grabbed Benson's shoulder. "I'm serious. You're not getting away with this."

Benson threw James off of him, then gave him a condescending grin. "You have no idea who you're dealing with." He tossed his head back and laughed before stomping down the hall in the opposite direction.

James just stared after him.

I hesitated. There was no easy way to make a graceful exit, unless I shuffled backward down the hallway.

Once Benson had exited the hotel through the far door, James turned around and spotted me. "Hey, I recognize you. You own Torte, right?"

"Guilty as charged." I raised my hands in surrender.

He came closer to shake my hand. "James—I manage food and beverage here at The Hills. You are a legend in these parts. I've seen you at a couple of the chamber meetings, but never had the chance to meet you in person."

"Nice to meet you. I'm Jules."

"You must be here to cheer on your barista. He's doing really well, especially for a first-timer." He continued to shake my hand, causing the lanyard around his neck to swing wildly. He finally let go and grabbed the lanyard. I wasn't surprised that James had once competed in the Barista Cup. His hipster skinny jeans and narrow goatee looked the part of coffee counterculture.

If he had suspected that I had overheard his argument with Benson, he gave no indication.

"Did you catch any of the first rounds?" He pointed to the ballroom.

"Yes. It's been amazing." I didn't mention Sammy's outburst, but I was curious about what I had overheard. "Benson is quite the character. I was worried at the beginning that Andy might have been out of the competition before it had even started."

James forced a smile. "Don't give Benson a minute of your time. He feeds on the attention. This is his thing. I'm convinced that he must spend weeks prepping insults to hurl at the contestants."

"Do you know him well?"

"No. I don't know him. Not at all. Thank goodness. Who would want to be associated with that guy? I feel sorry for Piper, though." He let out a quick high-pitched laugh. James seemed flustered as he unbuttoned the top button on his shirt, then buttoned it again. "I only met him a couple days ago when he and the other judges arrived. I'm sure you've had your fair share of chefs like Benson in your career. I could tell from the moment I met him that he had an ego the size of Texas."

Was James lying? From what I had just heard, it didn't add up that he and Benson had just recently met.

James tapped a smartwatch on his wrist. "Sorry to cut this short, but I need to go let the competitors know that the next round is going to start in twenty."

"I'll follow you in. I wanted to check in with Andy and make sure he ate lunch."

"None of them ever remember to eat," James said with a laugh. "They're too jacked up on caffeine and nervous energy."

We went into the ballroom together. The DJ had started the next playlist, and a few of the judges, including Piper, were chatting at the head table.

"I should go reconvene with the team," James said, taking his leave.

There was no sign of Andy. But something was definitely amiss. Diaz had his headphones on and his eyes were focused on an espresso machine. The only problem was—not *his* machine. He stood at Andy's station. What was he doing?

He must have felt my eyes on him because he looked up, met my gaze, and immediately jumped away from Andy's machine. He straightened his shoulders and danced his way back to his own spot, as if nothing had happened.

A strange sensation swirled in my stomach. Had he been tampering with Andy's espresso machine?

Jules, you're being paranoid.

The morning's events must have been getting to me.

I approached the competitor's area. Diaz ignored me as he jammed to his tunes.

Andy's station was neatly prepped and ready for the final round with bottles of spicy honey and ceramic tasting mugs lined in perfect rows. Upon closer inspection, I noticed something else. Dirt? Was that dirt on his table or maybe coffee grounds? It wasn't like Andy to have a messy work area. I resisted the urge to sweep the dirt or grounds away. I didn't want to accidentally do anything that might interfere with the competition.

"You haven't seen Andy by chance?" I asked Diaz.

"Huh?" He lifted one side of his headphones away from his ear.

"I was wondering if you've seen Andy."

"Nope." He flipped his headphones back over his ears.

I scanned the ballroom. Piper and Sammy were deep in conversation near the judges' table. I could only imagine that Sammy was likely giving Piper an earful. Since there was no sign of Andy, I hoped that meant that he had gotten outside for some fresh air or taken a lunch break. I went back to the other side of the hotel where Mom, Sterling, Bethany, and June were sipping coffee and sharing a plate of cookies.

"We saved a double chocolate marshmallow cookie for you, Jules," Sterling said. He pushed the plate toward me. "How's Andy holding up?"

"I couldn't find him."

"Don't worry, he'll be fine." Mom squeezed my hand. "Second place. He's doing great, and the next round is where he's really going to impress the judges. I tasted his signature drink yesterday and I was blown away."

"Right?" Bethany nodded with enthusiasm. "His hot honey latte is like the best thing I've ever tasted. I might forego a boyfriend for another cup of that deliciousness."

June's eyes twinkled. "Don't do that, honey. No coffee is worth it."

Sterling laughed. "Wise advice."

"Okay fine. Maybe not, but it was to-die-for good."
Bethany blushed.

We finished our dessert and made our way to the ball-room together.

Andy raced through a side door as we took our seats. He sprinted to wash his hands and get back to his station as James went over the rules for the third round.

"Folks, this is my favorite part of the day. Our world-class coffee judges have studied each of our barista's techniques and compared classic cups of cappuccinos and espressos. Now it's time for our baristas to show off their creativity. Welcome to the signature-drinks round!"

He motioned for more applause.

Andy made it to his station and tied on his apron. I wondered where he had gone. Hopefully, Mom was right. Maybe he'd gotten outside to clear his head and shake off his nerves.

"Get ready to see some of the most innovative flavor profiles on the planet," James continued. "Our contestants will be preparing signature drinks for our judges. Kale latte? Watermelon cold brew? Who knows? Their drinks will be scored on originality, the balance of the flavors, and, of course, on their technical skills. I'll be interviewing each barista as they make their drinks. They have twenty minutes for this round. Good luck and let's get brewing!"

Everyone cheered as the bell sounded.

James approached Diaz's station first. "Hey man, how does it feel to be in the lead?"

"Good. Not surprising. I knew I would be in first and that's not changing after this round." He flexed.

"That's getting annoying," Mom whispered.

"Wowza! Folks, how's that for confidence?" James let out a whistle.

Diaz shrugged as he tamped a shot. "It's called having a winning attitude."

"I like it. I like it." James clapped. "What signature drink are you brewing up for the judges?"

"This is my diablo chocolate. It's on fire and going to blow the judges' minds."

"That sounds spicy," James commented.

Mom leaned in and whispered. "Oh no, Andy's doing a spicy drink too."

"What's in your diablo chocolate?" James asked.

"Mexican chocolate—the best in the world—a combination of secret spices, and an avocado purée." Diaz reached for one of his avocados and tossed it in the air like ball.

James turned to the audience. "Folks, I wasn't kidding about crazy combinations. You heard that right. Avocado coffee. Can't wait to hear what our sensory judges have to say about that. Good luck, Diaz."

Diaz paused just long enough to pose for the crowd and soak up the applause.

James moved on to Sammy. "How's our reigning national champ doing?"

She glared at him. "Working."

"Right. I'll keep this short. Tell your coffee fans what you're brewing up for the judges."

Sammy didn't move. James had to thrust the mic toward her mouth as she poured milk into a steaming stainless steel pitcher. "I'm making a coconut-mushroom-infused latte with smoky vanilla and cardamom."

James bowed. "Okay, okay, folks. Let's all simmer

down. We're two drinks in and we've got mushrooms *and* avocados in the mix. Let's talk to our local boy, Andy."

Andy smiled.

"How do you feel being wedged in the middle of these top-notch competitors?" James held the microphone for Andy.

"I'm honored to be here."

"Awww. Did you hear that folks? I believe that's what you call humble."

Everyone let out a small collective "Awww."

"Does your signature drink involve mushrooms or avocados?"

Andy shook his head. "Nope. I'm going for a hot honey latte."

"Hot honey. Nice." James leaned over Andy's shoulder for a better look as Andy drizzled honey into the bottom of a ceramic coffee mug. He had warmed the honey for thirty seconds before adding it to the cup. I had memorized every step of Andy's process after watching him create the drink at least three dozen times at the bakeshop.

Diaz smirked. "Sounds like a grandma drink," he goaded Andy.

Andy had the perfect retort. "Actually, my grandma's in the front row and this drink is for her. She's my inspiration for this drink and the reason I'm competing in the Barista Cup." He waved to June, who blew him kisses as the crowd let out another "Awww" of approval.

James moved on to interview the other three contestants. One was making a strawberry latte, the other a red velvet mocha, and the last an herb inspired latte with rosemary and thyme.

Minutes later the final buzzer sounded and the round was over. The camera crew zoomed in for close-up shots of all the drinks. The strawberry latte was a beautiful pale pink with the outline of a strawberry in the foam. Diaz had hollowed out avocado shells. Rather than serving his drink in a mug, he had poured it into the shells. Andy's drink looked elegant with its dusting of chocolate shavings and flaked sea salt.

The volunteers served each sensory judge. Unlike in the first two rounds, each judge would share their thoughts about the drinks with the audience in real time.

Diaz was up first.

Benson looked at the avocado shell. "Am I supposed to drink out of this?"

"Yep. That's part of the sensory experience," Diaz replied, not sounding the slightest bit fazed by Benson's intense stare.

"How interesting." Benson lifted the avocado to his lips, closed his eyes, and tasted the drink. "Hmm. I'm getting touches of the sweetness of the avocado followed by that heat on the back of my tongue. Not bad. Not bad, but it's quite thick isn't it? And I don't want to be served in a discarded shell. I'm definitely docking you points for aesthetics."

Diaz shrugged.

Did nothing get to him?

The judges were unanimous in their critique of the red velvet latte—claiming it was cloyingly sweet.

Benson removed his glasses, squinting at the barista. "You call this coffee? This is a gut-bomb. This is liquid dessert. It doesn't deserve to be called coffee. How dare you offend my palate with this."

The crowd winced with the barista at Benson's caustic words.

The judges were split on the strawberry latte. Not surprisingly, Benson wasn't a fan.

"If I wanted a strawberry milkshake, I would order a strawberry milkshake. Where's the coffee in this? I'm not getting anything. This is a drink for a little girl in pink pigtails at the playground. Don't you dare call this coffee."

The reviews were mixed for the herbed latte as well. One judge called it "cutting edge." Benson, not surprisingly, deemed it a "coffee not even wild deer would stop to savor."

They moved on to Sammy's drink, and the reviews were gushing. Even Benson fawned over her creativity. "Mark my words, you're going to see mushrooms on the menu at every coffee shop in the county soon. This is brilliant. Nothing short of brilliant. Too bad you shot yourself in the foot in the first two rounds."

Sammy pouted.

Andy's drink was the last to be judged. Mom clasped her hand around mine as the first two judges praised his latte. They had wonderful things to say about his depth of flavor, the heat from the honey, and his latte art.

That changed once Benson picked up his cup. Like he had with the other drinks, he closed his eyes and took a sip. To my horror, he spit Andy's drink out.

Everyone gasped.

June clasped her hands around her bundle of yarn.

Mom clutched my hand tighter. "Oh no."

"This is vile! Foul." Benson's tongue hung from his

mouth. He fumbled for his water glass and waved to James. "I need a palate cleanser—stat."

James went to fill a fresh glass of water for him.

"How could he hate Andy's drink that much?" I asked Mom.

"I have no idea. The other judges loved it. Maybe it's not his favorite, but to spit it out?" Her eyes drifted to Andy, who hung his head.

"What did you put in this?" Benson repeatedly ran his tongue from side to side as if trying to rid his palate of the taste. He swished water in his mouth, spit it out, and did it again.

Andy rattled off the list of ingredients.

Benson wagged a finger at him. "Son, you're missing something. You made a grave mistake. A fatal error. There's at least a quarter cup of salt in this drink. Do you want to come taste for yourself?"

"No. That's not possible," Andy protested. "I added a tiny touch of flaked sea salt. That's it."

"You have a heavy hand with the salting, kid. This tastes like sea water. It's completely undrinkable."

Andy looked stunned.

James handed Benson the glass of water. "Folks, we'll take a quick break to tally up the scores and be back to announce who will be competing in the finals tomorrow."

Andy approached the judges' table. He said to something to Benson, and then picked up his drink.

"Is he tasting it?" Mom asked.

"I think so."

We watched as Andy tasted his signature latte and then, like Benson, spit it out.

Chapter Seven

My mouth hung open. I blinked twice. Had my eyes deceived me? It looked like Andy had spit out his own coffee, but that couldn't be right.

"Did you see that?" Sterling asked. He looked as shocked as I felt.

"Why would Andy do that?" Bethany wrapped a strand of her bouncy curls around her finger.

"I have no idea." June's serene face wrinkled in bewilderment. "That's so unlike him."

Andy took another sip and gagged it down.

There must be something wrong with his coffee.

He massaged his temples as Benson shouted at him. "You should be automatically disqualified for serving me this filth. You've fried my taste buds with this salt travesty. I might have to sue you."

The other two judges stepped in to defend Andy. One of them offered her drink for Benson to taste. He refused. She handed it to Andy.

We watched as Andy sampled the drink. He nodded emphatically after he tasted it. "This is what I served you, sir. Please try it."

Benson folded his arms across his chest. "I've already tasted and scored your drink. Nothing is going to change that. No amount of begging is going to persuade me to put that to my lips again."

"But, someone must have sabotaged my drink," Andy protested. "The other two samples are perfect."

"Sabotage?" Benson threw his head back and laughed. "Please, kid. You got distracted. That's what this competition does to people. It rattles your nerves. You weren't focused. You dumped a handful of salt in instead of a dusting. I've seen it again and again. You can't handle the pressure. This is the West Coast Barista Cup. This is where we separate the men from the boys. I've watched you sweat your way through each round. I'm not at all surprised this happened."

Andy looked crushed. He hung his head and shuffled back to his station to await his fate.

"Sorry," I mouthed to him.

He threw his hands up in disbelief.

James returned to the mic with the results. "Well folks, I warned you that things might heat up, and they sure did. I have the results of who is going through to the final rounds tomorrow. As the competition gets tighter, this gets harder and harder as we lose one contestant after another."

Andy buried his face in his hands.

"Poor Andy, he worked so hard for this." Bethany sounded heartbroken.

"In last place . . . I hate this part." James paused.

I didn't get the sense that he did hate it. He seemed like he was enjoying the spotlight and watching the contestants squirm.

"We are saying goodbye to a competitor who quickly won the hearts of our fans. His drinks were solid and steady, but unfortunately the judges agreed that his signature drink had some fatal flaws."

"It's Andy," Bethany said, fighting back tears.

I couldn't argue. It sounded like Andy's time in the competition was about to be done. I knew he wouldn't be ready to hear this anytime soon, but he could compete again next year. Making it through the third round on his first try was something he should be proud of.

"This was a squeaker, folks. Only one point separated fifth and sixth place, which tells us how great these baristas are. In the end it was red velvet that did him in. Cake in a cup did not resonate with our judges. Let's give it up for our barista leaving the competition."

"He's in! He's in!" Bethany clasped her hands together and grinned.

I couldn't believe it.

Andy glanced around him like he hadn't heard correctly.

"In fifth place, our local boy, Andy, made it through in a nail-biter."

We all looked to one another in stunned silence.

The barista who made the herbed latte landed in fourth, while the strawberry latte took third. Sammy was second, and Diaz maintained his position at the top. James gave everyone a brief overview of the rundown for tomorrow and encouraged us to peruse the vendor booths on our way out. The crowd dispersed.

We went to check in with Andy. Sterling embraced him in a man hug. Bethany kissed him on the cheek and made him pose for photos with his grandmother.

"You two are the cutest," she gushed, urging June and Andy to hug. "Everyone on social is going to eat this up."

Mom pressed her hands together. "I knew you could do it."

"Me too," I added. "See? All that sweat and worry for nothing."

"Not nothing." Andy shook his head. "You saw Benson spit out my drink, right?"

"It would have been hard to miss," Mom said, staring at the judges' table where Benson and Piper were arguing.

"What happened?" I asked.

Andy sighed. "I have no idea. I know for a fact that it wasn't because I was rattled or nervous like he said. I mean, yeah, I've been hyped for the competition, and I've been nervous, but not to the point that I would have mistakenly dumped a bunch of salt into my latte. No way. I told them that."

"Was it really bad?" Bethany bit her bottom lip.

"It was horrible." Andy shuddered. "Like, seriously undrinkable. Benson wasn't exaggerating, there must have been a few tablespoons of salt in there. I don't understand how. I made all three drinks in specific order. I warmed the spicy honey, then added some to each mug. I poured in shots of espresso, added the steamed milk, and finished them with chocolate shavings and flaked sea salt. There's no way I could have added that much salt. You guys saw me, right?" Andy picked up a ramekin with the flaked salt and demonstrated. "I did this. I literally sprinkled a few flakes on each drink."

"And you don't think Benson was showboating for attention?" I asked.

"No," Andy was adamant. "I tasted it. It was terrible. He wasn't exaggerating. I could barely swallow down a sip without throwing up."

"Did you get a good look at your mugs before you started pulling shots?" I asked.

Andy wrinkled his brow. "Why?"

I paused and looked to Diaz and Sammy, who were waiting for a word with the judges. "Do you think someone could have added the salt?"

"Yeah. Thank you for saying that, boss." Andy reached out to June for comfort. She rubbed his shoulder in sweet gesture of solidarity. "That's exactly what I've been thinking, but I was wondering if I was making myself crazy."

"Who would do something like that?" Mom asked.

"Diaz? Sammy? One of the other competitors?"

"Yeah, but why? I wasn't even in the lead. It doesn't make sense." Andy ran his fingers though his shaggy hair. "I think I would have noticed a bunch of salt in the bottom of one of the mugs."

"Would you?" I pressed. Benson could have a valid point. Andy was nervous. I didn't believe that he would have dumped that much salt into his latte, but could he have missed that there was flaky salt already in one of his mugs? That was more probable.

He scratched his head. "I mean, I think so. I guess it's a possibility. I was concentrating on timing my shots. I warmed the honey so it was thin and easy to incorporate into the milk. I guess I didn't spend much time assessing the mugs." He trailed off.

"Well, the good news is that you made it through."
As always, Mom shifted to the positive outcome. "To-morrow is a brand-new day and you'll wow them."

Andy forced a smile. "Thanks, Mrs. C." He stopped
and shook his head. "Old habits. Mrs. The Professor."

Mom winked.

"Do you have stuff to do tonight?" Sterling asked.
"Bethany and I were wondering if you wanted to grab
hamburgers? Steph said she could meet us at the Burger
Shack."

Andy looked to June.

Her eyes drifted to Bethany then back to him. "You
kids go have fun. I'm heading home. Thank you for such
a delightful day. You know you are always a winner in
my book." She patted his arm and left.

Andy blushed. "Yeah, burgers sound good. That
would be cool. Can you give me five minutes?"

"Sure. We were going to go check out the vendors
anyway."

Sterling, Bethany, and Mom headed for the foyer. I
hung back. "Is everything okay? Is there anything I can
do?"

Andy curled his hands into fists and then straightened
them. "If you're right, Jules, I want another shot. I want
to make my signature drink for Benson."

"But you're already through to the next round."

"Barely. The only reason I'm through is because I got
high marks from the two other judges. Benson gave me
a zero. A zero. That stings. I saw the score sheets. The
barista who made the red velvet latte scored a ninety-seven. I scored a ninety-eight. The only thing that saved
me was that none of them liked his drink. It was way

too sweet. Although was it? Maybe someone snuck a bunch of sugar into his drink."

"So what's your plan?"

"I'm going to make another drink for Benson. I want him to know what I'm capable of. I don't want to go into tomorrow with a zero." Andy brushed the dirt I'd seen earlier from the edge of his table.

"Do you think he'll go for that?"

Andy reached for a paper to-go cup. "There's only one way to find out." He began prepping another hot honey latte.

I left him to it. I wanted to warn him that I doubted Benson would be willing to give his signature drink another try, but he was right. He didn't have anything to lose. As I went to meet up with Mom and the team, I took one last look at Diaz and Sammy. Could one of them have intentionally ruined Andy's drink to ensure he wouldn't go through to the finals? I hated to suspect them, but it was the only logical explanation.

Chapter Eight

Mom and I spent some time exploring the vendor booths. There was a considerable showing of the latest coffee trends from equipment to independent coffee roasters as well as artisans who provided every accoutrement imaginable for coffee production and shops.

"It might be time to up our coffee game." Mom studied a pour-over coffeemaker and a porcelain coffee filter.

Even with the theatrics of the competition, attending the event made me think that we needed to work more trade shows into our future. It was critical to stay on the forefront of the industry. In fact, setting coffee trends was in Torte's DNA. When my parents opened the bakeshop back in the eighties, Torte had the first espresso machine in the Rogue Valley. Coffee had evolved at a breakneck pace over the last few decades, and I didn't want to get left behind.

"Maybe we need to budget to send Andy to more events like this."

Mom sampled a taster of macadamia nut milk. "You read my mind." I studied a refresh system that dispensed purified, sparkling, chilled water.

My phone vibrated. I removed it from my purse to see a string of texts from Carlos.

A BIG GROUP JUST ARRIVED. OKAY IF I SERVE THEM?

OF COURSE. I'LL GET A RIDE WITH MOM. MEET YOU AT TORTE IN JUST A BIT.

He answered with three heart emojis.

I knew that Carlos would never turn down an opportunity to serve guests. Service was in his blood. Much like Andy's speech to the judges, Carlos believed that sharing wine, food, and coffee was his life's mission. I couldn't picture him sending potential wine tasters away without offering them an opportunity to linger in the vineyard and regale them with his wine knowledge.

After the whirlwind of the competition, I wanted to check in at the bakeshop and clear my mind by kneading some dough or whipping up a batch of peanut butter brownies.

"Are you ready?" Mom asked. Her arms were loaded with samples of dark chocolate, pretty little packets of lavender latte instant coffee, and barrel-aged bourbon coffee beans.

"Let me help you." I took some of the items off her hands as we exited the hotel.

On our way to her car, I spotted Benson getting into a ride-share.

"Mom, look." I grabbed her arm and pointed to Benson. He was holding a paper coffee cup in his hand. "I wonder if that's Andy's drink? Maybe Andy was able to convince him to give him a second shot after all."

"If anyone could do it, it's Andy." Mom smiled. "How could you say no to his sincere face?"

I felt relieved. If Benson tasted Andy's drink without a handful of salt, I knew that he would love it.

Mom dropped me at Torte before going to meet the Professor for dinner. "We're meeting Thomas and Kerry tonight. They want some suggestions on their wedding plans." She glanced at A Rose by Any Other Name, which sat adjacent to the bakeshop. "Do you happen to know anything about Kerry's family?"

Thomas was my childhood friend. We had grown up together and dated through high school. Things ended between us when I left for culinary school, but when I had returned home to Ashland we had rekindled our friendship. At first, I had been worried that Thomas still had feelings for me. That changed when Detective Kerry arrived in town. Thomas had fallen for her—hard. They had recently gotten engaged, and I loved seeing Thomas so happy.

"No. Why?"

Mom frowned. "I don't know. I can't put my finger on it exactly. It's just a feeling. Doug doesn't know anything about her family or her past. When he asked about her parents—if they were coming to the wedding, that sort of thing—she got quiet. She said she doubted it, but didn't elaborate."

Kerry wasn't the most forthcoming person. In fact, when the Professor had hired her, I wasn't sure that her steely exterior was going to be a match for our warm and vibrant community. With time, I had come to have more appreciation for her less effusive style, and to understand that the walls she put up were protection. Thomas had found a way to break down some of those walls. Could part of Kerry's reserved nature be due to her past?

Come to think of it, I had never heard her speak of family or friends.

"I told Doug that I want to take her under my wing," Mom continued. "Can you imagine getting married without people who love you to stand up for you and support you? Doug and I want Thomas and Kerry to know that we will fill those roles for them."

"That's so sweet, Mom. I'm sure that Kerry will appreciate the offer."

Mom waved to an elderly couple sharing a malted shake at one of Torte's picnic tables. "I hope so, and I hope she'll feel comfortable sharing if she needs someone to talk to."

"Well, like you said about Andy, if anyone can put Kerry at ease, it's you." I kissed her cheek and hopped out of the car. "Say hi to everyone for me. See you at the competition tomorrow?"

"I wouldn't miss it for the world." Mom smiled as I got out of the car.

I had to stop for a minute and take in the bucolic sight of the plaza. Tourists meandered between the shops, their arms loaded with bags. Kids on scooters zoomed past me on their way to Lithia Park. A group of teenagers sat near the fountain in the center of the plaza, strumming on guitars. Two monarch butterflies fluttered between the potted Japanese maple trees in front of the bakeshop.

The only eyesore was the Merry Windsor Hotel, which sat on the far end of the plaza. Its fake Elizabethan façade and bellhops flanking the front entrance wearing pantaloons and puffy shirts tried to give guests the appearance of elegance. However, I knew that inside, the hotel was in dire need of updating with its green shag carpets and dated décor.

Just my luck. Richard Lord stood next to his ice-cream cart, peddling his wares like a snake oil salesman. He caught my eye and bellowed, "Juliet Capshaw, I want a word with you!"

Before I could duck into the bakeshop, he lumbered toward me. Richard was either an avid golfer or simply fully committed to bad fashion choices. I couldn't recall ever seeing him in anything other than ill-fitting golf attire. Today he wore a pair of aqua blue shorts with a shark pattern. His neon blue collared shirt had a similar collection of shark teeth. He completed the ensemble with sandals and black ankle-length socks.

"Not so fast, missy." Richard spat as he spoke. "You've been avoiding me for days."

"How have I been avoiding you?" I stepped away from his spray.

"You're jealous that my ice-cream cart is doing so well. Admit it." He shot a glance behind us at the streetside stand, aptly named Shakes' Screams, which in my opinion perfectly captured Richard's tacky approach to all things Shakespeare. The cart was designed to resemble an Italian gelato stand, except instead of red-and-white-striped awnings above the two-wheeled cart, Richard had opted for a brown and white Tudor-pattern canopy.

"I'm happy to hear that your new venture is a success." I plastered on a smile.

"Don't toy with me, Juliet. I know that you can't stand the fact that Shakes' Screams is seeing so much success. Look at the line over there now. What, did you and your mother think you were going to have a monopoly on ice cream in town? Sorry to prove you wrong."

"I never suggested we did." I shifted my body position, inching closer to the door. "Did you need something?"

Not only was Richard notorious for his outrageous golf outfits, he was also known for long, lengthy outbursts on his preconceived imaginary grievances.

"Yeah, I have a bone to pick with you." He wagged his finger in my face. "It's about Brady."

"What about him?" Brady had been hired to take over as head chef at the Merry Windsor after the hotel's previous chef had met an unfortunate and untimely death. Actually, to refer to any of the Windsor's kitchen staff as "chefs" was very generous. Brady was by far the best employee Richard had been lucky enough to land. I had taken him under my wing and given him some quick tips and easy recipes to implement at the hotel, not because of Richard but out of loyalty to Lance.

Lance was the artistic director for the Oregon Shakespeare Festival and beloved by the community not only for his visionary talent but also because he had a penchant for drama and for drawing everyone into his world.

"You've gotten into his head. He keeps insisting that his food budget isn't big enough. He wants to purchase produce at the farmers market. That's ridiculous. I told him that the Merry Windsor has had valued relationships with our regional distributors for decades. Being the incredible businessman that I am, I have negotiated the lowest rates around and I don't need you putting these crazy hippie ideas in his head, got it?"

I wanted to ask Richard how procuring locally sourced products and supporting family farms was a hippie idea, but I didn't have time to debate with him. "Noted. I'll be sure to recommend that Brady continue to order inexpensive, low-quality items from your distributor."

"Good." Richard gave me a gruff nod. Then he must have realized my meaning. "Hey, I don't buy low-quality items. We serve only the best at the Merry Windsor, and don't you forget that."

"Never." I moved even closer to the door. "Gotta run, Richard. Nice chatting with you as always."

I didn't give him a chance to respond before yanking the handle and scurrying inside the bakeshop before he could get another word out.

Torte was nearly empty. Sequoia and Rosa were wiping down tables and the coffee bar. I gave them a quick recap of Andy's performance, including the gory details about Benson spitting out his drink. While they finished cleaning upstairs, I went down to check on the kitchen. Marty had scrubbed every square inch of counter space. Steph was boxing up an order of two dozen lemon blueberry cupcakes. Sterling had already filled them in about Andy's roller coaster of a day via text updates.

"So our boy did well, except for a run-in with some salt." Marty tossed a dish towel into the hamper.

"He was great." I twisted my hair into a ponytail. "We all felt terrible about how things ended, but I think he may have convinced Benson, the judge who spit out his drink, to give it another try."

"He did," Steph said. She tucked in the edges of

our white craft boxes with the teal and red Torte logo stamped on the top. "Sterling texted. He said that Andy managed to get his drink in Benson's hands on the way out the door."

"That's great news." I knew it wouldn't change the outcome of his fourth-place finish, but I hoped that it would give him a confidence boost.

"I'm taking these across the street to city hall," Steph said, holding the box of cupcakes that had been frosted in a pale purple blueberry buttercream and topped with candied lemon slices. "Then I'm meeting everyone for burgers."

"Sounds good. Have fun. Make sure you give Andy a pep talk."

Steph snarled. "Yeah. You know me. I'm the pep-talk queen." Her darkly lined eyes gave the faintest hint of glimmer.

Marty chuckled as Steph left with the delivery box. "She puts on a tough face, but you know she's going to be cheering the loudest for him tomorrow."

"In her Steph way—yes. If that means internally screaming and externally acting as if she couldn't care less."

Marty reached for a bag of bread. "Yep. That sums up our Steph." His tone turned serious for a moment. "I can't thank you enough for giving me this job. I didn't realize how much I needed it. These young kids have breathed new life into me. It doesn't take away my sadness, but it sure is nice to be connected, so thank you." His voice cracked.

"Thank *you*, Marty." I placed my hand on my heart.

"You offer such wise guidance to our team. Everyone loves you." It was true. Marty's wife had died a few years ago, and I felt lucky that he had decided to come out of retirement. He was a grounding force in the kitchen and a fabulous role model for our young staff.

"What's on your agenda tonight?" I asked, moving to the sink and regretting that I hadn't thought to bring a pair of comfortable shoes to change into.

He patted the bread. "I'm making bruschetta for my neighborhood potluck."

"How fun. Your neighborhood has a potluck?" I took off my sweater and hung it on the rack with the aprons.

"It's a new thing. One of the women on my block thought it would be a way for us to get to know each other better. Nothing says 'get to know you' like bruschetta." Marty grinned.

"I will not argue with that." I returned his smile. "Have fun."

"You too. See you tomorrow." He headed for the back stairs.

I took a minute to soak in the quiet of the bakeshop. Marty's bruschetta had given me an idea. I would make a panzanella salad with fresh herbs and mozzarella for Carlos and me. I started by slicing a loaf of day-old bread into squares. Then I tossed the bread with olive oil and balsamic vinegar. I diced heirloom tomatoes, onions, garlic, and basil and mixed them in with the bread. Then I finished the salad with big chunks of mozzarella. The salad would be best after the flavors had time to mingle and permeate the bread. I set it aside and removed a pork loin from the walk-in fridge.

I massaged the tender meat with salt, pepper, olive oil, and more balsamic. Then I butterflied the meat, bundled some herbs with baker's twine, and placed it all in the center. I preheated the oven and set the roast to bake on low for an hour. The panzanella salad would pair well with the herbed roast. Now I needed something for dessert.

I checked our stock of concretes. There were tubs of ricotta with burnt sugar, dark chocolate with fresh mint, basil lime, horchata rum, banana pudding, caramel praline, and the current summer favorite—strawberry custard. Since strawberries were currently in season, Sterling had made a double batch of the strawberry custard concrete. I decided to make a twist on a classic strawberry shortcake with the rich and velvety ice cream.

I started making the shortcakes by combining butter, flour, and salt in a mixer. Then I added baking soda, sugar, and a splash of heavy cream and let the mixer do the heavy lifting. Once a dough had formed, I spread the batter into an eight-by-eight pan and slid it into the oven to bake for twenty minutes. Next, I sliced fresh strawberries and combined them with lemon juice and sugar. I would leave them to macerate while the shortcakes baked.

Soon the aroma of buttery shortcake filled the kitchen. One piece of advice I always offered new bakers was to trust their senses, especially when it came to smell. Most breads and baked goods emitted a wonderful scent when they were done. The artistry of baking relied on connecting to our sight, smell, taste, and feeling. A light finger tap in the center of a cake could easily tell me its doneness, as could a pie's bubbling juices, and a bread's fragrant aroma.

I checked the shortbread. It had risen nicely, with firm edges and a set center. I removed it from the oven and allowed it to cool. When it was time for dessert, I would assemble the shortcakes, layering the golden biscuits with strawberries and strawberry concrete.

Carlos arrived as I was taking the pork loin out of the oven. "Mi querida, what smells so wonderful? You have been cooking, si?"

"Si." I showed him our dinner. "Shall we plate up and go sit on the Calle next to Ashland Creek?"

"But of course. I want to hear about today and Andy." Carlos poured us glasses of wine, while I sliced the juicy pork loin and added generous scoops of the panzanella to our plates. We took our dinner outside to a creek-side table. Torte sits on the Calle Guanajuato, a cobblestone pathway running parallel to the creek. Most restaurants on the plaza had outdoor seating in the back. Dining on the Calle reminded me of Paris with its brightly colored bistro tables, a canopy of conifer trees, and the heady scents of climbing roses and wisteria.

As I took a seat at one of Torte's two-person tables, I spotted Mom, the Professor, Thomas, and Kerry dining al fresco at Puck's Pub not far down the pathway. They appeared to be in a deep conversation, I assumed about their upcoming wedding plans. I didn't want to interrupt them.

Carlos swirled his wine as I relayed the day's events. It was hard not to stare at him. He had rolled up the sleeves on his crisp white button-down shirt, revealing his naturally tanned arms. Hours spent tending to the vines had left his skin sun-kissed.

"This judge, he sounds like a terrible person. Who would take such pleasure in making Andy, or any of the competitors sweat? I am glad that I was not there. I would have had words with this Benson."

That I didn't doubt. Carlos wasn't confrontational in nature, but he was a champion of the underdog. If he saw an injustice in the world, he had to say something. Perhaps it was his Spanish upbringing. He was confident in both who he was in the kitchen and in the world.

"I think this man has no confidence himself. This is why he must put down others. I do not understand why the organizers allow it."

Before I could agree and elaborate on how odd I found the entire competition and Benson's role as a judge and organizer himself, a commotion broke out down the Calle. The crackling sound of walkie-talkies and the sight of Thomas, Kerry, and the Professor pushing back their chairs in unison and getting to their feet made Carlos stop talking.

In a blur, the police team raced past us.

Thomas held his walkie-talkie in his hand as he ran. "We are in route and responding!"

"What is this?" Carlos asked.

"No idea." I shrugged, trying to make eye contact with Mom who had gotten up from the table and was speaking to a waiter. After a minute she caught my eye, nodded, and came toward us.

"What happened?" I asked, hearing sirens erupt on the plaza.

"Benson." Mom looked stunned. "The call just came in from dispatch."

"What about Benson?" I asked.

Her walnut eyes were wide with disbelief. "He's dead."

Chapter Nine

How could that be?

"Mom, did you say that Benson is dead?"

She let out a sigh. Her lips parted as she nodded again and again in disbelief, as if trying to make sense of it herself. "Yes. He's dead. They found him in the back seat of the car he'd called for dinner."

"Is it wrong to say that I am not that sad after everything you have told me about this man?" Carlos scowled. "Sorry, that was not kind of me. Of course I do not want anyone to come to harm, but Julieta was just explaining how awful he has been to Andy. This is terrible."

Benson was dead. I couldn't believe it.

"That must mean they think it's murder?" I asked. My mind was already spinning with possibilities.

Carlos wrinkled his brow. "Why do you say that?"

"Doug and his team get called to the scene of any unnatural death," Mom answered. "It's his role to determine if an investigation needs to be opened, but I think what Juliet means is that if the call had been for a heart attack or something similar, Doug wouldn't have been summoned to the scene."

"Ah, si." Carlos nodded.

Had Benson died of natural causes or could someone have killed him? He had certainly amassed a growing list of enemies at the Barista Cup.

"Do they know anything more yet?" I asked Mom.

"No. You know everything I heard from Doug." Her voice sounded strained.

"Helen, please sit." Carlos held the wine bottle. "Would you like a glass?"

Mom glanced down the cobblestone path to the table she had abandoned. "That would be nice. I already asked the waiter to box up our meals. Let me go get them and settle the bill. Then I'll join you."

"Julieta, what is it?" Carlos asked. He had moved next to me so that our shoulders touched.

"Huh?"

"You are thinking something. I can see it in your eyes."

He had always been able to read my thoughts.

"I'm wondering if Benson's death could be connected to the competition. It seems like a strange coincidence, don't you think?"

Carlos shrugged. "I do not know. This will be up to the Professor to determine, but do not worry. It will be okay and it is probably better for Andy that this man will not be at the competition tomorrow." He massaged the back of my neck, flooding my body with a rush of calming energy.

If the competition even continues, I thought.

Mom returned with her half-eaten dinner and three to-go boxes. Carlos poured her a glass of wine. We talked about Uva. Carlos told her about his plans for a dinner in the vines. We tried to keep the conversation light, but I could tell that none of us were fully present. The sun sank behind the mountains. Waitstaff came outside to light votive candles and offer guests hot Irish coffees and blankets to warm their legs. I enjoyed June's cool evening breezes, but many tourists who visited Ashland were used to climates with warmer evening temperatures back home.

We polished off the bottle of wine. I took our dinner dishes into the kitchen and plated three servings of strawberry shortcake. Mom and Carlos devoured the dessert. The berries were ripe and juicy and Sterling's concrete was like tasting strawberries plucked fresh from the vine.

The dinner crowd on the Calle dispersed for the evening shows at OSF. We lingered over dessert and coffee, listening to the calming sounds of Ashland Creek and watching bats swoop above our heads snatching mosquitoes from the sky.

The Professor returned as the antique streetlamps came on, illuminating the cobblestone pathway with soft glowing halos of light. "Sorry to have left you stranded, my dear." He kissed Mom on the top of the head. He wore a lightweight sport coat and pair of khaki slacks.

"Don't give it a thought." She waved him off. "I had the better end of the deal. I've been drinking wine and eating Juliet's delicious strawberry shortcake."

"Can I get you a slice?" I asked.

He looked at the stack of to-go boxes. "Actually, I'm quite famished. I think I'll finish my dinner."

"Would you like a glass of wine with that?" Carlos offered. "I can open another bottle."

"No, no. Water will be fine." He nodded to the pitcher on the table.

Mom poured him a glass.

The Professor reached for her hand, clutching it like a crutch. "'From women's eyes this doctrine I derive: They sparkle still the right Promethean fire; They are the books, the arts, the academes, That show, contain, and nourish all the world.' Oh my dearest, Helen, what comfort and grounding I find in your gentle caress."

Mom massaged his hand. "Was it bad?"

He sighed. "Bearing witness to death is never something I take lightly, but I fear that it's becoming more and more difficult."

"This is understandable." Carlos exhaled deeply, shaking his head. "This work that you do, it is not for the weakhearted."

The Professor gave him a half smile.

"Do you have any idea what happened to Benson?" I asked.

"The medical examiner is quite sure that some sort of substance was involved. She'll be doing a formal autopsy, but we are in agreement that his death is unlikely to be from natural causes. The question will be whether Benson accidentally overdosed on something—be that prescription medication or illegal drugs—or whether he ingested something intentionally put into his food or drink. He was found with a coffee cup in the back of the car. We'll be examining the contents of the cup."

My stomach dropped. "Oh no."

"What is it, Juliet?" Mom asked. "Your face just went white."

"Andy. He gave Benson a cup of coffee right as we

were leaving, remember? You don't think that could have been Andy's drink?"

"Why would you assume that?" The Professor studied me.

"Did Mom tell you what happened at the competition?" I swatted at a mosquito that landed on my wrist.

He shook his head. "No. We met Thomas and Kerry for dinner and the conversation was focused on their wedding plans."

I gave him a condensed version of the day's events. "Andy made Benson another version of his signature hot honey latte after the competition was over. He was distraught that his first drink had been ruined. He wanted another chance to impress Benson. What if whoever added salt to his first drink slipped something into that one too?"

The Professor paused and removed a Moleskin notebook from the breast pocket of his linen shirt. He made a note. "Do you know when this was?"

"Mom and I left a little before five, right?" I looked to Mom for confirmation.

She nodded.

"You'll have to ask Andy, but it was around then."

"Excellent. I'll have a conversation with him first thing in the morning." He started to put the notebook away then changed his mind. "You mentioned that you believe someone tampered with Andy's drink. Can you elaborate more on that? Did you see anything suspicious? What about the other contestants?" He addressed both Mom and me. Carlos snuck off to get the Professor a slice of my strawberry shortcake.

"I did notice Diaz at Andy's station when I came back

from lunch." I explained that Diaz had quickly returned to his spot when he saw me.

"You know, come to think of it I saw Sammy, one of the other contestants, talking to Andy at his station right before the third round," Mom added. "She had one arm behind her back the entire time they were talking, which I thought was odd."

"Really?" I asked. "I missed that."

"You were talking with Bethany. She was taking thousands of photos. You know how she gets when it comes to posing the perfect picture." Mom squinted, as if trying to recall the scene. "I thought it was strange, because Sammy had been quite aloof when it came to interacting with any of the other baristas. She suddenly seemed interested in Andy's drinks, and kept fiddling with something behind her back."

The Professor cleared his throat. "Sammy was near Andy's coffees before they were delivered to the judges?"

"Yes, I'm sure of it. At the time I thought it was odd that she left her station. Actually, James—the MC— was there too. Did you see him leaning over Andy's shoulder when they were doing the close-ups?" Mom asked me.

"No." I shook my head. I was impressed that Mom had been so observant. Not that I had any reason to be surprised by that. She was naturally interested in people and a careful listener.

The Professor jotted down more notes. "Anything else you can add? Even if it doesn't seem monumental, you never know what might be important."

I thought back through the entire day as Carlos re-turned with a slice of shortcake and a cup of coffee for the Professor. "Oh, yeah, there was one other thing. I overheard James and Benson fighting. They were in the hallway and James kept saying, 'I'm not going to let you get away with this again.' I asked James about it and he brushed me off."

"Interesting." The Professor tucked away his notebook and took a bite of the shortcake. "Thank you, my most beloved women. This gives me a starting point for tomorrow. I'm much obliged."

We lingered a bit longer while the Professor finished his dessert. I was exhausted. The stress of the competition and Benson's death had caught up with me.

"Mi querida, let's go home. You cannot keep your eyes open." Carlos stood up and helped me to my feet.

I didn't bother to protest. Nothing sounded better than our comfortable bed at the moment. I wasn't sure what had happened with Benson, but I was pretty convinced that his death wasn't an accident. I needed a good night of sleep because, come morning, I intended to put every effort into making sure that my lead barista wasn't tied to his murder.

Chapter Ten

The next morning, I headed straight for Torte, leaving Carlos snoozing under the covers and ignoring the fact that not even the birds were awake yet.

To my surprise, Mom was already in the kitchen and had made a pot of coffee and a tray of sticky buns.

"You're here early," I noted, washing my hands and tying on an apron.

"Doug couldn't sleep. He was up most of the night researching the case on the computer. I kept seeing the glow of the blue screen in the hallway, and finally got up a little before four to ask him if he wanted to come into town. There's only so much he can do from his laptop at home, and when he's on a case like this, he always says that the first forty-eight hours are critical." She used a spatula to remove a glistening bun drizzled with caramel and walnuts from the tray. "Is everyone coming in this morning?"

"Yes. The events don't start until eleven, so Andy should be here in a half hour or so."

Mom handed me a plate with one of the rolls. "Coffee?" She held the pot.

"As if you need to ask."

She poured us both a cup.

"How is Doug feeling this morning? He seemed pretty shaken last night."

"I know. I'm worried about him." She twisted her wedding band. "Seeing death close up takes a toll. He's been trying to scale back, giving Thomas and Kerry more responsibility. We talked about it last night. He doesn't want to officially retire until after the wedding. He doesn't think it's fair to do that to them. They have a lot to focus on with planning a wedding, but he did promise that once the wedding is done and they're back from their honeymoon he's going to pull back."

"What does 'pull back' mean?" I took a bite of the morning bun. The yeast roll was springy and light. The caramel sauce and toasted walnuts gave it a gooey sweetness with a nutty finish. It paired perfectly with the dark French roast.

"Doug says that he's ready to retire, and I know that cases like this are becoming harder and harder for him. But I also think he might—no—he *will*—go stir-crazy being at home full time. Plus, we're spring chickens. Just because he *can* retire doesn't mean that he should. I think finding a balance is going to be the key for him. I suggested scaling back to two or three days a week. Ease into it. I know that working sixty-hour-plus weeks are wearing on him, but at the same time I think suddenly being at home twenty-four seven isn't the solution. Doug is a brilliant man, he's connected to the community, his mind thrives on puzzling through investigations. We're going to have to figure out a plan." Mom stretched her hands. She had developed mild arthritis from years and years of heavy lifting and kneading dough. Her doctor and physical therapist had suggested a stretching routine along with gentle yoga, walking, and water aerobics. It seemed to be working. However, she had a history of being less than forthcoming about her level of pain. I knew she didn't want me to worry about her. Our roles had slowly shifted over the last few years.

I felt the same way about her as she did about the Professor. I wanted her to take more time for herself and yet I knew that Torte was her happy place too.

"That's smart. Balance is a good goal." I stacked applewood in the pizza oven and started a fire.

"Thomas pulled me aside the other day and asked me to try and convince Doug to stick around in some capacity, even if it's consulting. He's worried that he and Kerry aren't ready to take over, but I tried to tell him no one is ever ready. We just have to dive into the deep end and start treading water sometimes."

"True." I thought back to my first days on the ship. Despite having graduated from culinary school, I had felt like I was diving into unknown waters when I had been thrown into the commercial kitchen, especially a large pastry kitchen at sea. I remember inching into the kitchen with my head half-down, and whispering my name to the head pastry chef, who immediately told me to square my shoulders, speak clearly, and hold on for dear life.

It had been good advice both literally and figuratively. Half the battle of working on a luxury cruise ship had been learning how to find a solid grip when the ship listed or we hit choppy seas. The other half had been learning how to trust my instincts when it came to baking. Pastry school may have taught me how to roll out layer after layer of buttery puff pastry dough or how to whip a light-as-air French chocolate soufflé, but the vast majority of my culinary skills had been honed from years of practice, fails and all.

"He might not know it yet, but Thomas is ready, so is Kerry. Doug has trained them well, whether they realized that or not. But most importantly they both care about our community. You can't ask for more than that—and as Doug says, you can't teach that. That piece of policing comes from the heart."

As Mom spoke a thought hit me that I had never considered before. "Who will take the lead?"

"What do you mean?" She chopped walnuts into fine pieces.

"Between Thomas and Kerry. One of them will take over the Professor's role at some point. I never thought about it, but I wonder if that could put a strain on their relationship?"

Mom considered my words. "I'm sure that Doug has accounted for that, and I think that when the time comes he'll work something out."

"I'm sure he will." I hadn't considered competing for a job with my husband. Fortunately Carlos and I had always managed different kitchens. We collaborated well together, but I never had to worry about him critiquing my technique for folding egg whites into a flourless chocolate almond cake or going after the same job. The pastry kitchen and the main kitchen were completely separate on the ship. We had our own staff, different hours, and unique challenges. Often we would sneak away for a late-night cocktail on the upper deck and swap stories about a sous chef who didn't realize that a fish skin must be dried before it goes into the sauté pan in order to achieve a beautiful crispiness, or a baker who had to be taught to crack eggs on the flat edge of the counter instead of on the rim of a bowl, where the eggs were more likely to break unevenly and end up in the bowl. However, we never had to answer to each other or provide anything other than support.

The thought gave me new appreciation for Thomas and Kerry's situation.

Andy arrived as I finished the last few bites of my sticky bun. "Good morning, Mrs. The Professor." He appeared to be in brighter spirits as he gave Mom a salute, and then turned to me. "Boss."

"Morning," Mom replied. "How are you feeling after the craziness of yesterday? I still can't get over how harsh the judging was. I told Juliet I was expecting the coffee version of the *Great British Baking Show*."

"Ha! I wish." Andy took off his baseball cap. "Sammy told me she wanted to murder Benson, and honestly I can't blame her. I had heard that he was arrogant, but I never expected anything like what happened yesterday."

Mom frowned. "Andy, you haven't seen Doug yet this morning, have you?"

"No why?" His eyes were lighter than they had been yesterday, but they were still puffy. "Is the police station even open yet?"

"No, but Doug is there. I'm guessing that means that you haven't heard the news?" Mom sounded concerned.

Andy scrunched his forehead. "What news?"

"It's about Benson." I said, stoking the fire in the pizza oven. The smoky aroma of applewood filled the kitchen.

"What about him? Is he dead or something?" Andy kidded.

"He *is* dead." I tried to keep my tone even. "And the Professor is sure that his death wasn't from natural causes."

Andy took a step away from us. "What? Wait, for real? Benson's dead? Are you pranking me?"

"No. He died last night. The Professor is coming over any minute to take your statement." I returned the iron fire poker to its hook.

"My statement?" Andy's brow creased more.

"It's standard procedure," Mom said. "And you may have been one of the last people to have contact with him."

"Me?" Andy pointed to his chest. "Why are you both acting weird? Is there something you're not telling me?"

I looked to Mom who gave me a half nod. "Andy, they found Benson dead in the back seat of an Uber. He had a coffee cup with him."

Andy's jaw dropped. "You think it was the latte I made him?"

"They don't know for sure. The Professor said that they were sending it to the lab to be analyzed."

As if on cue, the Professor appeared. He entered through the basement stairs. "Ah, how wonderful. You are exactly who I was hoping to find," he said to Andy.

"Hey, Professor." Andy didn't sound thrilled to see him. He took off his baseball cap and folded it in his palm.

"Shall we go have a chat?" The Professor ushered Andy over to the seating area attached to the kitchen.

"He can't think that Andy's involved, can he?" I asked Mom.

Mom stirred warm water and sugar with yeast. "Of course not, but he has to do his due diligence. He can't ignore procedure, and unfortunately there were hundreds of witnesses who saw Benson belittle Andy and spit out his coffee. You and I both know that Andy is one of the kindest people on the planet, but he has a very obvious motive for wanting to harm Benson."

"Right." I tried to concentrate on creaming butter and sugar for our cookie-dough base, but I couldn't stop staring at the couch where Andy and the Professor were talking. What were they saying? Had the Professor learned anything new?

I added eggs and a splash of vanilla. For our daily cookie specials we use the same base—a basic sugar cookie—and then add different ingredients. Today, I planned to add raspberries and white chocolate chips to one batch, chocolate and marshmallows to another, and oatmeal and raisins to the third. It was a quick and easy way to offer variety without having to spend hours mixing different recipes.

By the time I had dozens of cookies cooling on racks, Andy returned. The Professor asked to speak with Mom outside for a minute.

"How did it go?" I slid a giant six-inch raspberry white-chocolate cookie onto the rack.

"Not great. Not great at all." Andy rubbed his temples.

"What do you mean?"

"The Professor said he spoke with the lab and they

confirmed that Benson had my coffee. It was a honey latte and it was laced with sedatives."

"Sedatives?"

"Yeah, prescription strength." Andy's voice sounded distant. He scrunched his baseball cap in his hand. "It's bad. They think that's what killed him. He may have had underlying medical issues that exacerbated the issue, but that's why he died." I thought Andy might cry. "How did they get in the coffee, Jules? I didn't put them there. I don't even have sedatives. The Professor said they're going to have to search my house. I have to call my grandma and warn her. She's going to freak out when the police show up."

"Was anyone around when you made Benson's latte?"

"I don't remember." Andy sounded panicked. He ran his fingers through his hair. "I mean there were tons of people hanging around after the event, but I don't remember anyone right next to my station. I would have noticed if someone tried to touch the drink. I was super careful after the salt incident."

"I'm sure you were." I nodded.

Andy sighed. He flipped his baseball cap and put it on backward. "I'm going to go practice for the finals. Although who knows if they'll even happen now."

He went upstairs. I thought back to yesterday. While Andy had been making the latte, Diaz and Sammy were at the judges' table. Could one of them have slipped sedatives into the drink after Andy delivered it to Benson?

The Professor couldn't possibly consider Andy a suspect, could he? I refused to believe it. But Mom had a valid point. The Professor had to do his job. He couldn't simply write Andy off as a potential suspect just because he liked him.

Suddenly, Andy's status in the Barista Cup seemed secondary. If there was even the slightest chance that he was a suspect in the Professor's eyes, I knew that I had to do everything in my power to find the real killer and clear my young coffee protégé's name.

Chapter Eleven

The Professor interviewed Sterling and Bethany next. After he had taken their statements, he called me over. "Juliet, how are you fairing this morning?"

"Not well. You don't really think Andy could have been involved, do you?"

He strummed his fingers on the reddish gray stubble on his chin. "I'm following my heart's mission and the Bard's words: 'Love all, trust few, do wrong to none.'"

That didn't exactly answer my question.

He must have noticed I wasn't satisfied. "On a personal level, I do not believe that Andy spiked Benson's drink, but procedure must be followed." He paused. "It is unfortunate that Andy's coffee was the vessel for the murder weapon."

"So you're sure?"

"Indeed. I spoke with the coroner this morning and it has been confirmed. Benson was killed with an overdose of sedatives in the latte. They tested the remnants of the coffee. The evidence is conclusive, I'm afraid." His eyes traveled toward the wood and iron stairwell that led up to the dining room. For a moment I thought he was going to say more. Instead, he folded his hands and pressed his index fingers together. "The most imperative question for the moment is: How did the drug get in Benson's drink?"

"Could someone have slipped it into the cup without Andy noticing?" It seemed like a plausible explanation.

"Perhaps." The Professor didn't sound very convinced. "But, that's a highly unreliable method of murder. It's hard to imagine a killer leaving that up to chance. Andy could have made himself a drink. He could have handed that drink to dozens of other people. Unless we're talking about a serial killer hoping to kill at will, that doesn't appear to be the case in this investigation. And I have little doubt that Benson was the intended target."

"So you don't think there's any chance the drink was meant for Andy?" If nothing else that was a relief.

The Professor shook his head. "No. The one sure fact is that the drink contained a strong dose of sedatives. The coroner's report revealed some additional information that I'm not at liberty to share. My personal belief is that between the time Andy handed the drink to Benson and Benson entered the car, someone else added the sedatives. There's a possibility that the killer was aware of Benson's personal health history and knew that the sedatives would be fatal. There's also an equal chance that the sedatives were meant as a deterrent or warning of sorts without the intention to kill. My professional role is to prove or disprove every theory that comes across my desk. At this stage of the investigation, I can't, in good faith, dismiss any involvement on Andy's part without tangible evidence."

No wonder the Professor's tone was solemn and his face long. He had confirmed what I had feared—Andy was a suspect.

"I understand," I replied. "You might not be able to answer this, but it sounds like you suspect that Benson had other medical issues?"

"Unfortunately, I'm not at liberty to answer that." He sounded apologetic. "What I can say is that Benson had high levels of benzodiazepines in his system."

"What are those?"

"They are a class of sedatives typically prescribed for sleep and anxiety disorders." He removed a handkerchief from his pocket and dabbed his nose. "Allergies. I must admit that I've begun to wince at the stunning show of color right now. My senses embrace the beauty of summer's early blooms, that delicate yellow flush of St. John's Wort and the pink blossoms on the manzanita trees. But oh how my nose defies me." He folded the handkerchief and returned to the topic of Benson's murder. "What I can tell you is that we're pulling video surveillance footage from The Hills to see if we can piece together Benson's movements from when he left the ballroom to when he got into the car. We'll be interviewing the staff at the restaurant he patronized as well as the driver. We'll also be looking into whether anyone met him for dinner or interacted with him before his death."

"What does that mean for Andy?" I could hear his footsteps above us and the sound of coffee beans grinding.

"For the time being, nothing. He understands the severity of the situation and is fully cooperating. Not that

I expected anything less. I have no concerns about him being a flight risk."

"That's good." I let out a sigh. "What about the Barista Cup? Will it continue?"

"I'm on my way to The Hills now. Unless the organizers or James feel differently, we would prefer for today's events to continue as planned. It should provide an opportunity to watch some of our potential suspects in action, so to speak."

"Wait, does that mean that you have a suspect in mind already?"

"I have many." He lowered his voice. "I would like to beg a favor, if I might."

"Of course, anything."

"Your powers of observation are second to none. If it's not too much of an inconvenience, I'd ask that you observe today, specifically the competitors. Thomas, Kerry, and I will be watching and observing as well, but another set of eyes never hurts."

"Yes, absolutely. I'll be discreet and let you know if anything or anyone seems off."

"Much appreciated." He returned the handkerchief to his shirt pocket, then clasped his hands together. "I bid you adieu for the moment."

Once he left, I took a moment to collect my thoughts before going upstairs. This was not good news for Andy. He was already on edge from stress and exhaustion and now he was a suspect in a murder investigation. Observing the competitors would not be a problem. I would do anything to help my team. Andy was more than a barista, he was family. I couldn't sit idly by and do nothing.

With that resolve in mind, I took in a long breath and went upstairs. Sequoia had arrived as had Rosa and the rest of the team. Rows and rows of mini cream puffs, berry galettes, jam biscuits, and hazelnut-and-fig turnovers filled the glistening pastry case. Rosa tended to bunches of daisies on each of the tables in the dining room. A mix of classical and New Age music played softly overhead. I guessed that Sequoia had picked the selection. It matched the slow vibe of Sunday mornings.

Sundays tended to have an easy flow. We rarely had a long line waiting for their caffeine hit. Guests tended to arrive in waves. Usually the early exercisers, who stopped in for black coffee and egg-and-cheese puffs, showed up first. They were followed by the brunch crowd, who lingered over flat whites and shared plates. Last to arrive were college students, who never made an appearance for straight shots of caffeine until well after noon. I enjoyed the lazier rhythm of Sundays.

"How's everything going up here?" I asked Sequoia.

"Smooth and silky, just like my almond milk latte," she replied, pouring the creamy liquid into a steaming pitcher.

Andy was nowhere to be seen.

"Did Andy already leave?" I asked.

Rosa placed a vase of daisies next to the cash register. "Yes. He left with the Professor. He said to tell you he would see you at the competition."

"Got it." I glanced out the window and spotted Lance strolling across the plaza in our direction. Lance had become my closest confidant and friend over the last few years. As the Oregon Shakespeare Festival's artistic director, he had a pulse on everything happening around town and an uncanny ability for getting the latest scoop on gossip. Had he already heard about Benson?

I met him at the front door. As usual, Lance's outfit was meticulous. He wore a pair of slim gray slacks with a short-sleeve houndstooth shirt and a skinny black tie.

"Darling, don't you look absolutely ravishing this morning." He greeted me with a kiss on each cheek.

I glanced at my khaki shorts and simple gray-and-white-striped T-shirt, my typical bakeshop attire. "I think ravishing might be an overstatement."

Lance brushed me off with the flick of a wrist. "It's not always about the outfit, it's about those glowing, dewy cheeks. I must say that having your devilishly handsome husband in town has done wonders for your complexion."

"Thanks. I think."

"Don't scrunch your face like that. I mean it as a compliment." Lance was tall and thin with angular features and impeccable taste.

"You're up and about early. This seems to be a trend lately. I'm worried about you." I squeezed his wrist in jest.

"Don't get used to it. Arlo has daily doubles with the softball team and I promised him a coffee and pastry delivery, because that's the kind of guy I am."

"How are things going with you two?"

Lance had recently started dating OSF's interim managing director. Arlo had been hired to help steer the festival forward after financial setbacks because of wildfire smoke, as well as expand the company's commitment to diversity and giving voice to playwrights and actors from underrepresented communities. One thing that tourists who were new to Ashland's theater scene were often surprised by was the wide range of productions staged at OSF's indoor and outdoor venues. Shakespeare was a mainstay with at least two or three works penned by the Bard produced each season, but there was no shortage of other opinions for theatergoers—from musicals to experimental narratives and immersive interactive shows where audiences played a key role in developing the plot.

Arlo had caught Lance's eye from the moment he had arrived in Ashland, and Lance had been smitten ever since.

"Fine." Lance didn't elaborate, which was completely out of character.

"What can I get you?" I pointed to the pastry case.

"I already called in an order. You know me, I don't do lines."

I knew he was being sarcastic, at least in part. Lance enjoyed the fact that locals and tourists fawned over him.

"Do tell, what's the news this morning? I saw the Professor scurrying around the plaza. Something is amiss."

How did he know?

I considered my options. If I told Lance about Benson's murder, he wouldn't be able to let it go; but if he heard the news from someone else, he'd never let me hear the end of it.

"There's been a murder," I confessed.

Lance gasped and threw a hand over his mouth. "Murder? Did you say murder?"

I told him about the Barista Cup and Benson's suspicious death.

"What are we waiting for? We need to get to The

Hills—stat. We have a case, my dearest partner in crime."

"Not so fast."

Lance held up his index finger and cut me off. "Oh, don't even. You are the peanut butter to my jelly when it comes to investigating. Not to mention it is our civic duty, and you yourself said you're worried about Andy. There's only one way to solve that."

"Which is?"

"Which is to insert ourselves into this investigation and solve the case." He snapped. "I'll pick up my order. We can drop it off at the softball fields on our way to The Hills."

I stood in place, unmoving.

"Time is wasting. Snap to it." He made another, exaggerated, snap. "We have a killer to catch."

Chapter Twelve

Refusing Lance was futile, and it was true that I was mo-
tivated to clear Andy's name, so after I grabbed a few
things at Torte, I found myself driving to the collegiate
softball fields.

"I'll just be a moment," Lance said, as he picked up
the box of pastries from the back seat.

I watched him walk with a leisurely confidence to
the dugout and greet Arlo with a kiss on both cheeks.
Lance might not know it, but he had met his match with
Arlo. They made a handsome couple. Arlo was muscular with dark black skin and a bald head. He was taller
than Lance by a couple of inches. His genuine smile and
easygoing personality immediately endeared me to him.
As did the fact that Arlo wasn't interested in sucking up
to Lance.

I appreciated that Arlo held his ground when it came
to OSF's future. Lance had grandiose visions for the theater's evolution, one of the many things that connected
him to the company and the entire community. But
his artistic goals weren't always realistic when it came
to budgeting or in line with filling seats and attracting

new audiences. Lance's revolutionary lens came with a large price tag. He insisted that each production needed to stand out from the ordinary. "Dramaturgy" became his catch phrase for his exorbitant spending on special effects, intricate set changes, high-flying acrobatics, and massive song-and-dance numbers.

Thus far, Arlo had found a way to balance Lance's need to have the stage shape understanding while at the same time making sure that he didn't blow through his annual budget or alienate OSF's most loyal patrons. I didn't envy his position.

Lance returned to the car shortly. "Who's ready for an adventure?" He waited for me to respond.

"Me?"

"Uh, yes, *you*. Please, Juliet, a little more enthusiasm if you don't mind." He sounded put out.

"It's hard. I know you're teasing, but I'm worried about Andy." I bit my bottom lip and stared at the flaxen rolling hills on the far side of the valley. The sun illuminated the crest of Pompadour Bluff, casting an angelic light on the striking prominence.

Lance changed his tone. "Chin up. Consider this car your sacred space. No fear or worry shall consume us. We have a job to do. A duty to our beloved community and barista. Worry will only set us on a dark path. Today we shall shine a light on a killer. Understood?"

I couldn't not smile. "Understood. You're right, and I also know that arresting Andy is the last thing the Professor wants to have happen. I just wish it wasn't Andy's coffee that ended up spiked with sedatives."

"Exactly." Lance veered left to give wide berth to a family of deer nibbling on a dew-drenched grassy field. One of the many things I loved about living in the Rogue Valley was being entirely surrounded by nature. Within minutes of leaving the plaza, the landscape shifted from Elizabethan buildings and family neighborhoods to open pastures and organic farms to the east and dense evergreen mountain ranges to the west. "That will be our singular mission. Let's make a pact that we will discover who slipped something deadly into Andy's drink." He kept one hand on the steering wheel and held up his pinky on his free hand. "Pinky swear."

I did the same. "Swear. Do you know anything about benzodiazepines?"

Lance kept his eyes on the winding road. "No, why?"

"The Professor said that's what killed Benson. The class of drugs is used to treat sleeping issues and anxiety. I was thinking that if we could figure out if any of the other contestants or judges were taking sleeping pills or anxiety medication, we might have a lead on who killed Benson."

"I like the way you think." Lance made a clicking sound with his tongue. "Yes, let's do it. Let's see if we can figure out a subtle way to work some questions about medication into our queries. You know me, I'm the master of subtly so it shouldn't be difficult."

I couldn't contain my laughter. "Yep, that's we all say about you—the master of subtly."

"I think you jest," Lance sounded injured. "Just for that, I might not share any juicy discoveries with you."

"That, I highly doubt." I chuckled.

He scoffed as we pulled into The Hills parking lot. News vans and police vehicles lined the front entrance.

"Word has gotten out, I'll say," Lance noted as he parked the car.

"I wonder if that's going to make it more difficult for us to ask around?"

He turned to me and rolled his eyes. "Please. Remember who you're with, okay? I'll flash my pearly whites and we'll have every suspect eating out of the palms of our hands."

That sounded like a stretch, but I got out of the car and followed Lance inside. The hotel had a very different vibe from yesterday. Instead of high-energy pitches from the vendors in the lobby, many of the booths weren't open yet. The handful of vendors who had set up greeted us with restrained smiles and nods.

"Word has definitely gotten out about the *murder*," Lance whispered.

There was a palpable anxiety in the air. We walked past two uniformed officers stationed in the lobby and two more outside the ballroom.

"You'd think the queen was in town with all of this security," Lance commented.

After we showed our tickets to staff at the door, we went inside the ballroom and scored the same front-row seats. Most of the crowd had yet to arrive, but the competitors were already prepping their stations under the watchful eyes of the judges.

"Okay, give me the scoop." Lance crossed his lanky legs, revealing black and gray polka-dot socks.

"That's Diaz." I pointed to the station to Andy's left. Diaz wore his dark hair in another tight bun and moved to the beat of the music from his oversize headphones. "He came in first yesterday. That was a bit unexpected as Sammy was predicted to win. She's won the last three years." I nodded to Sammy who was prepping her work-station. Sammy rehearsed her speech under her breath as she arranged her high-end coffee gear.

"Got it." Lance focused his gaze on Piper. "Who's that?"

"She's the head technical judge. Apparently, she and Benson have been judging the Barista Cup for years." I gave him a brief rundown of the difference between sensory and technical judges.

"Interesting. What's your impression of her?"

I shrugged. "I don't really have one. She came to Andy's defense yesterday. She seemed to be able to ap-pease Benson at least in terms of the rules. They had a huge blowout too, though. He threatened that this was going to be the end of her. We need to confirm this today, but I'm pretty sure they were running the Barista Cup together. It's kind of murky. I'm not entirely clear on the business side of things."

"Hmm. We will have to get to the bottom of that, won't we? I think Piper is definitely someone we want to have a little tête-à-tête with."

James entered the ballroom. His shirt was untucked. His hair was messy like he had just woken up. "And, that I presume is our MC?" Lance asked. "Looks as if he might have tied on one too many last night. He could use a morning refresher—or two, don't you think?"

"Yep. He's top of my list." I told him about the fight I'd witnessed in the hallway.

"That gives us four suspects. I propose that we divide and conquer." Lance formed a plan. "I'll cozy up to the judge and our hungover MC, you take the baristas. You can go chat them up under the guise of seeing how Andy's doing."

"Now?" I glanced at the clock. The competition was due to start in less than thirty minutes.

"No time like the present." Lance tapped his wrist. "Let's get to them first. Make haste."

He turned on the charm as he approached Piper with a casual stroll and chummy three-fingered wave.

I knew that he would never let me hear the end of it if I didn't do my part, so with reservations I went over to Andy's station.

"How's it going?" I asked. Andy's setup reminded me of a chemistry lab. There were dozens of glass bottles with simple syrups and herb infusions, thermometers, scales, and an assortment of ceramic espresso cups.

Sweat poured from his forehead. His cheeks were stained with color. "It's okay, boss. I'm working on a few new techniques that I saw on YouTube last night."

Sammy, who had her back to us, made a grunting sound at the station next to us.

I had no idea she was listening to our conversation.

"You want some advice?" She set down a container of finely ground nuts and turned to Andy. "Look, this isn't the time to try something new. This is the West Coast Barista Cup. This is hallowed ground we're standing on. You don't mess around with YouTube demos. You come to compete. You come to win. Don't stray from what you know. Trust me on this." Her tone was condescending to say the least.

"Thanks." Andy tried to smile. His typical infectious grin was absent. "Yeah, you're right. I guess yesterday got in my head."

I moved slightly closer to Sammy's station. "I don't think we've officially met. I'm Jules. I own Torte, the bakeshop where Andy works his coffee magic."

She removed a pair of disposable gloves and extended a hand. Despite the fact that she oozed external confidence I noticed that her hands had the slightest tremble. "Sammy. Nice to meet you. I've heard good things about your bakeshop. I've been wanting to bring more artisan baked goods into my coffeehouse, Fluid. Everyone here seems to think that Torte is the place to go for pastries. Maybe I'll stop by and get some inspiration."

"We'd love to have you. Stop by anytime. Fluid is in the Spokane area, is that right?"

"Yep." She tossed the gloves into a waste bin and yanked on another pair. "Spokane now, but soon we're going be everywhere on the West Coast."

"That sounds like a big expansion." I watched as she tugged the gloves tighter and then measured dried chilies. "Smart move on gloves when you're dealing with chilies."

"I use gloves for everything. You never want to contaminate your coffee, not when even the tiniest adjustments can be tasted by the judges." She set the chilies on a cutting board and lifted a container of nuts. "My coffees are pristine. The slightest dusting of nut residue or chili powder that might linger on my fingers could stick to the rim of the mug and completely throw off the flavor."

Wow. And I thought *Andy* took coffee seriously.

"I'll go through more gloves than a surgeon in the process of crafting my lineup of coffees this morning." Her brown eyes gleamed with superior arrogance.

"What people don't understand is that the Barista Cup is a mental game too. We are being judged on our every movement. Every single second counts. The judges are watching. Doubt and hesitation have no room here. It'll cost you dearly. You have to think like a winner and act like a winner."

Sammy's statement made Andy sweat more.

It sounded like overkill to me.

Then another thought hit me. Sammy's stockpile of gloves could have been used to spike Benson's drink. If she had slipped the sedatives into his coffee with a pair of gloves on, she wouldn't have left fingerprints on the cup.

"That's cringey, bruh!" Diaz hollered from the other side of Andy. "Who wears freaking gloves to make a latte?" He tucked a loose stand of hair into his bun.

I could tell from the way he looked to me and then Andy that he was hoping for a reaction. I wasn't about to get in the middle of it. Instead, I used it as an opportunity to introduce myself.

I moved to his station and extended my hand. "Congratulations on your first-place finish yesterday. I try to stay in the loop on coffee trends, but I've never seen a latte served in an avocado before."

Diaz flashed me a cocky smile. "I get that a lot."

His workstation was the opposite of Sammy's. There were Tupperware, coffee beans, and splotches of spilled syrup everywhere. How had he scored high in the technical category when his workstation looked like a fraternity kitchen?

"I was telling your guy, Andy, that he can't be basic." Diaz ripped open a sealed bag of coffee beans and dumped them into the grinder. The scent of the intoxicating spicy roast made me crave another cup. "The judges have seen everything. You can't show up at the Barista Cup serving a vanilla latte. Boring. The judges are looking for innovation. They want to taste coffee like they've never experienced it before. You can't play it safe."

Was Diaz suggesting that Andy had played it safe? I would argue that his hot honey latte wasn't a typical offering on any traditional coffee-shop menu.

Diaz held up a large canister of coarse sea salt. "Like I told you yesterday, bruh, salt can be a game changer. If you do it *right*."

I didn't like the emphasis Diaz put on the last sentence or the darting glance he shot at Andy.

"Tough break yesterday, man." Diaz attempted to console Andy. His sarcastic tone suggested to me that he wasn't being authentic. "Salt can be tricky. Real tricky."

Andy didn't reply. It didn't help that Diaz appeared to be enjoying reminding Andy about yesterday's mishap.

"Are you making a drink with salt today?" I asked, noting the large container of flaked sea salt in Diaz's hands.

He almost dropped the canister, but caught it at the last minute and returned it to his messy countertop. "No. I'm not going with anything mundane. I have a new surprise in store, but you'll have to wait and see like everyone else. Can't give anything away in the final round." He pressed his index finger to his lips.

James announced that the competition would begin

in ten minutes. I returned to my seat armed with two pieces of what could be critical information. Sammy had access to gloves, and Diaz had a large canister of salt that he wasn't using in his drinks. Why would he have salt that he didn't intend to use? I couldn't be sure, but I had a pretty solid suspicion I knew the reason. Could Diaz have sabotaged Andy's drink?

Chapter Thirteen

"Do tell, what did you discover?" Lance asked when we both returned to our seats. I told him about Diaz and the salt, and Sammy's gloves.

He strummed his fingers together. "See, this is why we are an unstoppable team. Beautifully done. I too have uncovered some nefarious information."

"What's that?"

"I do believe that there's more to Benson and Piper's relationship than first meets the eye." He lifted one trimmed brow and cocked his head in Piper's direction.

She stood at Sammy's station, making notes on her clipboard.

"How so?"

"Her explanation of the business side of the Cup was thin to say the least, and as for her and Benson, I can't put it into words, but I'm quite confident there's more afoot than she's willing to say." He shrugged. "Call it a hunch."

"Speculation and hunches aren't going to clear Andy."

"Patience. Patience." Lance furrowed his brow and

shook his index finger. "O ye of little faith. I have a plan. There's only so much that can be said in a crowded ballroom. I invited Piper to meet us for cocktails later this afternoon. It's the least I could offer since it sounds like she and everyone connected to the event will be extending their stay in our hamlet until the Professor gives them the all clear."

That was news.

"You mean he's told her not to leave?"

A relaxed smile crossed Lance's angular face. "It appears that way, which must mean that our dearest Professor believes there are multiple suspects in this case." He tilted his head and sighed with satisfaction. "What do you say to drinks later? We can loosen her up with one of Puck's Pub's strong martinis and get her talking."

"Okay." I watched as James tested the mic. "What about James? Did you get anything out of him?"

"He's a tougher nut to crack." Lance flexed his fingers. "I didn't get far. Perhaps you'll have better luck with him as the fairer sex."

"The fairer sex?" I frowned. "Lance, please, this is the twenty-first century."

"And, I am your biggest champion. I'm simply saying that James might be more inclined to spill his secrets to the ever-elegant Juliet than to yours truly. Why? Who can say? Obviously, the man lacks character and taste."

"Are you suggesting that I flirt with him?" I flared my nostrils.

"Never!" Lance gasped. "Banish the thought. More like bat those lovely lashes and stick out the chest."

"You're the worst." I punched him in the shoulder.

"Hardly. I'm merely attempting to get to the bottom of this case. After all, it's your boy barista who we're doing this for."

James began making announcements. Lance and I would have to table our conversation for later.

The lineup for the day's events was similar to yesterday, with a few exceptions. The first was the police presence. The officers who had been at the front doors now flanked the competitors. Thomas, Kerry, and the Professor circled the ballroom. An average attendee would likely have no idea that a crew of detectives were on site, excepting Thomas, who wore his standard blue uniform and shorts. Kerry and the Professor blended in with the crowd in their street clothes. The second difference was that no one would be eliminated. The final five contestants would compete in three challenges. At the end of the last challenge their scores from each round would be tallied, and the first-, second-, and third-place winners would be named.

Before James officially kicked off the competition, he tapped the mic with his finger. "Folks, if I could get your attention. As I'm sure you're aware, tragedy struck our family of coffee lovers last night. I'd like us to take a moment of silence to honor the late, great Benson Vargas and his enduring contribution to the coffee culture. Benson was a controversial figure, but no one can dispute his coffee legacy. He's responsible for us being together here today in celebration of those wonderful roasted beans, so let's take a moment to remember him."

Everyone held the space for Benson. I couldn't tell if James's words were heartfelt, but I appreciated the gesture. It would have been weird to move on without acknowledging Benson's death.

The rest of the morning was relatively uneventful. A replacement judge had been called in to fill Benson's spot. He was much kinder and more effusive with his praise for the baristas' drinks than Benson had been.

Mom, Marty, and Steph came to lend their support to Andy. Marty had made cardboard cutouts of Andy's head and attached sticks to use as handles.

"Take one and pass them around," Marty said, handing me a giant prop of Andy's face. "I figured these should give him a good laugh and help ease some of the tension."

"These are hilarious." Mom hid her face behind the mask. "Team Andy!" she shouted.

We all did the same, waving Andy's face high. He turned in our direction and cracked up.

"Well done. Well done." Lance leaned down to catch Marty's eye. "I need the name of your vendor for these."

"Why?" I asked, and then immediately regretted it.

Lance offered me a conspiratorial wink. "I have my reasons."

"I don't want to know, do I?"

He patted my knee. "No, darling. No, you don't."

Despite Marty's attempt to cheer him up, Andy was off his game. He fumbled his way through the first round, spilling his first latte down the front of his apron, running twenty seconds over his allotted time, and forgetting to turn off the machine, causing extra espresso to flood over the top of his ceramic cups.

Mixing coffee and water seems simple, but there are so many variables that can drastically alter a shot. Andy often educated our customers while they waited at the coffee counter for their drinks. He would explain that the most relevant and understandable variable was that water dissolves the flavors within the coffee. The final product, these dissolved flavors, account for everything a guest tastes. Even running the machine for a second longer than intended could affect the flavor profile.

I couldn't blame Andy for being shaky. It had to be nerve racking to be surrounded by law enforcement, knowing that he was a suspect in a murder case all while competing for the title of the West Coast's best barista and a ten-thousand-dollar check. I knew that the money would go straight into Andy's savings account for his long-term goal—to open his own coffee roasting company.

"Keep your baby blues focused on those two," Lance commanded, nodding to Sammy and Diaz. "I'm watching our other suspects."

Nothing appeared to be out of the ordinary. The baristas concentrated on steaming milk and pouring shots. I wasn't sure what I had been hoping for. That Diaz would raise his hand halfway through the first round and confess?

Alas. Not so much.

There was also no way to tell how Andy was doing. The judges said nice things about every competitor's drink but wouldn't reveal scores until the grand finale later in the day.

"This is spicier than the closet scene from Hamlet," Lance commented as the buzzer started for the second round. "I dare say that I think my heart is palpitating a bit." He thumped his hand on his chest for effect.

"You should have been here yesterday," I retorted. "Benson brought a Polonius-like energy to the event."

"I'm sorry I missed it." He gave me a half clap. "And, well played on the Shakespeare reference."

Shakespeare was part of the ether in Ashland. I had grown up amongst playwrights, actors, dancers, artists, and a backdrop of Elizabethan culture. My father, like the Professor, would quote the Bard at will. He was one of the original founders of the Midnight Club—a late night band of merrymakers who staged impromptu performances and shared a mutual admiration of and obsession for Shakespeare's works.

James shouted out time warnings. "Ten minutes, baristas! Get those shots extracted and milk steamed!"

Steph who sat on my left, bounced her knee up and down.

"You're not nervous, are you?" I teased.

She gave me her signature scowl, her deep purple lips curling downward. "No."

"Okay, if you say so."

We watched in rapture as the competition continued, her toes continuing to tap on the floor.

I kept my eye on Diaz and Sammy, both of whom were singularly focused. Diaz swayed to the tunes the DJ was spinning, but unlike yesterday, he didn't stop to flex for the crowd or show off his dance moves. He had abandoned his headphones and used sheer force to grind his beans, pulsing them to a fine pulp. I wondered what that would do to the portafilter.

Sammy, on the other hand, treated her beans like a newborn infant. She had stored them on dry ice again. The billowing fog that escaped as she tenderly scooped the beans into the grinder made the crowd *oooh* and *aaaah.*

"Artistic illusion at its best, and well-timed I must say." Lance gave a nod of appreciation to Sammy's theatrics.

She didn't notice. She cradled her beans with both hands as if they might break. Wasn't that the point?

Meanwhile, Andy continued to sweat. He stopped twice to mop his brow and caught my eye.

You okay? I mouthed.

He shrugged and shook his head before refocusing on steaming a combination of almond, coconut, and oat milks. I knew that he had spent hours perfecting the ratio in order to achieve a delicate balance between the nondairy milks. I wished I could go rescue him or at least give him a quick pep talk, but the time continued to tick down.

"Five minutes, baristas!" James motioned for the crowd to cheer. "Five minutes until every offering needs to be cupped and ready for the judges."

The DJ played the *Jeopardy* theme song.

Piper took one last spin past each of the competitors' stations. She took great interest in Sammy's machine, bending over to study the settings. Sammy ignored her.

"Okay, let's count them down," James announced. "Ten . . . nine . . ."

Andy's face blotched with red streaks as he placed his alternative latte on the tasting tray. For this round, the baristas had to provide the judges with a nondairy latte, a chai latte, and a matcha latte. Sequoia had been an asset for Andy when he was prepping for this round. She had offered constructive feedback on how to warm the milk, whisk in the matcha powder to form a thick paste, and then steam the leafy, fragrant tea with the milk. She also suggested he add a dusting of matcha powder on the top for extra flourish and texture. By the looks of his beautiful green drink with a leaf made of foam, he had followed her advice.

At the end of the scoring, Andy stood in third place. A solid finish, but he didn't look happy.

When it was time to break for lunch, June—who had arrived with her knitting again—Mom, Marty, and Steph went to find seats at the buffet. Lance scooted off to have another go at James. The ballroom cleared out pretty quickly, except for Thomas, Kerry, and the Professor. I went to see if they'd made any progress and found them huddled near the judges' table.

"Any updates?"

The Professor broke off their conversation. "Ah, Juliet."

Thomas and Kerry turned around. Thomas wore a pair of khaki shorts and a navy polo with Peace Officer embroidered on the chest.

Ashland's small team of police officers were just that—peace keepers. They took a community approach to policing, getting to know anyone who might be at risk or in need of support and services, and then figuring out ways to connect them with that support. I knew we were lucky to have such a caring team helping to lift up our community.

Kerry was dressed in a sleeveless black tank top and matching narrow skirt. Her long auburn hair was twisted in a messy bun at the back of her narrow neck. Kerry was a minimalist in terms of style—I was too.

I'd rarely seen her wear jewelry, which is why my eyes traveled to the sparkling diamond engagement ring on her left hand. Thomas had shown me the exquisite ring before he proposed. I was thrilled for both of them, and crossing my fingers they would take us up on our offer to cater the wedding. Mom and I had discussed it—we thought it would make for a wonderful gift to be able to serve Thomas, Kerry, and their guests.

Kerry's ring made me acutely aware of my bare hand. During my separation with Carlos I had stopped wearing my wedding band; but when we reconciled, Carlos insisted he wanted to give me something new.

"We are starting fresh, mi querida," he had said, caressing my naked finger. "We both need new rings to signify our commitment again. This is a new life we are beginning together in Ashland. It will be a chance to renew our vows, si?"

I had agreed. Not that I needed a ceremony or a ring to convince me that I'd made the right choice, but there was something to be said for the symbol of merging our lives in Ashland.

Kerry waited for me to respond to the Professor.

"Sorry, I didn't mean to interrupt." I started to back away.

"Not at all. I was hoping for a word with you as fate would have it." The Professor stopped me. He removed his notebook from his shirt pocket. "I noticed that you were able to get a moment with the other competitors and wondered if perhaps they revealed anything of interest?"

Thomas followed the Professor's lead and took notes on his iPad mini.

"Maybe." I told them about Diaz's salt canister and Sammy's gloves.

"Noted. Anything else?" He waited to see if there was more. I wished I had more to share.

"No. I didn't get much out of either of them. They were prepping for the competition." I wished I had thought of a way to bring up the subject of sleeping pills with either of them. It wasn't exactly casual conversation. *So, are you taking anything to help you sleep?* I would have to ponder a more subtle way of approaching the topic.

A uniformed officer interrupted us. He held a thumb drive for the Professor to see. "Here's the information you requested."

The Professor gave him a grateful nod. "Many thanks."

What was on the drive? I wanted to ask, but Thomas beat me to it.

He clicked off the iPad and pointed to the thumb drive. "Is that the surveillance footage?"

"Indeed. We'll see if The Hill's cameras were able to capture anything of interest. I'm optimistic and yet also a realist. I fear that our killer likely considered the placement of cameras. It wouldn't have been difficult to maneuver around them, but we can hope." He handed the thumb drive to Thomas.

"What's Lance up to?" Thomas asked.

I held my breath. Oh no, what *was* Lance up to? I followed Thomas's gaze to the far corner of the ballroom where Lance was laughing loudly with James. I could tell that he was intentionally trying to draw attention, from the way he threw his head back and let out a booming laugh.

"Who knows? Being Lance?"

The tiniest glimmer of amusement crossed Kerry's face before she narrowed her eyes. "Define 'being Lance.'"

I shrugged. "Your guess is as good as mine."

Another officer approached us. He whispered something to the Professor, who in turn motioned to Kerry and Thomas. "That's our cue. Juliet, excuse us please, and thank you for the information."

I watched them leave the ballroom in a hurry.

What was that about?

There was no sign of Andy or Sammy, but Diaz was at his station listening to music. I decided to give it another shot.

"Good job this morning," I said.

He lifted one side of his headphones away from his ear. "Huh?"

"I said 'good job.' You did well this morning."

"Yeah, thanks." He took off the headphones.

I stared at the slew of ingredients at his messy station.

He must have noticed my eyes linger on the container of salt because he grabbed it and stuffed it into a paper grocery bag.

"Oh, are you using salt in one of your drinks this afternoon?"

He threw the grocery bag under the table. "Why do you care?"

"I just wondered. After what happened with Andy yesterday I thought maybe salt would be taboo."

He glared at me. "Don't you own a coffee shop? You should know that you never want to be underprepared. Better to pack more than you need than not enough."

He had a fair point, but I didn't trust him and my gut was telling me that he was lying. I should have dropped it, but I couldn't stop myself.

"I was just talking to the police. They're looking into who spiked Andy's first drink with salt." That wasn't fully true, but the Professor hadn't actually said that they weren't looking into that possibility.

Diaz clutched the edge of the table. "Oh yeah?" He tried to sound casual.

I knew I should leave it, but I might not have another chance to speak to Diaz alone. "They think that whoever sabotaged Andy's drink could have done it again, with deadly consequences."

"What?" Diaz threw his hand to his chest. "Nah, no, that's not what happened."

I couldn't believe it. Was he about to confess?

Diaz smoky eyes narrowed. He glanced around us. "Look, you know the police here, right? You were just over there talking to them."

"Yes, I know them." I could feel my heart rate speed up. What was he going to say?

"You have to talk to them for me." His eyes shifted. They were wide with fear. "You have to tell them that I didn't kill Benson."

"I didn't suggest that you did."

He cracked his knuckles. "You know about the salt."

I played innocent. "What do you mean?"

He reached into the grocery bag and slammed the salt on the table. "This. Okay, this. I admit it. I tossed a bunch of salt into Andy's drink."

I'm sure my face reflected my shock. Not that Diaz had done it, but that he was claiming responsibility.

"Look, I need the money, okay? Do you know how expensive it is to live in San Francisco on a barista's salary? My tip money barely pays for my gas. I don't have health insurance. I'm bumming on my friend's couch. Ten grand would help a lot."

"That doesn't make it okay to sabotage another competitor. And why Andy? Sammy seems like she was the one to beat." The reality of Diaz's confession had started to sink in. I felt my internal temperature rise.

"I was going to slip something into *her* drink too." He shook his head. "Don't look at me like that. It's not like it was deadly. It was just some salt. These competitions have gotten bigger and bigger with fat payouts. I was just trying to get a leg up. You're looking at me like I took some kind of a drastic measure. It was just salt," Diaz repeated.

It was more than salt, but I kept quiet.

"Sammy doesn't need the money," he continued. "She's a YouTube star. She makes serious cash on her coffee videos. I found out what each of the contestants was serving for the signature round and I came up with a plan to taint their drinks. I didn't mean to throw that much salt into Andy's cup, but you spotted me. I had to hurry."

So he had been tampering with Andy's coffee when I'd seen him yesterday. "And what about Sammy?"

Diaz shuffled his feet and fidgeted with his hands for a moment. Then he bent down and removed a plastic tub from beneath his table. "I had a plan in mind for her coffee too, but she never left her station." He lifted the lid.

I leaned closer for a better look. "Is that *dirt*?"

"Yeah. She was making that ridiculous earthy mushroom coffee. I figured a sprinkling of dirt would add too much earth. I had to stick with flavors they were already using in their coffees, otherwise it would be too obvious. I had to add just enough to throw off the balance. That was the brilliance of the plan. Two of the judges would get great drinks. They would argue with the third judge who would claim something was off, but things went south."

That dirt must have been what I had seen on Andy's station. "I don't understand. How did you target Benson?"

"I didn't. That was the luck of the draw. It didn't matter who got the drink. I just needed one judge to disagree with the others and I'm in first place." He put the lid back on the tub of dirt and stuck it under the table.

How should I respond?

Diaz had admitted to cheating. That would exclude him for the competition. But the bigger question was, could Diaz also have slipped deadly sedatives into Benson's drink?

Chapter Fourteen

"You're going to tell the police, aren't you?" Diaz pounded his fists on the table, causing his headphones to fall to the floor. He bent over to pick them up. "Bruh, I'm such an idiot. I should have been more careful. If I hadn't tossed that much salt into Andy's drink I would have gotten away with it. It was just salt. What's the big deal?"

The big deal was that he had ruined Andy's placement in the competition yesterday at best, and at worst, he might be the one who killed Benson with a latte.

"Listen, Diaz, *you* need to go talk to the police—now. I'll take you to the Professor, our lead detective here in Ashland. He's one of the most intelligent men I know. He'll hear your side of the story, but this is a murder investigation. If you don't go talk to him then, yes, I will."

"But, I didn't kill him. You don't understand. It was nothing. A way to ensure that I would at least have a shot of getting into the finals. I need the cash. I wasn't going to do anything today. I knew that if I could make it to the finals, I had a good chance of winning, and even second and third place pay some serious cash."

"This is everything you need to say to the police," I insisted. The ballroom was starting to fill in. People trickled to their seats. The DJ started the music and the judges had reconvened at the main table.

Diaz fiddled with the chord on his headphones, twisting it around his hand like a tourniquet. "They're going to think I killed him. I didn't touch the new drink that Andy gave Benson. I wasn't even here when Andy was making it. I was up at the judges' table waiting to have a word with Benson."

I nodded and let him continue, but internally I made note to share that fact with the Professor. Standing at the judges' table when Andy delivered Benson the second hot honey latte gave Diaz the perfect opportunity to spike the drink.

"I swear, I only wanted to level the playing field. I was going to flex on everyone. I wanted a shot at the money and the title. That's all. I didn't kill Benson. I didn't even know the guy." He tossed the headphones onto the table.

"All the more reason to share this with the police now. The longer you withhold information, the more you'll look like a suspect."

Diaz groaned. "Okay, but I'm going to tell them that the person they should be looking into is James, not me."

"James?" I wished I had a better poker face. I was sure my mouth was hanging open.

"Yeah. He and Benson went head-to-head yesterday. I thought he was going to punch the guy. He might have if Piper hadn't jumped in between them."

"When was this?"

Diaz shrugged. "I don't remember. Late. After the

competition was over. It was dead in here. I was packing up my stuff when they got into it."

"Do you know what they were fighting about?"

"No, but it sounded like an old grudge. James kept saying that Benson wasn't going to do this again. He threatened him."

I had heard a similar argument between the two men yesterday, which made me more inclined to believe that Diaz was telling the truth—at least about that.

"Should we go find the Professor?" I asked.

"Do I have a choice?" Diaz expelled an audible breath.

"You don't have to come with me, but like I said, if you don't tell them what happened, I will and I think it will be much better coming from you."

He pounded his fist on the table a final time. "God, I'm such an idiot. I should have kept my mouth shut."

We didn't talk more on the way to the lobby. I spotted the Professor speaking with a woman at the reception desk.

"Wait here," I said to Diaz and went over to the Professor.

"Can I snag you for a minute?" I asked, pointing to Diaz, who stood near the front door. I half wondered if he was considering making a quick escape.

The Professor excused himself and came with me. "You already know Diaz. He and I were just talking and he has something important he needs to tell you about."

I left them to talk, wondering what might happen to the Barista Cup now.

Lance was in line for coffee. He spotted me and waved.

I joined him.

"Well, do tell. Obviously you had success." He titled his head toward the Professor and Diaz.

"Diaz admitted to sabotaging Andy's drink," I whispered, then proceeded to tell him about my conversation while we waited for coffee.

"The plot thickens." Lance rubbed his hands together. "He doesn't exactly strike me as the killing type. Does he?"

I scowled. "No. I don't know. I don't want to make any assumptions at this point, but I think I believe him. He seemed sincere. Don't get me wrong, I think it's terrible that he ruined Andy's drink and cheated, but he swore he didn't kill Benson. Plus, what would his motive have been? Benson's feedback had landed him in first place. How would killing him have helped his chances at winning the competition?"

"Excellent point. Excellent point."

We made it to the front of the line. "Two iced mochas, please. Heavy on espresso, easy on the mocha," Lance said to the barista.

"Easy on the mocha? What does that mean?" I tried to wink but my face scrunched together.

"She knows, right dear?" Lance addressed the barista. Not waiting for her answer, he pulled me to the side. "Here's what you need to know—James was very cagey. As in squirming like an antsy toddler."

"How so?"

"I asked him directly about his relationship with Benson, after I tried to butter him up with box seats and a backstage tour. He said, 'Live theater isn't my thing.'" Lance threw his hand on his forehead. "Imagine the horror. Who would utter such hurtful words?"

Classic Lance. "I don't know, but what did he say about Benson?"

Lance took our light-on-the-mocha drinks from the barista and handed me one. "He said it was none of my business and to stay out of it. If that isn't an admission of guilt, I don't know what is."

We sipped our drinks on the way back to the ball-room. "I'm not sure about that theory. Maybe he's pri-vate and doesn't feel the need to talk about his personal relationships with a stranger."

Lance stopped mid-stride. "A stranger? Moi? I hap-pen to be the artistic director of the most prestigious repertoire theater this side of the Mississippi. How dare he."

I was used to Lance's antics. I knew he was kidding, but I did wonder about James. I had seen him arguing with Benson, and Diaz had witnessed a similar interac-tion. There had to be more to their relationship. He had specifically mentioned "not getting away with it again," which led me to believe he and Benson had a past.

"I'm telling you, you'll have to try to work your charms on him," Lance continued. "I have a feeling he'll be more willing to spill his secrets to you."

When we returned to our seats, Mom, Marty, June, and Steph were waiting for us. "You missed lunch," Mom said, offering me a croissant club sandwich with a side of fruit salad and kettle chips. "We brought a plate for you too, Lance."

Lance blew her a kiss. "Helen, you are a saint among women."

Piper and James were huddled with the other judges along with Detective Kerry near the head table.

"Oooh, things are getting even more interesting." Lance took a drink of his creamy mocha. "I can't believe I almost missed this."

Kerry called the contestants over. I wondered if she was breaking the news that Diaz had cheated. She held them off for a moment while taking a call on her cell.

"What do you think she's saying?" Lance leaned forward.

I took a bite of the light and airy croissant sandwich. "If Diaz confessed to the Professor, I'm guessing she's telling them what happened. The question is, will the competition continue or are they going to call the whole thing off? Between a murder and sabotage, this is getting out of hand."

"Or better yet, something I should put on the stage. Shakespeare couldn't have scripted this theatrical farce." Lance raised his brows in quick succession before taking another drink.

My thoughts drifted to Andy.

Poor Andy. He had worked so hard preparing for the Barista Cup. Although at least he would be vindicated. Everyone would know that his drink had been tainted.

"Something feels off," Mom commented.

"I agree." I chomped on the crunchy kettle chips and polished off my sandwich and fruit salad. I had no idea I was hungry, but my empty plate said otherwise.

After about fifteen minutes James addressed the crowd. "Folks, sorry for the delay. Thank you for your patience. There's been a development that is going to change the outcome of today. We're going to need you to sit tight for a while longer as we talk through some different options. Again, please accept our apologies for this unexpected delay. The café is open and there are complimentary snacks and pastries along with our delicious coffee cart available for you in the lobby. If you want to get up and stretch again this might be the time to do that. I'm hoping we'll have an update for you in about thirty minutes."

"Thirty minutes," Lance scoffed. "That's longer than intermission." He had finished his lunch as well.

"Yeah, but they probably have to talk through whether they allow one of the contestants who got eliminated yesterday back into the competition, or maybe the Professor wants them to cancel the entire thing?"

Lance glanced at his watch. "Alas, I have an afternoon meeting with a group of high-end donors in town from Southern California that I absolutely cannot cancel." He sighed. "I'm going to miss the fun. You must promise to fill me in on every detail later."

"Deal." I nodded.

"And, we're on for happy hour, right? Bring that devastatingly handsome husband of yours and we'll see what we can get out of Piper. Puck's, five o'clock sharp."

He waved with his fingers, said goodbye to everyone, and made his exit.

I wasn't sure what to do. Mom excused herself to go check in with Doug. Marty and June went off together in search of dessert, and Steph had put in a pair of earbuds and was watching a baking show on her phone.

I didn't want to sit in the ballroom for a half hour, but there wasn't enough time to head back to Torte. I decided to take a walk around the property. Stretching my legs would feel good and maybe it would clear my head too.

The Hills' extensive grounds included tennis courts, a pool, multiple patios with lounge chairs, and their signature collection of bright orange bikes to tool around the hotel or pedal into town on. I wandered along a small pathway bursting with yellow primroses and fragrant jasmine. The path led past a turquoise pool with burnt orange lounge chairs and tan umbrellas to the backside of the property. I drank in the afternoon sun and the smell of the warm grasses mingled with a hint of chlorine wafting from the pool.

I continued on until I came to a collection of lounge chairs with views of the bluff.

This is just what you need, Jules, I told myself.

A few minutes relaxing under the sun would be good for my soul and a way to gather my thoughts. I sat down and adjusted the chair so that I was facing the sun. The glow quickly warmed my cheeks, but relaxing was a challenge. I couldn't stop my mind from churning over every potential possibility. Diaz, James, Sammy, maybe even Piper and the other contestants. Everyone in the ballroom had the potential to be a killer. The question was who?

Chapter Fifteen

I must have dozed off, because the next thing I knew a text message buzzed on my phone. I sat up and pulled my phone from my shorts pocket. The text was from Andy.

WHERE R U?

OUTSIDE. I texted back. Then I stood up. Bad idea. Spots burst like fireworks in my field of vision. Dizziness assaulted my body.

I took a minute to refocus. My arms had turned a light shade of pink under the heat of the mid-afternoon sun. It was a good thing Andy had texted. If I had slept much longer I would likely look like a lobster. Having fair, pale skin meant that I needed to be extra careful not to burn.

My phone buzzed again: YOU SHOULD GET IN HERE.

I retraced my steps to the ballroom. Before I had even entered, I heard the buzz of the crowd.

James stood near the competitors, mic in hand. "As promised, folks, I have an update for you. I think you're going to want to sit down for this one." He waited for a few spectators to take their seats. Then his tone turned solemn. "It has come to our attention that one of the contestants in yesterday's rounds cheated. For those of you who were with us yesterday, Ashland's own, Andy with Torte, had a rough time in the third round. Benson gave him the lowest score possible, which we now understand was due to another contestant."

Murmurs erupted from the crowd.

"I regret to inform you that Diaz Mendez, our top contender and first-place finisher yesterday, has been disqualified from the West Coast Barista Cup."

Everyone gasped.

"I can't go into any further details as this is a pending investigation. We have discussed options with the judges and remaining contestants and decided to postpone this afternoon's finale until tomorrow. That will allow us time to invite yesterday's last-place finisher back into the competition. We will repeat this morning's events and finish with a finale tomorrow afternoon. I know that it's a workday for some of you, and I apologize for that. I also know that many of you are here on vacation and had intended to stay on to see plays and experience the bounty of our beautiful Rogue Valley. We decided that since the theater is dark tomorrow night it is our best timeframe for moving forward. We apologize for any inconvenience this may cause you, but we're excited for the competition to resume tomorrow when we'll officially be able to crown a new West Coast barista champion."

There was more talk amongst the crowd.

James turned to the baristas. "Contestants, I need you to stick around for a mandatory meeting. For the rest of you folks, thanks for your support and understanding. I promised you a doozy of a show from the start, and we've certainly had that! We'll see you back here tomorrow. Doors will open at three o'clock. I've tasked my staff here at The Hills with creating some special bonus treats for you. The competition will kick off an hour later at four. Looking forward to seeing you all then."

No one moved. People talked in hushed tones and their eyes darted around the room, as if expecting that James would say, "Never mind, you've been punked."

One of the You Mocha Me Crazy T-shirt women who had been sitting next to me yesterday, tapped my shoulder. She and her friends were in the row behind us. Today they had matching hats that read Better *Latte* Than Never.

She slowly began to gather her things. "I can't believe it. Can you? Diaz was so good. And so sexy. He was destined to win. Why throw all of that away? What a waste."

I wondered where Diaz was now. He hadn't returned to the ballroom since the announcement. Was that due to embarrassment or had the Professor made an arrest?

Andy came to talk to us before his meeting with the judges. "Nice cutouts, guys." He pointed to Marty, who twisted the cardboard version of Andy.

"We thought it might lighten the mood," Marty said. He held the fake Andy next to the real one. "I have to say you two look alike."

"Ha!" Andy laughed and pointed to his chest. "Except this guy is much hotter, right?"

Steph rolled her eyes.

June pinched his cheek. "You were great today. Don't

worry, you'll be even better tomorrow. Consider today
your practice round."

Mom wrapped him in a hug. "Your grandmother is
right. I'm so sorry about the competition. You've gotten
more than I'm sure you expected out of this experience,
but now that Diaz has confessed, you can focus on winning."

"That's for sure." Andy gaze went distant. He gave
his head a slight shake. "It's weird. I thought I would
feel more relieved. I mean, don't get me wrong, I am
glad that the judges know that Diaz ruined my latte yesterday, but at the same time the whole thing feels just
gross."

"That's understandable." Marty clapped him on the
shoulder.

Steph clasped and unclasped one hand into a tight
fist, revealing her black-and-purple-striped nails that
matched her eye shadow and lipstick. "You want us to
rough someone up? I can put my pastry posse together."

That made Andy laugh harder. He knelt over and
clutched his stomach. "Steph, I would love to see your
pastry posse."

"Okay. I'll go get them." Her deadpan expression
didn't waiver.

Marty checked his watch. "Yeah, we should probably
head back to the bakeshop. There's work to be done and
an angry mob to incite."

Mom chuckled. "I see a friend, I'm going to go say
hello. One request before I go, though. I never heard this
plot for pastry shenanigans." She stuffed her fingers in
her ears and walked away.

"Can I give you a lift back to Torte?" Marty offered.

"Thanks, I think I'll walk."

He and Steph left together.

"I'm going to head out as well dear." June squeezed Andy's hand. "See you later tonight. Go have some fun."

Andy hugged her tight. Seeing his tenderness with June the past couple days had made him even more adorable.

"Jules this is crazy, huh?" Andy looked at the competitor's area. "I need to start packing up."

"I'll help."

We walked to his station and began pulling boxes and tubs from beneath the draped table. "Can you believe that Diaz spiked my drink with salt?"

"No." I didn't tell him about my conversation with Diaz or that Diaz had also intended to ruin Sammy's drink. I knew that he was stressed and didn't want to burden him more with undue worry now that Diaz had been removed from the competition. "How are you feeling?"

"Good. I mean, I guess. It's still weird that Benson is dead. The reality of the Barista Cup is not at all what I had built it up to be in my head. I never thought I would have to worry about another barista trying to mess with my drink, but I'm glad he admitted it. I told you I didn't put that much salt in my coffee."

"I know." I thought for a minute as I stacked wooden stir sticks in a box. "Hey, has being here today triggered anything?"

"What do you mean?" Andy dumped used spoons and steaming stainless steel pitchers into a tub.

"I just wondered if being back in the ballroom might have made you remember something—anything else that happened." I stared at the lighting overhead. Large industrial spots and floodlights were positioned to feature the barista arena. Heat poured down on us. No wonder Andy had been sweating, it was baking underneath the studio lights.

He sighed. "No, nothing."

"Don't worry about it." I felt bad for pushing my agenda.

"Um, what about tomorrow?" He asked, packing up tins of spices.

"What about it?"

"I'm supposed to work the afternoon shift at Scoops."

"Oh Andy, don't give it a thought. I'll rework the schedule and get someone to take your hours. Trust me, that won't be a problem and should be the least of your worries." I handed him a box of napkins and another with a variety of crystallized sugars.

"You're the best, boss." He winked.

That was the Andy I knew and loved.

"*You're* the best, and I can't wait to watch you tomorrow. In fact, maybe we'll close Torte early and bring the entire team over to cheer you on?"

"Really?" Andy perked up.

"Yeah, why not?" As I said it out loud, I liked the idea even more. After the insanity of the weekend, Andy could use all the encouragement possible.

"That would be so cool."

"Consider it done." I saw that the other baristas had begun to congregate. "You should get back to the meeting.

Don't come in tomorrow. We'll all see you here—and try to get some sleep tonight."

He saluted with two fingers. "You got it, boss."

I left the ballroom and began to walk back to Torte. It was only about two miles to town and I could use the exercise. Not to mention the late June weather was near perfection. Come mid-July, afternoon temps tended to swell into the nineties. Our proximity to the Siskiyou Mountains meant that even if temps climbed in the afternoon, they tended to cool off quickly in the evening. We typically had three or four weeks of hot summer days before the first touches of fall would begin to show.

There was no sign of the Professor or Diaz in the lobby or parking lot as I left The Hills. I had no idea if that meant he had taken Diaz into custody.

To return to town, I had to cross the overpass that stretched above Interstate 5. The densely forested Siskiyou Mountains with their varied shades of green stretched as far as I could see. I traveled past the YMCA, where young kids squealed with delight as they chased soccer balls through the grass. Farther down the street was the cemetery with ancient gravestones and deer nestled in the grass, taking siestas under the shade of madrones. The native trees had begun to shed their yellow leaves. Tourists often asked whether the exotic trees were eucalyptus imported from Australia, due to their red bark, which was as smooth as a baby's skin. The long-lived trees flourished in Ashland's rocky soil and wooded slopes.

As I walked toward the plaza, I reviewed everything

that had happened thus far. Diaz was definitely at the top of my list. He had sabotaged Andy's coffee to get ahead in the competition and had intended to do the same to Sammy, but that still didn't explain why he would want Benson dead.

I really wanted to see if I could learn anything more from James. He had been tight-lipped about his argument with Benson and had claimed they'd never met. Something told me he was lying.

Hopefully, drinks with Piper later this evening would be revealing. She had worked with Benson the longest and their exchange yesterday had been painful to watch. What had Benson meant when he had said that she was finished? Did he have the power to fire her? And if so, could that give her a motive for murder? If nothing else, she would hopefully be able to provide insight into who might have wanted to harm him.

Then there was Sammy. I didn't know much about the reigning national Barista Cup champion, but she had been furious with her third-place finish. If I hadn't witnessed the competition myself, I would have blown off the idea that a low placement for Sammy could be motive for murder, but now I wasn't so sure. Her intensity when it came to coffee was like nothing I'd ever seen. She had mentioned that she might stop by Torte. I would have to cross my fingers that she would make an appearance at the bakeshop, or I would have to figure out a way to track her down. I hoped that she would show up at Torte so I could butter her up with some of our delectable lemon rosemary shortbread cookies and see if she might be more forthcoming.

Doubtful, Jules, I said to myself as I passed the vast

green lawns and impressive line of cherry trees on the Southern Oregon University campus. Summer school students lounged on beach blankets and tossed Frisbees. A group of cheerleading campers wearing matching blue T-shirts practiced pyramids on the grass. SOU hosted a variety of camps throughout the summer from cheerleading to theater—staffed by OSF actors—to science, held in its labs. I always enjoyed watching young campers trot around campus. The thought brought a slight tightness to my chest.

Lately I'd been thinking more and more about children of my own. I wasn't ready yet. That much I knew for sure. Carlos and I needed time together to rebuild our relationship before we considered having a baby. We had just found our way back together, I didn't want to throw the stress of starting a family into the mix.

The problem was that I didn't have unlimited time. Yes, women were having babies well into their forties these days, but not without risk. If Carlos and I decided to take the plunge into parenthood at some point, I wanted to be young enough to enjoy the experience. The other looming question was whether Carlos was even interested in having more kids. He already had Ramiro, who was now fourteen years old. Was Carlos open to the idea of providing Ramiro with a sibling?

I brushed the thought out of my mind as I continued down Siskiyou Boulevard toward the plaza. Carlos had been in Ashland for only a couple of months. Now wasn't the time to broach the subject. However, I couldn't put it off forever either.

You don't have to add that to your list of worries, Jules, I told myself as the creamy rooftop of Ashland

Springs, the plaza's only skyscraper, came into view. I had a tendency to overthink everything for better and for worse, and I didn't need to ruminate on my future at the moment.

When I arrived at Torte, every outdoor table was taken. Families enjoyed cold brew and our concrete milkshakes under large red and teal umbrellas mounted on each table. Banners advertising the upcoming Juneteenth celebration and Fourth of July parade hung from the antique streetlamps. Next door, at A Rose by Any Other Name, large tins with poppies, reedy grasses, and stargazer lilies sat in front of the window, which was draped in white with bridal bouquets in pale blushing palettes hanging from twine. I made a note to talk to Rosa and Steph after Andy finished the competition about doing a bridal showcase for our window display. It was hard to believe, but wedding season was upon us.

Inside the bakeshop there was a line for pastries and generous scoops of concrete in our house-made waffle cones. "Hi Sequoia, I'm back. Do you need a hand?" I called.

Sequoia had her dreadlocks twisted in a loose braid. Her hands flew in a choreographed rhythm as she poured shots over ice. "Nope. I'm good. Rosa could probably use some help, though."

Rosa stood behind the pastry case taking orders and payments, scooping creamy concretes, and boxing up pastries.

I squeezed past the line and tied on an apron. "It looks like the afternoon rush came early."

She brushed her hands on her apron. "Only within

the last few minutes. It's been steady all day and then boom—it exploded! Everyone came at once."

I helped box and plate orders. Then I did a sweep of the dining room, refilling coffees and taking away empty dishes. Within twenty minutes the line had died down.

"Thank you." Rosa wiped her brow with the back of her hand. "That was quite the rush."

"Agreed." I rearranged a stack of our diner-style mugs.

Rosa closed the ice-cream cooler. "I was laughing with Carlos the other day. It's funny to compare his Spanish to mine. You know there are many differences between the Spanish spoken in Spain versus Mexico. Take 'ice cream' for example. I would say 'nieve,' while Carlos calls it 'helado.'" She emphasized her accent.

"You told him your pronunciation was right, though?" I teased.

"Yes. I let him know that he is absolutely butchering my native language." Rosa's face lit up when she smiled.

Bethany came upstairs balancing two trays of black and white cupcakes, strawberry shortcakes, pecan shortbread, mini rhubarb pies, and lemon champagne cakes. "This is the last of it. Customers have gone through the pastries like crazy today."

"How's everything in the kitchen?" I asked, making room for her to slide the trays into the pastry case.

"Good. Sterling is finishing the last of the lunch orders. Marty is packaging the rest of the bread for delivery, and Steph and I are almost done with custom cakes. How did it go? No one has told me a word yet.

We got caught up in the rush as soon as Marty and Steph came back. Actually, come to think of it, why are you all back? I can't believe you're already here. Is the competition over? Does that mean Andy didn't win?"

Since there was a lull in the line, I filled everyone in on what had happened.

"Oh my God! I can't believe it. Poor Andy. I hope Diaz gets in serious trouble for ruining his drink. Did they arrest him?" Bethany scowled. She twisted one of her curls around her finger. It was her tell. She had harbored feelings for Andy for a while. I wasn't sure if he reciprocated the interest. Not because he wasn't attracted to Bethany, but because he had been obsessed with coffee and the Barista Cup. Once the competition was over, I wondered if he would let some of the pressure he'd been putting on himself go.

"I don't know, but he has been kicked out of the competition." I explained how the event was being rescheduled for tomorrow. "What do you think about closing up shop and having all of us go cheer him on?"

"That would be awesome!" Bethany beamed. I could count on her for never-ending positivity. "We could even livestream it on social. That would be cool."

Sequoia and Rosa agreed that attending together would be good for Andy but also a fun team-building exercise.

"Yeah, come to think of it, I'll call James and see if I can get a reservation for dinner. We could do a late dinner after the event outside on the patio. What do you think?"

"Count me in," Bethany said.

Rosa and Sequoia seconded her.

I was excited about the possibility. Not only would it be nice to spend the evening with my hardworking staff outside of Torte, but it would also give me a reason to get in contact with James.

I was about to go downstairs to fill Sterling, Marty, and Steph in on my plans when Sammy came in the front door.

She wore a black leather biking jacket and a pair of dark sunglasses. A large cargo purse with coffee pins and badges was tucked on her arm.

What luck.

"You made it," I said when she stepped up to the counter. "What can I get you? A coffee—dare I ask how you take it?"

"How I take my coffee?" Sammy didn't remove her sunglasses.

"Yeah."

"Seriously. I take my coffee seriously."

I laughed. "I have no doubt about that. But, seriously what can I get you? It's on the house."

"I wasn't kidding. Coffee is my life." She frowned, staring at me from behind the gray-toned lenses. "And, you don't need to do that. I can pay my own way."

"No, I insist." I glanced over to the windows where a booth had just opened up. "In fact, why don't you go grab that booth? I'll bring you an assortment of pastries for us to taste. You mentioned expanding your baking options, so I'll grab some of everything we have in the case today."

"Uh, I guess." She sounded unsure. "I wasn't planning on hanging out for long. I have a lot of practicing to do."

"You should give yourself a little break. I told Andy the same thing." I cut a slice of the lemon champagne cake that was layered with lemon curd and champagne buttercream. Then I added a pecan shortbread bar and a mini rhubarb pie. "Sequoia, will you make a couple of special drinks? I'm going to deliver this to Sammy." I lowered my voice. "By the way, she's one of the baristas Andy has been competing against. She's won the last three years in a row, so make whatever you're in the mood for."

"I'm totally down with that." Sequoia reached for a gallon of almond milk. "I know just the drink."

"Great." I took the pastries and joined Sammy. "Here's a sampling of our baked goods."

"Impressive." She had taken off her jacket and pushed her sunglasses on the top of her head. When she reached for a fork and took a stab of the champagne lemon cake, I couldn't help but stare at her tattoos. They were all of coffee—coffee cups, coffee art, coffee beans, coffee sayings. It was impossible to tell where one tattoo began and another ended. Her skin reminded me of the tattoo sleeves the costume shop down the plaza sold for the Halloween parade.

After savoring the lemon cake for a minute, she looked at me. "This is good. Like big-city level good. Not bad. I'm impressed."

"Thanks." Sammy's perspective didn't surprise me. Many tourists who visited Ashland for the first time were shocked at the plethora of top-notch restaurants in town. For a small community, our food scene was on par with any major city on the West Coast. It was one of the many reasons I loved being a part of Ashland's thriving downtown.

Sequoia brought over two iced coffees. "This is our special today. It's an iced almond milk latte infused with house-made simple almond syrup, vanilla, and a pinch of cocoa. You'll see I went heavy on the froth."

She wasn't kidding. Our drinks had nearly three inches of frothed foam on the top.

"Cool. Cool." Sammy gave her a nod. Whether it was of approval or disdain was difficult to tell, given that Sammy made Steph look effusive.

"So you're from Spokane," I asked. "What's the coffee culture like there?"

"It's small, but there are about ten or twelve indie shops doing pretty cool stuff. My place, Fluid, has been there for almost a decade now. We started when there was no one doing artisan coffee." She rummaged through her purse looking for something.

Sammy couldn't be more than twenty-six or seven. When had she gotten in the business?

She stopped searching her purse. She must have sensed my confusion. "I started working there part time when I was going to school at Gonzaga, and then once I graduated, I bought out the owner."

"That's quite a feat for a recent college grad." Now it was my turn to be impressed.

"I had help. It was my parents' graduation gift." She sounded nonchalant.

Nice gift, I thought.

"When did you start competing?"

She thought about it for a moment. "Probably five or

six years ago. Right after I bought the shop. It was Benson who got me into the Barista Cup."

I tried to keep my expression neutral. Benson had gotten Sammy into the Barista Cup? Clearly they had had a lasting relationship. The question is, what did that mean in terms of his murder?

Chapter Sixteen

"How did Benson get you involved in the Barista Cup?" I asked, hoping my tone matched my passive expression.

"He recruited a bunch of us back in the day." Sammy pushed her purse to the side. She rubbed her forearms repeatedly as if we were in the middle of a Siberian snowstorm.

"Is everything okay?" I asked.

She took another bite of the cake, stabbing her fork with force to break off a piece of the light and airy slice. "I can't find my medication. My doctor prescribed a pill that helps me relax during competitions."

That wasn't a shocker. Sammy's fierce approach to the Barista Cup would definitely fray her nerves. What I did wonder was whether the missing medication could be linked to Benson's murder.

"It's missing?"

She rubbed the back of her neck. "Yeah, I must have left them at the hotel."

I dropped the subject for the moment. "Anyway, what were you saying about Benson encouraging you to compete?"

"That was the way things went when the Cup started. Listen, this is when the coffee scene was underground. You had to know the right people or get invited. It wasn't the free-for-all it is now. There were no newbies. The Cup was reserved for the best of the best. I'm talking about baristas who lived and breathed coffee and understood the science, history, and culture that goes into each cup. I mean, any barista from Starbucks, or one of the big corporate coffee chains, can compete today, which is total crap if you ask me."

"Really, so Benson recruited baristas?" That seemed odd. Why would a judge recruit contestants? I didn't bother to respond to Sammy's commentary on who should or should not be allowed to compete in the challenge. I could tell that she and I likely had opposing viewpoints on that issue. Although her words may not have completely spelled it out, I suspected she her choice of "newbie" was a dig at Andy.

Sammy answered my question before I'd had a chance to voice it. "He started the Barista Cup, you know that, right? It's common knowledge."

"No, I didn't know that." That wasn't entirely true, but I wanted to hear what she had to say.

"Yeah. It was his baby." Sammy stopped short of saying *duh*.

"It sounded like it still was his baby."

"Yeah. He was pretty protective of the Cup. But he deserved to be. He built it from nothing to what it is today. You could say that he helped make coffee a trend. He was the *Seattle Times* food critic for years. Seattle was the hub of the coffee scene then. That's where

Starbucks started. Seattle's Best, Tully's, Caffe Vita. All the big players in coffee originated in Seattle. Once that trend started to take off, Benson began writing and reviewing coffee shops just like restaurants. He was one of the first critics to make the shift."

"I had no idea." I took a drink of Sequoia's frothy almond milk latte. The almond milk gave the coffee a light texture and brought out the nutty undertones in the roast.

"Yeah, a good review from Benson could put you on the map, and a bad review could kill you. I had a bunch of friends who lost jobs because of his scathing reviews." Her sunglasses slipped from her head. She readjusted the dark frames, using them like a headband to hold back her jet black hair.

Losing a job could be motive for murder. I also found it interesting that she had used the word "kill" to describe getting a bad review.

Sammy continued. "Benson did a five-part piece for the *Seattle Times* about Washington's coffee regions. He came to Spokane and was pretty impressed with what we were doing at Fluid. It was a big deal for us. At the time, we had a faithful crowd of locals, but Benson helped put us on the map. People came from all over to try our coffee thanks to Benson's write-up."

"How did that translate into competing?" I swirled the ice in my coffee.

She scrunched her forehead in concentration. "I don't really remember exactly. We kept in touch via email. Anytime he was in the area he would stop into Fluid to see what we were doing next. He kind of took me under his wing. I think he saw my potential. At some point when he and Piper decided to start the Barista Cup, he sent an email to a bunch of us asking if we'd be interested in competing."

"Wait, did you say he and Piper started the competition?" The line was starting to pick up at the counter. Sequoia placed four drinks on the bar and was working on the next order, while Rosa sent people off with bags of our house-made granola and pistachio cream pies. If the crowd continued to grow, I would need to excuse myself to go help them.

Sammy tapped her fork on the edge of her cake plate in rhythm, like she was playing the drums. "Yeah. They were a thing for a while. I think they lived together."

Woah. That was major news. Piper and Benson had been a couple?

"When was this?" I asked.

Sammy frowned. "I don't know, I think six years ago, maybe five."

I wish I had a notebook with me. I tried to memorize everything Sammy was telling me. "And, you've been competing ever since?"

"Basically. If you want to take competing seriously you have to treat it like a job. I'm lucky to be the sole owner of Fluid. I can dedicate my time at the coffee lab to practicing. I hired a coach after I went to nationals the first time. I finished in seventh place—not where I wanted to be. I knew I needed to level up. Ever since, I've made it my singular mission to win the Barista World Cup. That takes hours and hours of practice." She took a taste of the drink and moved her head from side to side as if trying to decide if she approved of

Sequoia's creation. "Benson was good to me at the beginning." She trailed off.

"Did something change?"

She cleared her throat. "No, not at all."

Was she lying?

"Did Benson continue writing reviews for the *Seattle Times*?"

"No. He gave that up a few years ago. There was a lawsuit. I don't know the details, but a coffee roaster sued him for ruining their reputation and lost revenue."

That was interesting. "Do you know who?"

"Nope. I don't even know if that is true. It was rumored, but I never heard more about it."

I made another mental note to look into Benson's past articles in the *Seattle Times*.

Sammy finished the slice of cake. "I can't eat all of this. It's really good, but if I finish it, I'll be in a sugar coma, especially since I'm already jacked up on caffeine."

"Let me box up the leftovers for you. You might want a midnight snack later."

"Thanks. This coffee isn't bad either. Tell your barista, good job."

I started to stand, but stopped myself. "You know, that reminds me. You were so upset about finishing in third place, which seems pretty impressive to me."

She held up three fingers. Her ombré nails in multiple shades of blue reminded me of a cascading waterfall. "Third? Third is not good when you've won the National Barista Cup and have gone to Worlds. Third is terrible."

Debating her status in the competition wasn't my goal. "You seemed particularly upset with Benson, though."

Sammy's lip curled. "No. No I wasn't. That's the way these events go. The intensity of the challenges gets to everyone. It's no big deal."

Maybe. Or maybe Sammy was trying to downplay her outburst now that Benson was dead.

"Hey, can I get your number? I might have a couple questions to ask you about the pastry market, if that's cool?"

"Sure." We exchanged numbers. Then, I went to package up her pastries and added a few bonus cookies for later. "Here you go," I said returning with a Torte box. "I hope you enjoy these later, and good luck tomorrow."

She grabbed her purse and took the box. "I won't need luck now." With that she walked out the door.

Things seemed to be getting weirder by the minute. What did she mean by that? Now that Benson was dead she was confident that she would win? I hated suspecting anyone of murder, but I couldn't rule out the possibility that Sammy was involved.

I went downstairs to fill the rest of the team in on my plan and to bake. I needed a distraction. As expected, the kitchen was running as smoothly as a ship on still waters. Everyone was excited about the idea of getting to see Andy compete and having a team dinner. I washed my hands with lemon rosemary soap and went to the walk-in for ingredients. Since I had a few hours before Carlos and I were due to meet Lance and Piper, I decided to make dinner for later—a pasta salad packed with flavor, which would keep in the fridge.

I loaded my arms up with red onions, carrots, cherry tomatoes, chicken, and three kinds of cheese. Next I grabbed a container of pasta, olive oil, vinegar, garlic, and an assortment of fresh herbs and spices. I set a pot of water to boil on the stove and started with a marinade for the chicken. I diced garlic and mixed it with the olive oil, vinegar, and spices. I set half of it aside to dress the pasta salad and poured the rest into a gallon Ziplock bag along with the chicken. The chicken could marinate for hours. I could grill it right before I was ready to serve the pasta.

With that done, I began chopping red onions, carrots, tomatoes, and Colby-Jack, Irish cheddar, and Swiss cheese. My water had come to a rolling boil, so I added the pasta and set a timer for eight minutes. Pasta is best served al dente. There's nothing worse than limp, soggy noodles. To ensure a well-cooked yet firm pasta, I always boil it for two or three minutes less than the time recommended on the packaging.

Once the pasta had cooked and cooled, I added it to a large bowl along with veggies and cubes of cheese. I poured the remaining dressing over the noodles and mixed everything together. Then I covered the bowl with plastic wrap and placed it in the walk-in. The flavors should mingle and develop with a little rest. I had made a triple batch. Not only could Carlos and I have some for dinner, but there was plenty to serve for tomorrow's lunch special.

I still had an hour before I was due at Puck's, so I went to my small office and put in a call to James. He answered right away.

"The Hills, this is James."

"It's Jules from Torte, I wanted to see if I could make a reservation for a large party tomorrow night."

"How many people are you thinking and what time? If it's during the competition, things might be pretty tight during regular dinner hours since we had to push the Barista Cup finals back."

"I was hoping for after the competition." I told him my idea about a spontaneous staff party.

"Oh, sure, I love it. Yeah, we can definitely accommodate that. You want to sit outside on the patio?"

We made the arrangements. Before I hung up, I asked him one more question. "Hey, I heard that Benson used to be a coffee critic for the *Seattle Times*. Did you know that?"

He went silent.

For a minute I thought he had hung up or that we'd been disconnected.

"Hello?"

"Yeah, I'm here. What about Benson?"

"I was just wondering if you knew that he was a coffee critic."

"Where did you hear that?"

I didn't want to throw Sammy under the bus. "I don't know who I heard it from. Word is going around."

"Why are you asking me?" He sounded irritated.

Had I hit a nerve?

"You've been in the business so long, I wondered if you had known Benson when he was writing for the *Times*."

"Listen, I have to go. I have, like, a dozen fires to put

out, but I have your reservation. We'll see you tomorrow night." He hung up.

I couldn't be sure, but from the almost instantaneous shift in his tone, I had the sense that James knew more about Benson than he was saying.

Chapter Seventeen

An hour later, I left Torte and walked a few doors down to Puck's Pub. The restaurant was designed to resemble the forest scene from *A Midsummer Night's Dream* with snaking ivy, twinkling lights, and tiny fairies tucked into nooks and crannies. Tourists frequented Puck's for its whimsical Shakespearean atmosphere and craft beer served in pewter steins. Puck's was also a favorite hangout for locals, especially during the off-season when the popular pub offered open mic nights for musicians, actors, and spoken-word poets.

Carlos was standing at the bar when I came inside. He wore a pair of navy chino shorts, a gray-and-white-striped T-shirt, and Top-Siders. With his tanned arms and the slight wave in his dark hair, he looked as if he had spent the afternoon on a catamaran. When he saw me and flashed me his dazzling smile, my knees went weak. "Mi querida, I was going to order for you. What would you like?"

Puck's summer cocktail menu featured a variety of delicate and refreshing drinks. I opted for Love at First

Sip, a blend of rum, fresh strawberries, lime, and a splash of bitters.

Carlos ordered a London mule with gin, lavender, lime, and ginger beer. "Lance is outside. He found a table on the patio."

We took our drinks and wound our way through the restaurant and out the back exit. Like the other restaurants on the plaza, Puck's had outside seating on the Calle. Like its interior, the rustic outdoor tables that sat parallel to the creek continued the fanciful vibe. They were each made of old-growth wood and hand carved. Instead of providing shade for guests with colorful patio umbrellas like the other restaurants nearby, Puck's had installed dark green sails that stretched in varied angles to mimic a forest canopy.

Lance was seated at a four-person table adjacent to the water. He waved with two fingers. "Over here!"

Piper hadn't arrived yet.

I inhaled the scent of jasmine and the sound of the gurgling creek.

Lance pounced the minute we sat down. "We don't have much time. What's our strategy?" He strummed his fingers together.

"Strategy?" Carlos looked confused.

"You haven't told him?" Lance gave me an exasperated sigh.

"I just got here. I've been at the bakeshop."

Lance dismissed me and gave Carlos his version of the morning's events. Never one to pass up an opportunity to add extra flourish, Lance embellished every detail, making it sound as if the Professor had tackled and cuffed Diaz for owning up to sabotaging Andy's latte.

"What? Andy's coffee was tainted by this contestant Diaz? This is terrible. How could someone do such a thing?" Carlos's hands flew in the air as he spoke.

"Yes, yes, it's a travesty, an absolute travesty, but we have to think of Andy. We have to focus for his sake. It's all connected. It has to be." Lance clapped twice. "Piper is on her way here now. We have an opportunity to figure out what she knows. I'm convinced that there's more to her and Benson's relationship."

"How?" Carlos sounded skeptical.

I took a sip of my cocktail infused with summer flavors. The sourness of the lime paired beautifully with the sweet strawberries.

"I don't have anything firm to go on yet, but she and I had a chat this morning, and I know enough about body language, movement, and what our eyes say when our lips are saying something else from my years directing to know that she was definitely holding back."

"That could be true." I told them about my conversation with Sammy.

"Most enlightening. Well done." Lance raised his cocktail in a toast to me. "Further proof that we need to make the most of this happy hour. Let's dazzle Piper with our enchanting personalities and see if we can get her to spill some secrets."

Carlos frowned. "You two and your schemes, I do not understand how you get involved in a case like this."

Piper arrived, saving me from a lengthy explanation. Without her judge's apron and clipboard, she looked less severe. She wore her copper curly hair long and loose. Yellow-tinted sunglasses replaced the frames she'd been wearing earlier.

"Hi everyone. Thanks for the invite." She placed a glass of white wine on the table and sat down next to Lance. "When I travel for these competitions, I usually end up having dinner alone at the hotel bar, so this is such a treat—especially after this weekend."

Lance introduced her to Carlos. "You met Jules at the competition, right?"

"Nice to see you again." Piper clinked her wineglass to mine. "I'm sorry about your barista, Andy. In all the years I've been judging the Barista Cup and now hosting the event, we've never had anything like this happen. The entire weekend has been a train wreck."

"How well did you know Benson?" Lance didn't hesitate.

Piper swirled her wineglass. "Benson and I go way back. I can't say that we always saw eye to eye, but the man had a meticulous palate. No one had talent like Benson. He was a coffee sommelier. He could tell you in just a few sips everything from the origin of the beans to the roasting-and-brewing process used. He could distinguish every aroma and flavor in a cupping," She stopped for a minute. "That's the technical term we use, in case you aren't familiar. Anyway, he could give you the perfect food pairing for every cup too. Watching him dissect coffee was truly a work of art." Her voice trailed off for a moment. She shook herself from the memory. "If Benson liked your coffee, chances were solid that everyone would like your coffee."

"Yeah, I heard something about him being a critic for the *Seattle Times*." I found it curious that Piper made no mention of her personal relationship with him.

"That's true." Piper ran a finger along the rim of her

wineglass. Her nails were polished in a thin clear coat. I noticed that there was a tan line from a missing ring on her right hand. "Benson was one of the leading voices in the industry for many years. A good write-up from him could make you and a bad review could break you."

"And you knew him then?" I asked.

She nodded. "Yes. You have to remember that the coffee industry has exploded in the last couple of decades. For many years there was a relatively small group of us in the artisan coffee world, but once the trend took off, the numbers of indie shops has skyrocketed. Back in the day most of us knew everyone by name. East Coast. West Coast. It didn't matter."

"Were you a coffee writer too?" Lance asked, as he took a drink of his cocktail.

"No. Not me. I worked for an Italian importer. I would help small independent shops install espresso machines and train them how to use it. That's where my technical expertise comes from. Benson was more about taste and flavor, whereas I know how machines should be operated and maintained."

"It sounds like you two had complementary skills," I said, hoping that might prompt her to say more.

She stared at her wine for a moment before answering. "You could say that. We had some good times in the early years."

"That sounds ominous." Lance chuckled.

"Not really. We started the Barista Cup. Did you know that?"

"Please enlighten us. We'd love to know more about its origins." Lance laid it on thick.

"It was Benson's idea." Piper adjusted her sunglasses

as the light cut through the sunshades. "It was a way to highlight some of the incredibly talented baristas, especially coffee artists who lived in more remote regions. He pulled me in for my technical knowledge. The first few years were nothing like now. We had five baristas. They were held at different coffee shops. No vendors. The only spectators were the other shop employees and maybe a handful of faithful customers. Then the competition started to take off. We got vendor sponsorship money and were able to give cash prizes and host the event at bigger venues. Each year it's grown exponentially."

"That sounds like a success." Carlos spoke for the first time.

"It was. It was fun. I enjoyed seeing baristas gain regional and national attention. That was the best part for me. We weren't making much money in those days. It was about the coffee and the community." Her voice held a sense of nostalgia and longing.

"Did something happen with you and Benson?" Lance asked what I knew we were all thinking—why was Piper being closed lipped about her personal relationship with him?

"No. Not exactly. We just had different visions for the future. He wanted to continue to grow the competition and I felt like we'd maxed out our capacity. It's become a full-time job to organize the event—competitors, judges, advertisers, ticket sales, marketing. Benson wanted to do even more. He was pushing to host monthly, quarterly, and then an annual competition. I didn't have the capacity to make that happen, but he didn't want to hear it. He had a vision and was used to getting his way. The other issue was the way he was treating the baristas. At first it was kind of a joke. We would say that he was the Simon Cowell of the coffee world, but lately it had gotten ugly. The fun in his teasing had disappeared. It became mean spirited. We have amazing competitors. None of them deserved to be ridiculed by Benson. Maybe he didn't like a particular coffee, but there were no terrible drinks. If a barista makes it into the Cup, they've already proven themselves."

Piper was much more forthcoming than I had expected.

"Let me guess, Benson didn't take kindly to any feedback about his brash style?" Lance asked.

"No. That made it worse. I stopped trying, because if I said anything, he would take it out on the contestants. That wasn't fair."

"This Benson, he does not sound like a very kind man," Carlos noted.

"He wasn't." Piper knocked back her glass and drank half the wine in one long swoop. "I can't say I'm heartbroken that he's dead. There were days later in our relationship that I have to admit I wished he were."

Lance kicked me under the table. I had to bite my bottom lip to stop myself from saying *ouch*.

I didn't need to make eye contact with him to know what he was thinking. Piper and Benson definitely had a contentious relationship. Did that mean she could have killed him?

Chapter Eighteen

Piper regained her composure. She sat taller and tossed her hair over her shoulder. "I'm sorry. I know that saying that about Benson must sound crass. I would never want anyone to die. We had a complicated relationship, that's all."

I decided that this was my chance to probe deeper. "Were you and Benson romantically involved?"

She snorted with a dismissive laugh. "He liked to think that. We had a fling that flamed out fast. I broke it off long ago. I should have done it sooner, but you know how that goes. Men! You can't live with them and you can't live without them!"

"I'll drink to that." Lance touched his glass to hers.

A waiter came by the table to ask if we wanted to order anything or have our drinks refreshed.

Piper stretched and massaged the side of her eye. "I would love to stay longer, but I don't sleep well in hotel rooms and I have an early, early meeting with James tomorrow morning to go through final details." She reached into her purse and handed the waiter a twenty-dollar bill. "We should do this again soon. I may be sticking around longer, so next time maybe dinner—on me?"

"Wonderful." Lance stood to shake her hand.

Carlos followed suit. Piper looped her purse over her arm and left with a wave.

"That was enlightening, wasn't it?" Lance asked after she was gone. "I most certainly picked up a wistful quality in her tone when she was reminiscing about her past with Benson. Agree?" He raised an eyebrow.

"I was thinking the same thing."

Carlos frowned. "What? You asked her about her past and she gave you an honest answer—why is this a problem?"

"Ah, such an innocent and trusting mind." Lance reached across the table and patted Carlos's hand. "Don't worry, Juliet and I shall teach you the Ashland ways of the world, won't we, darling?"

Carlos being painted as innocent made me chuckle. "What ways?" I bantered back.

Lance threw his hand to his forehead. "Must I do everything around here? Carlos, if Juliet and I have learned nothing in our time assisting the police in their investigations, it's to trust no one. I repeat—*no one.*"

Carlos laughed, which only encouraged Lance.

"You think I jest, my friend, but do not say that I didn't warn you. Our Ashland might appear to be bucolic and charming, but there's a dark underbelly in this hamlet that your stunning wife and I have seen on more than one occasion."

Carlos couldn't keep a straight face. "Si, si. Thank you for telling me, my friend. I will take your warning to heart." He placed his hand over his heart and winked.

Lance scoffed. "Mark my words, Piper is not being entirely forthcoming. I don't trust that woman. I can't pinpoint what it is, but let's not allow her easy dismissals to blind us to the truth."

I sighed. "I wish I had a sense of the truth. Everything is muddled. Piper, James, Diaz, and Sammy all either had a reason to want Benson dead or an argument with him. I'm more confused than ever."

Carlos leaned over and kissed the top of my head. "Mi querida, do not let this worry you. This is the job of the police. The Professor he will take care of this."

"Yeah," I agreed.

Lance caught my eye.

As our friendship developed, we had come to have an understanding between us. Most of the time we didn't even need to speak. I could tell what Lance was thinking. His quick glance told me everything—we would continue this conversation later.

He took a few bills out his wallet. "This round is on me, you two love birds. I have a date, which means I must go freshen up. Juliet, we're on for our coffee date per usual tomorrow morning, yes?'"

"Uh, yeah." Lance and I didn't have a standing coffee date.

"Thank you for the drink. We will return the favor next time." Carlos extended his hand and got to his feet.

"I know you will." Lance gave him a Cheshire cat grin and stood too.

"Before we go, did Julieta mention the dinner in the vines?" Carlos asked.

Lance looked miffed. "No. No, she did not. *Julieta*, are you holding out on me?"

I rolled my eyes. "No. It slipped my mind. There's been a lot going on." Even though Lance had insisted on being a silent financial partner in Uva, Carlos and I liked to loop him in on our plans and vision. Lance trusted us implicitly. As he had said when we signed the paperwork making our collaboration official, "I'm in it for the free wine and the company."

He claimed that he enjoyed being treated like royalty whenever he graced Uva with his presence, but I knew that he had swept in to save the small, organic vineyard from being bulldozed and turned into a gated community out of the goodness of his heart and for me. Recently Lance had opened up and shared pieces of his childhood and family story; memories that had been painful and kept close to his chest for decades. It had made us closer and given me a glance into his deeper character that he didn't let many people see.

"Fair enough." Lance turned to Carlos. "Do tell."

"You remember we had discussed the idea of hosting dinners at the vineyard?"

"I do."

"Julieta and I think we should host the next Sunday Supper in the vines. I will prepare a five-course meal and pair a wine with each dish. I think she may have told you about our themed dinners on the ship?"

"Yes, yes. They sounded fit for the stage." Lance rubbed his hands together.

Carlos smiled at the compliment. "We did not want to do a food color pairing, but we thought it would be nice to have the guests dress in the same color—white. It is summer and everything is fresh and warm and breezy. What do you say? Do you like the idea?"

"Yes! Absolutely, yes." Lance bounced on his tiptoes. "I say let's book a date. Count me in. I happen to look ravishing in white if I do say so myself."

"What do you think?" Carlos asked me. "Next week? Is that enough time to get the word out? I have been playing with the menu the last few days, so that will not be a problem."

"Torte's Sunday Suppers are legendary. If you put the word out the morning of the event, you'll have the dinner booked in five minutes," Lance said.

"That might be a bit of an exaggeration," I replied.

"My point is, next week is excellent and my Sunday happens to be free, so I vote yes."

"Si, it is a date." Carlos beamed.

I knew he was excited about getting to share his love and knowledge of food and wine with his new friends and family.

We parted ways with Lance.

"I made dinner, if you're hungry." I said to Carlos as we walked toward Torte.

"Si, I am famished."

The bakeshop was empty. My staff had left it sparkling and spotless.

"The kitchen is cleaner than on the ship. You have taught the team well, Julieta." Carlos ran his finger along the marble countertop.

"They are pretty amazing. Aren't they?" I went to get the pasta and chicken from the fridge.

"What can I do?" Carlos washed his hands.

"Can you grill the chicken?" I set the bowl of pasta on the counter and gave it another toss.

Carlos warmed olive oil in a pan.

"Speaking of our staff, I want to treat everyone to dinner after the competition tomorrow night. What do you think?"

"That is a wonderful idea." Carlos seared the chicken breasts. "I will talk with Sterling and Marty about the menu for the Sunday Supper. I would like their help."

"They'll be thrilled." Carlos had taken Sterling under his wing last summer when he and Ramiro had come to celebrate Mom and the Professor's wedding. Sterling and his father had endured a strained relationship, so watching him and Carlos build an easy and natural rapport had made me happy. Likewise, Carlos and Marty had become fast friends. They shared a mutual love of corny jokes and enjoyed playing pranks in the kitchen. Carlos believed that a happy kitchen was an efficient kitchen. I didn't disagree, but I had found myself holding my breath on more than one occasion, waiting for a fake snake to pop out of a flour canister or finding plastic spiders mixed in with raisins. Thus far Carlos had been restrained, but I knew that there was no chance he had given up his impish ways, and I wondered if part of pulling Sterling and Marty in on the menu planning was also going to involve some kitchen antics.

Once he had grilled the chicken, he cut it into long, thin strips. I poured us glasses of water, plated the pasta salad, and buttered some rolls. "This is incredible. I must cook for you, Julieta. You have been doing so much cooking for me. Are you trying to fatten me up?" He ran his hand over his taut waist.

"No. I've needed a brain break, that's all. I was so worried about Andy, but after today I'm feeling more confident that suspicion has shifted away from him."

Carlos held my gaze. "This is one of the reasons I love you, mi querida. You care so much for everyone around you. Sometimes to your own detriment, si?"

"I know." That was fair. I did tend to get wrapped up in investigations like the mystery surrounding Benson's death and worry about my staff's personal lives and well-being. I blame it on a combination of my inquisitive nature and genetics. I had recently learned that my father, who died when I was young, had assisted the Professor on his first murder case, a previously unsolved hit-and-run. In a strange way it brought me comfort and a new point of connection with my father to know that the Capshaw bloodline had always been intrigued with puzzling together clues and trying to restore justice. I knew that Carlos didn't fully understand my obsession. He seemed resigned to the knowledge that I wasn't going to abandon who I was at my core for him. That didn't mean that I needed to rub it in his face, though. I tried to be tactful and low key about my involvement.

Carlos dove into his pasta salad and changed the subject. "Okay, Sunday it is. I want to make sure that our Uva wines are the star of the show. Every course will be designed to enhance and elevate the flavors of the wine. I will work with Marty and Sterling, but I am hoping that you can find the time to brainstorm the dessert course."

"Absolutely." I savored the tangy flavors in the cold salad. The chicken was tender and juicy. "What wine are you thinking for the dessert course?"

"At first I was thinking the rosé because it's light and sweet, but I want to start the salad course with that and work our way through the deeper wines. What do you think about a dessert pairing with the Cab Franc?"

Our Cab Franc was a heavy and bold red wine with dense notes of blackberries and spice. Immediately, I thought of a pavlova, a chewy and crisp marshmallow-like meringue we could serve with berries steeped in the Cab Franc, vanilla bean, lemon zest, and vanilla. We could finish it with a scoop of our vanilla concrete or hand-whipped cream.

When I finished telling Carlos my brainstorm, he dabbed the side of his lips with a napkin. "This is making me drool. It is perfection. For the other courses I want herbaceous salad, bread and cheeses with dipping sauces and olives, a cold soup, and then grass-fed beef. I don't know yet how we will serve it. Marinated steaks? Or perhaps thinly sliced and slathered with pesto. So many choices. I will see what Marty and Sterling have to add, but this dinner it will be beautiful."

"What about décor?"

"Could we ask Janet to make some simple white flowers for each table? What else do you think we need?"

"Sure." Janet, Thomas's mom, owned A Rose by Any Other Name and had an exquisite eye when it came to floral design. Our families had partnered for years. Janet and her staff brought table bouquets to Torte every week and would stop by unannounced to touch up their flower arrangements.

"That's where Bethany and Steph will come in. For sure we should do flowers along with white table linens and candles, but I know they'll have some other great ideas. Bethany has an amazing talent for framing photos for social media."

"This is good." A wide grin spread across his face.

"This is what we need. If we can take pictures and share them, this will bring in even more tourists."

We agreed on the remaining details. I would send an invite out to our Sunday Supper email list and task Steph with designing some posters to display at Uva and by the pastry case. We finished dinner, cleaned up, and headed for home. Carlos made us Italian-style espressos and we sat on the deck watching the sunset. I took comfort in being cocooned in Carlos's arms beneath a canopy of waxy oak trees and towering ponderosa pines. The sun put a show on for us as it illuminated Grizzly Peak and painted the hills a brilliant blushing pink and eggplant purple. We lingered until the stars made an appearance against the black night sky.

He didn't mention anything more about Benson's death. I appreciated the reprieve. In the morning, Lance and I would meet for coffee and map out a plan of what we'd do next.

Chapter Nineteen

The next morning was Monday, which meant that Torte would likely be busy all day. I wanted to get an early start since we intended to close the bakeshop to cheer on Andy later in the afternoon. I left Carlos snoozing in bed, pulled on a pair of white shorts, tennis shoes, a simple V-neck shirt, and a thin sweater. I opted to walk down Mountain Avenue and along Siskiyou Boulevard. My morning walks were a moving mediation. A way to clear my head and center myself before the mixers whirled to life and the ovens pumped out heat.

Despite the hour, the plaza was starting to come to life as I made my way through town. A city crew watered hanging baskets; shop vendors placed sandwich-board signs on the sidewalk, touting specials and sales; and morning exercisers headed toward Lithia Park with yoga mats and tennis rackets. During the summer season, most shops and restaurants offered extended hours for tourists who might take a stroll through Lithia Park and stop for a coffee or breakfast on the Calle before perusing Ashland's many family-owned boutiques. I waved to a few fellow business owners on my way to

Torte. A gorgeous white lace summer dress with a darted waist and flirty chiffon skirt caught my eye in the window at London Station. It was perfect for our dinner in the vines. I would have to stop in once the three-story mercantile was open and see if they had it in my size.

I continued on to the bakeshop, passing the blue awnings of the police station. As always there was a water dish for dogs and a bucket of chalk for young street artists sitting next to window boxes brimming with heliotrope and salvia.

When I crossed the street to Torte, the bakeshop was still dark. That must mean I was the first to arrive, which was fine by me. I unlocked the basement door, flipped on the lights, and went to work warming ovens, proofing yeast, and mixing cookie batter.

One of my favorite tricks to bring butter up to room temperature quickly—an essential step for baking—is to fill a Mason jar with boiling water. Then I would dump the water into a stockpot to use later and place the steaming jar directly over a stick of butter. After two minutes the stick was smooth and silky. The softened butter could be cut easily with a plastic knife. I used the technique to soften a few cups to use as the base for my lemon rosemary shortbread. The cookies were a popular item with their crisp, buttery texture, bright citrus flavor, and just a touch of rosemary to add an interesting herbal layer. The shortbread only used six simple ingredients: butter, sugar, flour, salt, lemon, and rosemary. I would cut them into pretty daisy shapes and dust them with lemon-infused sugar.

The pasta salad that Carlos and I had shared last night could be one of our lunch specials, but I needed to marinate some more chicken. By the time I had four trays of lemon shortbread baking and a vat of chicken marinating, Andy, Steph, and Sterling arrived. Steph and Sterling had recently moved in together, so I wasn't surprised to see them, but I was shocked to see Andy.

"What are you doing here?" I scolded. "I thought we discussed that you were *not* coming in today."

"I know, boss, but I have some news that I think you're going to want to hear."

Steph twisted her violet hair into two small pixie-like braids. Sterling unzipped his gray hoodie and hung it on the rack near the row of clean aprons.

"News about the murder?" I asked.

"Yeah." Andy nodded. His eyes weren't as puffy as they'd been yesterday. I hoped that meant that he'd finally gotten a good night's sleep.

"Are you going to leave me hanging?"

Andy chuckled. "I am because I need a coffee—bad. I'll run upstairs and make us some and then I'll fill you in."

My curiosity was piqued, but I couldn't turn down a coffee, and I figured pulling shots of espresso was probably as therapeutic for him as kneading bread dough was for me.

"Smells like you're baking," Sterling said, peering into the industrial ovens.

"Lemon rosemary shortbread," I told him.

"Nice." He gave me a nod of approval before folding the top of his apron over so that he could wear half of it around his waist. He grabbed a pristine white kitchen towel and slung it over his shoulder, a trick that he had learned from Carlos. "Any special requests?"

"I made a pasta salad last night." I showed him the marinating chicken. "There should be plenty for individual portions."

"That sounds great. I was thinking of doing a cold carrot and cilantro soup for lunch and Marty had a couple of ideas for handmade naan with a side of hummus."

"Am I drooling?" I teased. "What about you, Steph? Anything you need?"

She clipped two new custom cake orders to the wall near the decorating station. It was the height of wedding season, so we had a systematic approach to ensure that every cake was completed in a timely fashion. Orders in process were displayed on the left side of the wall, pending orders were stored by delivery date in a hanging folder, and completed orders ready for delivery or pickup were clipped to the right side of the wall.

Wedding cakes were very labor intensive. Most took at least a week to produce from start to finish. Plus we still had a lengthy list of custom orders for birthdays and anniversaries along with our regular daily items for the bakeshop.

Steph removed the top order. "I should have the lettering finished on the chalkboard cake in the next couple hours. Then I'm going to work on the three small party cakes that are due to be picked up this afternoon."

"Sounds like a plan." The chalkboard cake had been fun to watch come together. It was a four-tier chocolate cake draped in black fondant to resemble a chalkboard. Steph had been piping quotes about love provided by the bride and groom in white buttercream on each layer. The top of the unique cake would be adorned with a bouquet of flowers. One of the quotes that made me smile each time I had seen it was from Albert Einstein: "You can't blame gravity for falling in love."

True, I thought, as Andy made his way into the kitchen balancing a tray of iced lattes.

"I brought one for each of you." He passed around the cold drinks. "Don't get too excited. It's nothing fancy—a standard iced latte. I've got to save myself for this afternoon."

"Thanks, man." Sterling took one of the glasses. "I'm sure it's awesome and you definitely need to save your best stuff for later."

"Do you want to go sit down?" I pointed to the seating area adjacent to the kitchen.

Andy hesitated. "As long as I'm not keeping you from anything?"

"Not at all."

We took our lattes over to the couch. "What's going on?"

Andy rubbed his hands on his thighs. "I heard a rumor last night. A big rumor that might lead to an arrest in Benson's murder. I'm going to call the Professor first thing, but I wasn't sure when was too early to call him." He looked to the clock. It wasn't yet six.

"That's thoughtful of you, but I know that he would take your call anytime, especially if it's related to a murder investigation."

"Yeah. I'll call him after this." Andy took a long drink. "It's about Sammy and, like I said, I don't know if it's true. It might just be a rumor, but even if it is, I think there's still major implications."

I could feel nervous energy vibrating through me. What had Andy learned?

"Did you know that Sammy owns her shop, Fluid, in Spokane?" He looked particularly young this morning in cargo shorts, graphic Star Wars T-shirt, and baseball cap.

"Yes, she told me that yesterday."

"That's pretty impressive for someone her age." Andy sounded wistful.

"Definitely, but don't let that discourage you. She also told me that her parents bought her the shop as a graduation gift."

"Really?" Andy perked up. "I hadn't heard that."

"What *did* you hear?" I tried to get him to refocus.

"Right." He nodded twice. "Yeah, I guess the rumor is that she's planning to expand Fluid. She wants to open franchises all up and down the West Coast, something like a hundred shops in the next five years. Her goal is total world domination when it comes to coffee."

"Wow. That is ambitious to say the least." I knew enough about franchising to know that it is a serious undertaking I had no interest in. Thankfully, neither had Mom. We were quite content in Ashland.

"You probably know more about this than I do, but apparently there are huge costs with trying to scale up a brand, even if it's just a regional expansion."

"Absolutely." I gave him a brief history on what I had learned about the process in culinary school. There were dozens of factors to consider, including the cost of leasing property, building out sites, supplies, staffing, and marketing—just to cover the basics.

Andy stirred his latte with his paper straw. "So, if it's true, Sammy would have needed a lot of cash and financial backers, right?"

"Unless she's independently wealthy, yeah."

He plunged a straw into his coffee. "Here's where it gets interesting. According to what I heard, Benson was one of her backers. He was planning to invest in the chain. Her vision is not only an expansion of Fluid coffees shops throughout Washington, Oregon, and California, but also a bunch of drive-through locations. That's just the start. After she establishes her dominance on the West Coast, she wants to go nationwide and then even international. I guess she tells people that she's going to be the new Starbucks, only way better. She hates corporate coffee and wants Fluid to make artisan drinks mainstream."

The drive-through coffee market had mushroomed in the last ten years. It was nearly impossible to go to any small town and not have multiple choices for coffee-on-the-go options. In Ashland alone we had five exclusive drive-through shops. It was a risky market. Yes, rents tended to be lower, but the competition was fierce and sales were dependent on variables like proximity to freeways. Mom and I had been approached a while ago about taking the Torte brand regional with a collection of drive-through shops. That was another proposal we declined.

One glaring issue with Sammy's expansion plan was that artisan coffee, like what we served at Torte, was meant to be served slow. Drive-through coffee chains had their place in the market. I had frequented many of them on road trips to the coast or wine country, but their model was to produce consistent coffee products quickly and efficiently. Drive-through coffee shops relied on volume, not customers staying to savor a complex cup of a custom roast or lingering for lunch. I wondered how Sammy intended to scale Fluid, given her voraciousness about her intentional, studied approach to coffee.

"Sammy doesn't solely want to be the Barista Cup champion. She wants Fluid to be a household name. From what I heard, she doesn't care about who she takes down in the process. There are more rumors about her circling some mom-and-pop shops that are struggling, like a vulture, waiting for them to go under and then swooping in and devouring the carcass."

"That's a graphic analogy." I drank a long sip of coffee trying to get the image of vulture tearing up its prey out of my head.

"Sorry." Andy's cheeks tinged pink. "I guess that is kind of dramatic. The point is that Sammy is cutthroat and ruthless—if the rumors are true."

"Where did you hear these rumors?"

"You won't believe it—James."

"James?" I sat up straighter. "How would James know?"

Andy shrugged. "He didn't say."

Why would James tell all of this to Andy? Something seemed off.

I tabled that thought for the moment and moved on to the next thing that was bugging me. "I don't understand though. If Benson was planning to invest in Sammy's shops, that wouldn't give her motive to kill him. In fact, that would be the opposite. She would want him alive if she needed his cash."

Andy's lips thinned. "Right? You would think, but here's the kicker. Apparently, they had a big blowup and Benson told her that he was pulling all of his funding. According to James, that happened the night before Benson was killed. He overheard the whole thing. Sammy and Benson were on the pool deck, and when Benson told her he was withdrawing his offer, Sammy told him that he would never get away with it and that he had better watch his back."

If Andy was right and if James was telling the truth, that changed everything. Suddenly, Sammy had a very viable motive for murder. Not only that, but she had a weapon too. She had admitted yesterday that her anti-anxiety medication was missing. Was it really missing or had she used it to spike Benson's drink?

Chapter Twenty

Andy watched my reaction. "Right? That's crazy isn't it? I mean if Sammy thought she was going to get a huge financial investment from Benson for Fluid's expansion and then learned that he wanted out, that's motive for killing him, don't you think?"

"That's exactly what I was thinking." I took another drink of the milky latte. "What I don't understand is why James told you all of this information. Why wouldn't he have gone to the police?"

"I don't know. I didn't think about that." Andy thought for a minute. "He and I were going over the plan for today when Sammy stormed out for some reason and he said, 'Don't mind her, she's upset about something else' then he proceeded to tell me everything I just told you. I guess at the time it seemed kind of off the cuff, like he was trying to explain her behavior, but now that I think about it, it *is* weird."

"You should really call the Professor." I glanced at the clock. It was after six now. Even if it wasn't, Andy had critical information to share.

"Okay." He stood.

"Do you need his number?"

"No, I've got it." He reached for his phone. His case was plastered with ski stickers.

I returned to the kitchen. Sammy wanting to expand her coffee empire and Benson investing in it was a huge piece of information. The question that kept pounding on my head was why James had shared this news with Andy. It didn't make sense. Unless he was lying, maybe trying to push suspicion onto someone else?

I wondered if there was any way I could learn whether Sammy really was planning a West Coast rollout for Fluid. Could she be trying to inflate her sense of worth in the coffee industry to intimidate her fellow competitors?

I also wanted to find some time to see if I could read through some of Benson's old reviews in the *Seattle Times*. I wasn't sure whether James's information was trustworthy, but it certainly gave me more incentive to find time to get him alone at some point today.

The rest of the team arrived shortly after my discussion with Andy. The kitchen hummed to life. I found myself busy running trays of pastries upstairs and making sure we were ready to open the front doors by seven. When the time came to flip the sign from Closed to Open, there was already a small line of customers eager for affagatos and flaky cherry almond croissants. I worked the counter with Rosa. At least once or twice a week I opted to spend a few hours upstairs in the dining room. It was an important way to stay connected with our loyal clientele and welcome tourists. When my parents had started Torte, they had made it their mission to create a space where anyone who walked through the front door was treated like family. If I succeeded in no other way, I was committed to carrying on that part of their legacy.

Selfishly, I enjoyed watching people ogle over our mint chocolate macarons or salted caramel tarts. It was such a delight to see kids press their faces close to the glass for a better peek at fluffy marshmallow cloud cupcakes, raspberry bars, and vanilla sugar cookies with rainbow sprinkles. It never got old to observe a customer taking their first sip of our cold brew or soak in the aroma of our spicy chai latte.

Sometime after nine, I spotted a familiar face in the dining room—Lance.

"You *are* here early," I noted, greeting him with a kiss on the cheek.

Lance was a night owl. We had opposite schedules. I rose before the sun to bake, whereas he greeted audiences at the evening show and lingered for cast parties long into the early hours of the morning.

"Don't remind me." He massaged his temples and sighed. "The things I do for you. The sacrifices I make. I gave up two hours of beauty sleep for our coffee date."

"We don't have a coffee date."

He tilted his head to one side. "I beg to differ. I'm here. You're here. In a *coffee* shop. I smell coffee. I see coffee. I need coffee."

I chuckled. "Oh, Lance, what would I do without you?"

"Perish the thought." He looped his arm through mine and dragged me to the espresso bar.

We ordered coffees and took them to a booth by the front windows.

"Okay, dish." Lance leaned closer. "I know you were trying to downplay your involvement for the sake of Carlos, but it's just the two of us. Time to come clean. Confess. What else do you know?"

"Not that much," I replied.

Lance pursed his lips together. "Please. It's me. I can read every muscle in your face. You know something, and you know that we make a perfect team when it comes to sleuthing out whodunit. You need me."

I wasn't sure if I *needed* him, but it was nice to have someone to toss ideas off of, and I could count on Lance to listen to any theory—regardless of how far-fetched it might be.

"I did hear a new piece of information from Andy this morning that may or may not be connected to Benson's death."

"I knew it." Lance snapped. "Continue."

"Andy told me that Benson and Sammy were going into business together. They were planning to expand her coffee shops throughout the West Coast, but apparently Benson pulled out of the deal right before he was killed."

Lance let out a low whistle. "Color me intrigued. Now *that* sounds like motive for murder if I've ever heard it."

"Maybe, but it's just a rumor." I told him about Sammy's claim that her anxiety medication was missing and how James had been the one to relay everything to Andy.

"Hmmm. That leaves us with two possibilities. James is lying or Sammy is a murderess."

"I'm not sure it's that simple."

Lance scoffed. "Don't get caught up in details. We have to interrogate both of them."

This was exactly the reaction I had expected from Lance. There was no arguing that he loved to bring a touch of dramatics to any conversation. "The Professor, Thomas, and Kerry might frown on us 'interrogating' them, but I do agree that I'd like to find a way to talk with them. I think I have a good excuse with James. I made reservations for a staff party tonight. I could go to The Hills under the guise of wanting to talk about dinner."

"Wait." Lance held up his index finger. "I don't recall receiving an invite to this bash. I'm hurt, darling. Hurt."

"You want to come to our staff party?"

"No." He rolled his eyes. "I want to be invited, though."

"Consider this your invitation."

He pressed his palms together. "Thank you. I just may take you up on the offer after all. Now, back to our investigation. You go scurry off and see what you can glean from James." He was about to say more, but he stopped and gasped. "Ah, fate!"

"What?"

"Look." He pointed out the window across the plaza by the Lithia bubblers. "Speak of the devil."

Sammy sat at a bench near the famed fountains. She had a sketch book and set of pencils with her.

"That's my cue." Lance brushed his hands together and got up.

"What are you going to do?"

"I'm simply going to gush over her performance at the competition and dazzle her with my winning personality." He tapped his wrist. "Shall we reconvene at The Hills? Say thirty minutes before the espresso starts to fly?"

He didn't give me a chance to reply before blowing a kiss and dashing out the front door.

I went downstairs to check on progress in the kitchen. Steph was using a palette knife to paint bright red, yellow, and orange buttercream in messy streaks on a cake.

"Ohhhh, I'm loving that," I said kneeling to get a look at the artistic cake from another angle.

"Embrace the mess." Steph slapped more buttercream on. "It's been one of our most requested cakes this summer. Everyone wants a painted cake for their barbecues and birthday parties."

The sweeping brushstrokes of buttercream gave the cake the feel of a textured oil painting. If I didn't know that there were luscious layers of our white almond pound cake beneath the colorful frosting, I could have been convinced that Steph's painted cake was actually canvas.

"I don't blame them." I turned to Bethany, who was working at the station next to Steph. One of the upgrades we'd made during the basement renovation was to install dedicated decorating stations. The intricate task of hand-pipping ten dozen cookies or a showpiece wedding cake required good counter space, access to tools like our ever-expanding sprinkle collection and flat spatulas in every size possible, and great lighting. Lighting was essential. We had installed track lighting as well as magnifying spotlights on swiveling arms that could be moved in any direction so our cake designers didn't have to squint to see what they were doing when it came to the fine details.

Bethany worked on a two-tone gray and navy tiered terrazzo cake. The design was also on trend for the summer. It gave the cake a dramatic effect of resembling wall or floor tiles, made with colored fondant, flecks of gold, and sugar paste.

Marty and Sterling were leafing through cookbooks while watching butter sizzling on the stove.

"Marty, can you keep an eye on things? I'm going to run over and finalize our dinner at The Hills. Remember, we're going to close early this afternoon. I've posted signs on the front door and at the counter, and Bethany shared on social media."

"No problem." He tucked a pencil behind his ear. "Carlos called to tell us about the dinner. We've got some ideas, don't we, Sterling?"

Sterling nodded. "Yeah, but don't tell her yet."

"Never." Marty grinned. "A chef never tells his secrets."

I shielded my eyes with my hand. "I promise I won't look." I walked over to the decorating station and filled Bethany and Steph in our vineyard dinner plans. "Can you two put your creative brains to work on decorations; and Steph, I was hoping maybe you could design some fliers to post at the winery and upstairs?"

They were already chatting about possibilities when I left for The Hills. I wasn't sure if James would be available to talk with me, but I had to give it a shot. I didn't want to get my hopes up, but it felt like we were starting to close in on Benson's killer.

Chapter Twenty-One

The Hills lobby was still set up for the Barista Cup when I arrived. Vendor tables lined both sides of the spacious mid-century room with its angled ceiling and exposed beams. I walked to the reception desk and asked if James was available.

"Do you have an appointment?" the young woman behind the welcome desk asked. A massive peace sign made from ferns and foliage hung behind her.

"No. I'm Jules with Torte. We're having a staff dinner here tonight after the competition and I happened to be on this side of town and thought I might be able to get a few minutes with James to chat about menu options and pre-pay."

"Let me check." She made a phone call. "He said to give him five minutes. He's in the ballroom. He'll meet you in his office. Do you know where it is?"

"No."

"Right down that hallway." She pointed in the opposite direction of the ballroom. "Second door on the left."

"Thanks." I walked through the hotel until I found the

door that read CATERING AND SPECIAL EVENTS. It was partway open, so I went inside.

James's office was tidy. His desk had a variety of plastic organizers with brochures for weddings and events, menus, and pricing sheets. A variety of magazine articles about The Hills had been framed and hung on the walls. I read one of the features from *Sunset* that touted James's skills as a chef. The article raved about Ashland, as well as the hotel's modern design, stunning views, and world-class food. I was about to take a seat when the tag line under a photo of James wearing his chef coat, caught my eye. "Former Seattle barista trades coffee culture for hotel couture."

James had been a barista in Seattle? That couldn't be a coincidence.

"Hey, sorry to keep you waiting." James came into his office.

I startled and moved away from the article. "No problem. I had some errands on this side of town, so thought it might be easier to chat about tonight's dinner before things get busy with the competition."

"Sure. Have a seat." He walked around his desk.

I took a seat across from him. The article from *Sunset* was my perfect entry. "I didn't realize you were a barista in Seattle." I pointed to the framed magazine.

"Huh? Oh yeah. That was a lifetime ago."

"How did you make the switch from coffee to catering?"

Was it my imagination or was James starting to sweat?

He ran his wrist along his forehead. "I wasn't a barista for long. After I left the coffee shop I'd been working at in Seattle, I got a job as a line cook for a hotel and, you know how the story goes—I worked my way up until I was the assistant catering director."

That was impressive. Most catering directors I knew had gone through culinary school.

"Catering is a better match for me. Too many angry customers in the coffee world, if you ask me. I think it's because people are crabby until they get their caffeine fix."

I wasn't sure that I shared his sentiment. Yes, we had a few outliers at Torte. A handful of customers who had no interest in making small talk while they waited for their drinks, but they were the exception. The vast majority of our clientele was friendly and engaging.

James reached for an order form and changed the subject. "I have tables reserved for you on the patio starting at eight tonight, although we can adjust earlier or later if the competition goes longer."

"That's great. My staff is coming to cheer Andy on, so we'll all be here."

"What else did you want to discuss?" James asked.

"I wondered about menu options. Is it better to have everyone order off the standard menu or do you prefer to have a limited offering for bigger parties?"

"Either way is fine with us." James tapped the pencil on the paper. Was he in a hurry to get back to work, or was he nervous? He grabbed a menu and handed it to me. "Take a look at this. It's our catering pub fare. We can do a few options from it if you want. That might make it easier on the kitchen, but really we can handle standard ordering too."

I reviewed the menu and tried to think of a way to bring up what Andy had told me about Sammy and

Benson without it seeming too obvious. "Everything sounds delicious. Let's do the fried chicken with bacon gravy and Brussel sprouts, tomato and herb flatbread pizza, and the summer salad with fresh berries, goat cheese, walnuts, and grilled salmon."

James made a note. "Got it. The pub menu also comes with a selection of our desserts. We can do a couple platters of chocolate brownies, cookies, and mini carrot cakes."

"Perfect."

"What do you want to do about drinks? I can put together a craft beer list and offer a choice of red, white, or sparkling wine." He leafed through some paperwork, looking for the bar list.

"That would be lovely." I wanted to splurge a bit and celebrate the team's hard work, but I didn't want to spend a fortune on cocktails. "If anyone wants a cocktail or more expensive glass of wine, can they order that directly?"

"Of course."

There wasn't much more to discuss. I needed to work up the courage to ask him about Sammy, but I couldn't figure out the right way to broach the subject without seeming pushy. But if I didn't do it now, I was going to lose my chance.

"You mentioned payment?" James asked.

"Right. I forgot to ask if you need a deposit or prefer pre-payment." I handed him the menus.

He returned the menus to their spot on his desk. "I think I know where to find you if you try to sneak out on us."

I smiled.

"No, actually this isn't anything out of the norm for us. You're not even that big of a party. You can pay the server at the end of the dinner. We add a customary gratuity for parties your size."

"Sure, no problem."

"Was there anything else?" James asked. He glanced briefly at his watch.

"Actually, I have an off-topic question for you."

His jaw tightened ever so slightly. "What's that?"

"It's about Sammy."

Again he flinched. "What about her?"

I decided my best option was to tell a little white lie. "She stopped by Torte yesterday and we had a nice chat about the business. It sounds like she's planning to go big with Fluid. As the owner of a small coffee shop myself, I'm impressed with her vision."

"Yeah, I heard something about that." He didn't offer more.

"Did you hear anything about Benson being her financial partner?" I hoped that my tone sounded innocent.

"The coffee world is still small. Word gets around pretty quick and Benson wasn't known for being discreet."

"Oh really?"

James softened his shoulders. "The guy had such an inflated ego. Even if he wanted to be discreet, he couldn't. He had to be the center of attention. He bragged to everyone about all of his business ventures. He liked to make it known that he was the most successful guy in the room. I'm sure you know the type."

Richard Lord came to mind.

"Did he brag about investing in Sammy's shops?"

James cleared his throat. "I don't know. I tried to keep my distance from the guy. We didn't see eye to eye, if you know what I mean."

"He seemed harsh, for sure." Maybe if I mirrored James's tone he would keep talking.

"Harsh doesn't even begin to scratch the surface. He was intentionally cruel. He took pleasure in tearing people down. The guy was evil."

I had clearly hit a nerve. James had a fist clenched. I noticed for the briefest moment his face turning toward the mounted magazine article. I was going to ask him more, but he coughed and rolled his shoulders before standing up. Yet again, I couldn't help but wonder if there had been more to James and Benson's relationship.

"Sorry, I have so much to do. I need to cut this short and get back to work." He moved toward the door. I had no choice but to follow him.

"Feel free to call if you think of anything else, but otherwise we're looking forward to having the Torte staff here for dinner later." James held the door open for me.

"I think it will be fun. Thanks for your help." I felt his eyes on my back as I walked down the hallway to the lobby.

My first order of business was to do some research into James's past. If he had been a barista in Seattle, odds were good that he and Benson's paths had crossed. Both Sammy and Piper had mentioned that the coffee scene had been small. James and Benson must have known each other. Could that have given him a motive for murder?

Chapter Twenty-Two

At Torte, I did a quick check-in with the team before heading to my office. There were multiple things I wanted to look into, but the first was James. I searched his name, and the first few links took me to the *Sunset* article along with numerous stories I'd seen in his office about his new position at The Hills. As I scrolled further, a headline caught my eye: "Seattle's Star Satellite Barista Receives Scathing Starless Review."

I clicked on the link.

Jackpot!

My jaw dropped as I read the *Seattle Times* column written by none other than Benson Vargas. He had systematically eviscerated James's first coffee shop, Satellite, in a front-page feature in the Food Section.

"The famed Satellite had me wishing I could launch myself into orbit and jet into a different galaxy to escape the lifeless sludge barista and owner James is trying to pawn off on hopeless customers. My thirty minutes at Satellite is time I'll never get back. I call foul on James calling himself a barista. He had no knowledge of the bean's origin or the brewing process. Rather

*than freshly grinding the roast, he simply stuffed the
portafilter with stale pre-ground beans. Tragic! James
not only squandered my precious time but he assaulted
my palate with his lackluster, watered-down dirty-
bathroom sediment that he claims is coffee. Let me
tell you, sir, that what you're serving is not coffee. The
smeary mocha made me wonder if one of the baristas
had had an unfortunate accident and rather than rush-
ing to the bathroom they opted to defecate in my cup."*

Woah.

I couldn't read on. It was too painful. Benson had
gone for the jugular. No wonder James had no love for
him.

I clicked away from the article and did a little more
searching. Subsequent stories written after the review
had been published painted a sad picture. Benson's vile
words about Satellite appeared to leave a lasting mark.
The coffee shop shuttered its doors for three months
after the review originally ran. Poor James. I had a new-
found empathy for him, and yet this was tangible proof
that he had a clear motive for killing Benson. Could
James have been involved in the lawsuit that Sammy
had mentioned?

I copied the stories, pasted them in an email, and sent
them to Thomas. It was highly likely that he, the Professor, and Detective Kerry were already investigating
Benson's previous columns, but it wouldn't hurt and I
had made a promise to the Professor to share anything
I learned.

Next, I shifted gears and found Sammy's website and
social media. Fluid's online presence matched Sammy's
haughty attitude. There was no mention of franchising

anywhere on her website. However, there were numerous photos of her and Benson posing together at barista competitions and at her shop, and even links to the glowing articles he had written about her.

The contrast between his adoration for her talents versus his utter disgust with James was revealing. What did it mean in terms of his murder?

I was becoming more convinced that James might be the killer. He had motive and he certainly had the opportunity. I'd witnessed a nasty argument between him and Benson. Had James tried to give Benson one last warning? Is that why he'd told Andy about Sammy? Was he trying to make sure that suspicion shifted to her and away from him?

In some way, I couldn't blame James for being upset with Benson—not that I condoned murder. I played out different scenarios in my head. Maybe James hadn't expected to see Benson here. He had started a new life in Ashland and put the coffee world behind him. What if seeing Benson brought back memories he had buried? Could he have snapped? That was certainly a possibility. But there was another one. What if Benson's murder was premeditated? Since James managed the catering department for The Hills, he must have been involved in planning for the Barista Cup. Could he have seen Benson's picture or bio on the publicity materials and decided this was his opportunity to exact his revenge?

I didn't have a ton of time to stew over other possibilities as the lunch rush picked up. I returned to the kitchen to help plate my pasta salad and Ruben sandwiches grilled to perfection on our house-made rye bread, brushed with Russian dressing, and oozing melted Swiss cheese. Sterling's carrot and cilantro soup was a hit too. The same was true for Marty's buttered and blackened naan served with creamy hummus and summer veggies.

The afternoon breezed by. Soon it was time to close up and caravan to The Hills. Steph had finished her trio of party cakes. One was a silky simple two-layer buttercream cake with fancy rainbow sprinkles. Another was an ice blue cake with a wreath of buttercream succulents, and the last cake had been designed with layers of chocolate, vanilla, and strawberry buttercream with a chocolate drip spilling over the edges and an ice-cream cone made entirely of cake smashed on the top.

"Those turned out great." I complimented her creative efforts.

She returned the praise with her signature half shrug. "Thanks."

"I'm going to head over to The Hills a little early to hold seats for everyone. How are we on deliveries?"

Steph folded cake boxes together. "We're going to deliver the ice-cream cake on our way. The other two are due to be picked up in the next half hour."

"Perfect. Does anyone need anything else from me before I go?" I looked to Sterling and Marty, who were finishing lunch cleanup.

"Nope. We'll see you there soon." Marty plunged a stockpot into soapy water.

"Be sure to get front-row seats again," Bethany added as she positioned the succulent cake in the center of the counter to take a picture.

"I'm on it." I waved and left for the hotel. In truth, I

did want to get good seats, but I also wanted a chance to swap notes with Lance.

He was already waiting for me when I arrived. He had placed white sheets of paper with the word RESERVED on every seat in the first two rows.

"How did you manage to reserve us an entire section?" I asked, setting my purse on a chair.

"Don't ask questions. I have my ways."

I didn't doubt that.

He looked around us. A few staff members milled about, but there was no sign of the judges or competitors.

"Where is everyone?" I asked.

"They just went into the adjacent room for a meeting, so let's not dally. Do tell, what did you learn?" He crossed one leg over the other.

I told him about James's former career as a barista and how Benson's review was responsible for the death of that career.

"You must send me that. It sounds like excellent bedtime reading." Lance winked.

"It was painful and cringeworthy to say the least." Spectators began filing into the ballroom. "What about you? Any luck with Sammy?"

"She's a shady one, that girl. I'm not sure about her. I would bet money that there's something she's not saying, but I couldn't get it out of her. She did admit that she had financial backing from Benson, but I'm not sure that's earth-shattering news."

"How did you get that out of her?"

"As if you need to ask. Please." He tapped his fingers

together. "Let's just say that I might have tossed out the possibility of the festival being on the hunt for a new coffee vendor."

"Smart."

"I know." He soaked in the praise, motioning for me to keep it going.

I punched his arm. "Did she say anything about Benson pulling out of the deal?"

"Not a word, and that's why I'm not so sure she's trustworthy. She skirted answering that question faster than an actor trying to get out of a fitting after a weekend of imbibing. And that girl should cut out the caffeine and take up meditation. She's as jittery as an ingenue on opening night."

Carlos arrived, followed shortly by the rest of the team along with Andy's grandma June, and Mom and the Professor. We put our conversation on hold.

Andy and the remaining contestants entered the ballroom to "Eye of the Tiger." He spotted us and beamed.

We must have looked like an official cheer squad. Our team filled two entire rows and erupted in applause for our favorite barista. Marty had made enough cutouts of Andy's head for everyone, and Bethany started a Torte chant.

James went through his introductory routine with a bit of a tweak. He informed the crowd that one of the competitors had been disqualified and that yesterday's sixth-place finisher would be returning. "You can't script this, folks! The West Coast Barista Cup has had it all this year, and by the end of the day we're going to crown a winner, award a ten-thousand-dollar cash prize, and send this year's champ on to Nationals. Hold onto to your seats, because it's about to get wild in here." He pointed to the DJ, who blasted a dance mix.

James pumped up the crowd, then he made a slicing motion across his neck to cut the music. "All right, let's get serious. Since we had to eliminate a contestant and make some last-minute changes, today's rounds will freestyle. That means that none of our baristas have had a chance to plan or prepare for what's to come. The judges decided this was the only way to level the playing field."

He caught Piper's eye. She pushed her leopard-rimmed glasses to the bridge of her nose and gave him a curt nod.

Sammy threw her hands over her face. "Wait, what? You can't do this. I've spent months preparing my talking points and each drink offering. Freestyle?"

"I'm afraid so." James put one hand out in front of him and held the mic with the other. "You're going to have to think on your feet. The judges came up with a list of traditional espresso drinks found on any coffee shop menu. You'll have fifteen minutes to come up with a concept and then an additional fifteen minutes to prepare and present your offerings in each round. Got it?" He looked to the baristas.

Sammy ran her fingers through her hair and shook her head in disgust as the other baristas, including Andy, nodded their approval.

"Okay, let's get this party started." James reached into a clear vase with folded up pieces of paper. He took extra time unfolding and reading the paper he chose. After a minute, he grinned and directed his words to the baristas. "How are you feeling about blended drinks? Break out those blenders and stock up on ice because for this first round, the judges want you to present not one, not two, but three blended coffees. You have fifteen minutes to think about what you want to blend—and your time starts now!" He snapped and the countdown clock and music started.

While the baristas frantically searched through their stockpile of supplies and began sketching out recipes, my thoughts turned to Diaz. Where had he gone? Had he left town? Would the Professor have allowed that?

I'd been so focused on James, Sammy, and Piper that I'd forgotten that Diaz had been my top suspect just a day ago. On a hunch I surveyed the ballroom. Sure enough, Diaz was slumped in a chair in the very back row. He wore a black baseball cap low on his forehead in an attempt to conceal his face. What was he doing here?

I was surprised he'd been allowed to return to the building. Did that mean that the Professor had eliminated him as a potential suspect? Or could there be another reason he was lurking in the back?

I made a note to try and have a word with him before the night was over.

James returned to the mic. "That's it, baristas! I hope you've blended up something amazing in your mind. Time's up for your prep. How are you feeling about your frozen concoctions?"

Sammy pushed the mic away when James approached her for comment. "I don't have time for this."

So much for her speech to Andy about the mental game. Lance wasn't exaggerating about her lack of composure.

"Ouch! Someone's feeling the pressure." James moved on to Andy's station. "How about you? Care to entice the crowd with what you're going to blend up?"

Andy spoke with ease and confidence. It was like he and Sammy had swapped personalities over the course of the competition. "Sure. I'm going to start with a tiramisu-blended coffee that will be Italian espresso infused with dark chocolate, almond extract, heavy cream, and a splash of Grand Marnier."

The audience let out collective "ooohhh."

"Yeah, what they said." James clapped Andy's shoulder. "Save me a sample of that, okay, kid?"

Andy's boyish grin had returned to his face.

Carlos leaned in. "I think that this is good for Andy, si? He does well under pressure. This is because of his training at Torte. He isn't rehearsed. He's tapping into his heart center and his creativity." He pressed his fingers to his chest.

I agreed. Andy's cheeks had color and his eyes twinkled as he explained that his second blended drink would be his take on a Thai iced tea with shots of strong spiced chai, and that he would round out his tasting tray with a classic coffee milkshake featuring Torte's coffee concrete and a Guatemalan roast, served with spiced whipped cream and chocolate shavings.

"He is going to win this no problem." Carlos leaned against his chair and reached for my hand. "You watch and see."

"I hope you're right." I crossed my fingers.

The bell rang to announce that it was time for the contestants to start blending their drinks. I got swept up in the excitement. Andy performed like a champ. I had a feeling his massive squad had given him a boost. As Carlos had predicted, he ended the round with top marks. Sammy pouted when James announced that she was holding steady in second place.

After a quick break, it was time for the second round.

"Who's feeling nervous?" James asked. "Those blended beauties were frothy and fun, but what will your next assignment involve?"

The DJ played a clip of ominous music.

"Is this even legal?" Sammy folded her arms across her chest.

"Legal?" James turned to Piper. "Does our technical judge want to weigh in on that?"

Piper took the mic from him and addressed the baristas. "I understand that this situation is less than optimal, and I wish there was another solution, but after many hours of discussion and deliberation we decided the only fair way to proceed was with this random method since four of you already presented drinks yesterday. In terms of legality, the answer to your question is yes. The rules clearly state that the judges reserve the right to make changes as necessary without warning. I'd advise you to read the fine print."

"She is not open to debate, is she?" Carlos asked.

"Doesn't sound like it."

"All right, on that note, let's see what you're going to brewing for us next." James reached into the vase again. "Simple syrups! The judges want three Americanos where a simple syrup is the star of the show. You ready? Let's countdown fifteen minutes for you to come up with a concept."

"Andy has this for sure," Mom said. "His simple syrups are the best around. Customers are always asking if we'll bottle and sell them."

She was right. He breezed through the second round with another first-place finish. Before I knew it, James was reviewing the rules for the final round.

Andy had a chance at winning. I couldn't believe it. Not that I had a single doubt about his talents, but after the way the weekend had started I never would have imagined that he might be a contender to be this year's West Coast Barista Cup Champion. When James announced that the final round would be latte art, my sense of hope only expanded.

"Latte art! This is my favorite category, folks. The judges want to see what our dream team of baristas can create from nothing more than foam. A quick note here—food coloring is not allowed in this round. The judges want you to mastermind an amazing design with nothing more than frothy, frothy foam!"

"He's got this," Bethany voiced what I had been thinking. She turned to the team. "Let's get a chant going." She clapped three times. "We love Andy!"

Marty was the next to chime in and then our Torte crew was on its feet cheering for Andy. It warmed my heart to see such a show of solidarity. We quieted down once the bell sounded and watched with bated breath as Andy delivered three stunning lattes with unique designs inspired by Ashland—Mt. A., a black-bear paw, and the pièce de résistance: Shakespeare's bust. Piper took meticulous notes, and the judges offered no feedback after studying the lineup of gallery-worthy coffees.

Andy's voice came out strong and solid as he shared

his connection to the latte designs. "I wanted to leave you with a piece of me. This is Ashland, the place where I was born. The place I love. Your first latte design represents Mt. A. Ever since third grade, I would board the ski bus in the winter after school and hit the slopes. Skiing comes second only to coffee. The next latte is a bear paw, because I started as a Cub and graduated as a Grizzly. Go Ashland High!" He paused to pump his fist. "It's not just a middle- and high-school mascot. We get bear visits nightly, especially when I forget to drag the garbage cans inside. Right, Grandma?" He turned to June.

She pretended to scold him.

"Lastly, I had to give you Shakespeare, because Ashland." Andy laughed. "When you grow up in a place as great as this, you can't take it for granted. I learned that through coffee, believe it or not. It's Torte, the bakeshop where I work, that has made me appreciate how special Ashland really is. But one last fun fact—Shakespeare never drank coffee. What a shame."

The audience clapped.

I caught Lance blinking rapidly. "Your eyes aren't misty, are they?"

"I'm not crying. You're crying," he bantered back.

"Folks, we'll be back with the results in five minutes. Sit tight. I can feel the tension building and I can tell you this is going to be a close one." James set down the mic and went to the judges' table.

"Did you know he could do that?" Mom asked me.

"Shakespeare in coffee? No! I don't know when he practiced that, but it's going to have to go on the menu."

June gleamed. "That was my idea. Everyone loves Shakespeare."

"True." Lance leaned forward to give her an air high five.

While the sensory judges huddled, Piper headed for the back of the ballroom. I tried to be discreet as I observed her and Diaz talking. Unless I was reading her wrong, Piper appeared to be trying to convince Diaz to leave. She thrust her index finger in his face and then toward the exit doors.

Diaz ignored her, folding his arms across his chest and smirking.

Under normal circumstances I might have thought that she was simply worried about appearances and not wanting a contestant who had been caught cheating on the premises. But these weren't normal circumstances. My mind spun with a new slew of possibilities. What if they'd been in it together? I hadn't considered the possibility that more than one person could have killed Benson. They could have teamed up to take out the crotchety judge.

"Okay folks, are you ready to crown this year's West Coast Barista Cup Champion?" James interrupted my thought.

The crowd cheered.

"In fifth place . . ." he paused for effect before announcing the competitor who had been eliminated prior to Diaz getting caught tampering with Andy's drink. Then he went through fourth and third places, the strawberry and the herbed-latte baristas.

That meant Andy would finish no worse than second place.

"In second place . . ." James continued, waiting even longer. "We have Sammy. Which means this year's champion is Andy from Torte!"

Everyone around me erupted.

He had done it.

Andy had won the West Coast Barista Cup!

Chapter Twenty-Three

"He did it!" Bethany shouted into her phone and then spun around to show the crowd's reaction. Confetti fell from the ceiling. James popped open a bottle of champagne. Piper handed Andy a two-foot-tall silver trophy in the shape of coffee cup. The other judges gathered for a photo op and a celebratory glass of bubbly. Bethany captured everything on her livestream.

Mom dabbed tears from her eyes "I'm so proud of him. My heart is bursting."

"Me too." I squeezed her in a long hug.

June went down the row of seats hugging and high-fiving the entire team.

Sammy fumed as she was awarded the second-place trophy. She couldn't mask her disappointment. It was obvious from her scowl and the way she eyed Andy's larger trophy that she was practically ready to snatch it from his hands. Again, her intensity gave me pause. As ludicrous as it seemed that someone would kill over a coffee competition, it wasn't out of the realm of possibility for her—in my opinion.

After everyone had posed for photos and toasted with

champagne, Piper brought out a four-foot-long check with Andy's ten-thousand-dollar winnings. This made everyone cheer again.

Andy basked in the attention. June joined him for pictures, pinching his cheeks and repeating, "That's my boy!"

Once the crowd began to disperse, we went to congratulate our star barista.

"Everyone squish together," Bethany said, directing us on either side of Andy. She handed her phone to Piper. "Can you take a group shot of us?"

"Of course." Piper held the camera. "Say West Coast Barista Cup Champ!"

"West Coast Barista Cup Champ!"

She gave Bethany her phone back.

I scooted over to Piper. "Are you done now?"

Piper tucked her glasses in her purse. "Pretty much. We have a wrap-up meeting with the judges. We'll be sharing out Andy's win to our newsletter subscribers and on our social media channels as well as announcing next year's locations. So I'll finish that up and then I plan to stay in town for a few more days. I haven't had a chance to take in a show at OSF yet. Lance was kind enough to give me complimentary tickets to the Elizabethan Theater for tomorrow night." Her purse slipped from her arm and its contents spilled on the floor. She bent down to gather up lipsticks and her sunglasses.

I helped her pick up her things. My hands landed on a prescription bottle.

Piper snatched it from me. "Thanks."

I nodded. "You'll love the theater. It truly is a one-of-a-kind experience to see a production outside, and the weather is perfect right now. Not too hot. Not too cold. Here's an insider's tip, be sure to stop by the pillow booth for a seat cushion and blanket—it might get chilly for the second act." I glanced to where Diaz had been sitting. He must have taken off. "I saw you chatting with Diaz a while ago. He's still around too?"

She twisted a silver bracelet around her wrist. "The police have asked all of us to stay, at least for another day or two."

"Right." She hadn't answered my question. "I'm surprised that Diaz showed up after getting kicked out."

"That's exactly what I told him. When I saw him sitting in the last row, I immediately went over to explain in no uncertain terms that he is *not* welcome here. He made his bed and he has to lie in it. We won't condone cheating in the Barista Cup."

"Did he say why he was here?"

Piper yawned. "Sorry. I didn't get any sleep last night." She stifled a second yawn. "Yeah. He claimed that he wasn't planning to cause a disruption. He gave me a sob story about feeling guilty and wanting to apologize to Andy. I didn't believe a word of that. He came here to make a scene. He doesn't have an empathetic bone in his body. How could he? He sullied the Barista Cup name by cheating. I know the real reason he came here today. He wants another shot at next year. I've been around long enough to know truth from fiction. He wanted to butter me and the other judges up in hopes that we would change our minds."

"About what?"

"Next year." She sounded irritated. "Diaz can't complete next year. He's been banned for life."

"I didn't realize that."

She stretched her neck in a semicircle. "We can't have a competitor with a tarnished reputation competing in the Barista Cup. I've worked too hard and too long to build the competition into the prestigious event it is today. I will not let Diaz Mendez trash the insane amount of effort that has gone into creating a world-class event. He didn't like hearing that, but frankly that's not my concern. He should have thought of that before he made such a huge error. The Barista Cup is a worldwide brand, and I will not have him ruin our reputation or good name."

Suddenly Piper sounded like Benson.

Her expression was tight and her lips flattened as she continued. "Diaz has no place here. I'm going to see to it that he will never work in the industry again."

I knew that I had a tendency to want to believe the best about people. Part of me felt sorry for Diaz. If he had been desperate for the cash, I could understand how he might have felt the need to cheat. That didn't justify his actions, but it did make me feel empathy for him, especially if Piper was serious about trying to ostracize him from future employment.

On the other hand, I couldn't rule out the possibility that Diaz had done more than try to sabotage his fellow competitors. There was a good chance that he could be a killer.

"Are all of the competitors staying here at The Hills?" I asked Piper.

"Yes. The competitors and judges have a block of rooms. Fortunately, we had some surplus in the budget, so we'll be able to cover the cost of a few additional nights."

I wanted to ask her if she knew anything about Benson's partnership with Sammy, but Bethany was waving me over for another group photo. "Stop by Torte tomorrow before the play. I'll hook you up with some pre-show pastries."

"That would be wonderful." Piper attempted a smile, but it fell short. "I need to go and try to get some sleep."

After at least a dozen photos and group hugs, James came over to tell me that our table outside was ready.

"Who's hungry?" I asked

"I thought you'd never ask, boss." Andy grinned. He clutched his trophy and check. "I don't think I've eaten more than a couple bites in a week and suddenly I feel like I could eat everything on the menu."

"Let's get you some food then." I led the way to the patio. The hills blushed with pink light, and a nearly full moon rose above the forested mountainside. One long table had been set with twelve places. A waiter stood at the ready to take drink orders. The mood was light and vibrant. Andy walked everyone through each stage of the competition. There were gasps, ooohs, and ahhhs at all of the twists and turns. He was a natural storyteller, which made the experience that much better.

"Andy, you have to tell us how you made Shakespeare out of latte foam. You were already going to win, but that put you over the edge." Bethany had positioned herself in the seat next to Andy. I was sure that wasn't a mistake.

"I want to know that too," Mom said from across the table. "Shakespeare. Wow! You've been holding out on us."

Andy grinned. "That was my grandma's idea. She said I needed a secret weapon. Something that no one else would do. I've been practicing it at home every night."

June sat on the other side of him beaming with pride. "I told him that he had the winning combination—talent and heart."

"Salud." Carlos stood and held up his wineglass.

We toasted with sparkling cider, hoppy beers, and aromatic wines. Lance ended up staying after all. He sat next to Carlos and me, sipping a glass of champagne.

"Torte's ascent to fame continues. You can now officially claim that you have the best barista on the entire West Coast. Let's take a moment to imagine Richard Lord's face when he learns the news." Lance threw his head back and cackled.

"You sound like a movie villain."

"Intended, darling." He lifted his champagne flute.

Dinner involved lots of sharing and tasting bites from one another's plates. By the time the wait staff brought out platters of desserts and carafes of coffee, the sky had gone dark and we continued the conversation under a blanket of stars.

Carlos wrapped his arm around my shoulder. "This is so good for the team. I'm glad you thought of it."

"Me too." I leaned into his embrace and listened to the happy sounds of laughter. Our staff had an easy chemistry despite their very unique personalities. They had become an extension of me—my Ashland family. I decided on the spot that we needed to do more of this. Hard work deserved rewards. An idea began to form about a new staff outing—an adventure on the Rogue, a trip to Crater Lake, something special. I'd have to brainstorm with Carlos and Mom later.

For the remainder of the evening I drank in the glow of the moonlight and the infectious spirit of my staff. A chill began to descend as the night grew longer.

Mom rubbed her arms. "I think these goose bumps are my cue to head to bed. Well done, Andy, and thank you to everyone. We have the best team in Ashland—in the world for that matter. Smooches to you all. See you tomorrow." She blew a kiss and left with the Professor.

Lance stretched. "A nightcap with a tall drink of bald beauty is calling. Ta-ta."

Everyone else departed. I still needed to settle the bill. When our waiter came by to clear the table, I asked for the check.

"Oh, James told me that he needs you to meet him in his office. He has the bill for you there."

"Okay." I was surprised that the waiter couldn't take my credit card, especially after my conversation with James earlier.

"Do you want me to come with you?" Carlos asked. "Or, I can pull the car around to the lobby."

"Yeah, do that. I'll go find James and meet you out front in a few minutes." I went inside. The lobby was deserted. A single front-desk clerk stood behind the large reception area. "Is James in his office?" I asked.

The young guy frowned. "I don't think so. I thought he left a while ago."

"The waiter told me that he had our bill for our large party outside."

"Weird. You can check his office, but I could have sworn he left."

A strange feeling assaulted my stomach as I walked

down the corridor to James's office. The door was shut. I knocked twice.

No answer.

I knocked again.

Still no answer.

I twisted the handle, expecting it to be locked. To my surprise it turned with ease. I opened the door to find James's office pitch-black.

"James? Are you in here?" I asked, knowing it was highly doubtful I would receive a response. Why would James be in a dark office?

I ran my hand along the wall on the left side of the door until I found a light switch.

My heart rate sped up as I flipped on the lights.

Something felt off.

Was I being set up?

Maybe this was a mistake. What if James was the killer and he had lured me in here? What if he was hiding next to the door with some sort of weapon? He could smack me on the head and disappear.

Jules, don't be ridiculous.

I braced myself against the wall.

There was no one lurking in a corner. Everything appeared to be in place. There must have been a mistake.

I let out a long sigh of relief.

But that relief was short lived as I caught sight of James's desk. A large sheet of white poster board had been taped to the top of the desk. YOU'RE DEAD was lettered in blood-red paint.

I stifled a scream and raced to the lobby.

Chapter Twenty-Four

"Are you sure James left?" I asked the desk clerk.

"I think so. He said goodbye like an hour ago and I'm pretty sure he walked out those doors." He pointed toward the lobby.

"Okay, thanks." I hurried outside to find Carlos waiting in the car.

"Julieta, is something wrong?" He paused. "Why do you sound like you are out of breath?"

"Because I am. It's James. I went to find him and instead found a threatening note in his office. I have to call the Professor."

"What?" Carlos puffed out in a protective position.

I called the Professor's phone. Mom answered on the first ring. "Hi, honey it's me. Doug's driving."

I told her about the note, then listened as she repeated my words to the Professor.

"Okay, hang on. We're turning around. We are only halfway home, so will be there in less than ten minutes."

We hung up.

Carlos frowned and reached for my hand. "Do you think that James is in danger?"

"I don't know. I'm so confused. Honestly, I've been wondering if he could be the killer, but now I'm sure I must have gotten that wrong." I sighed.

"Unless the note was for someone else." He caressed my hand.

"Who?"

Carlos stared at me.

"Me? Why?"

"What if James thought you suspected him? You and Lance have been snooping around. You know that I love you, Julieta, but you two are not exactly discreet. Could he have left this note as a warning for you? You said that you were told to go to his office to pay, and you thought this was strange. It *is* strange. You must consider your safety, mi querida. I do not like this."

Was Carlos right?

Could the warning poster in James's office have been meant for me? I supposed it was possible, but there were so many other ways he could have tried to scare me. He could have left a threatening note at Torte. Why leave something like that in his office for anyone to see?

Blue, red, and white police lights cut through the dark night sky, followed by the sound of sirens. Thomas zoomed his squad car into the parking lot and pulled in next to us. He and Kerry got out of the car and walked over to us. Carlos rolled the window down.

"I take it the Professor called you?" I leaned across Carlos.

"Via your mom, yeah." Thomas removed a flashlight from his belt. "Where did you find the threat?"

"Inside. Do you want me to show you?"

Carlos grunted his disapproval.

"It's okay," Kerry said to him. "You can come too."

Kerry offering to allow a civilian to join her investigation? That was out of the ordinary to say the least. "It's a poster, right? You didn't find a body, did you?"

"No." I shook my head and opened the passenger door.

The four of us headed inside.

"Let us take the lead, Jules," Thomas said, with one hand on his holster.

I showed them to the office.

Thomas directed us to wait in the hallway. I tried to sneak a peek at what he and Kerry were doing. Had I gotten it wrong? Could James be in danger?

Kerry clicked photos. Thomas made a call.

Mom and the Professor arrived a few minutes later. The Professor went into the office.

"You found a threatening note?" Mom asked.

"Yeah. It's so weird, because the waiter told me that he couldn't take payment. He said that James had the invoice waiting in here for me, but there was no sign of him and the front-desk clerk told me he left an hour ago."

"That doesn't make sense." A flash of concern crossed Mom's face.

Carlos jumped in. "Si, I can tell you are thinking the same thing, Helen. What if the note was meant for Julieta?"

"But why would James lure me to his office and leave a warning poster on his desk? That seems like a weak way to threaten me."

Mom agreed with Carlos. "I don't know, honey. Why wouldn't our waiter take payment? Something feels off about this situation. I'm glad you called Doug."

As the words left her lips, the Professor stepped into the hallway.

"Well?" Mom looked to him.

He tapped his chin with his finger. "I find the Bard's lines running through my head. 'Let every eye negotiate for itself and trust no agent.'"

The Professor had a quote for any occasion. Tonight his words sent a chill down my spine.

"Carlos, will you please escort Juliet home? I'm going to send a squad car to drive by your house a few times as a precaution."

"A squad car?" I couldn't keep the shock from my tone. "Are we in danger?"

"Call it an abundance of caution," the Professor replied.

Carlos put a protective arm around my shoulder. "I will stay up tonight."

"I don't think that's necessary. The squad car will do a few drive-bys. If they see anything out of the ordinary, they'll stick around and notify me. I'm sending a team of two highly trained officers. Their job will to be to keep watch so that you and Juliet can have a restful night's sleep."

Right. Like there was any chance that would happen. Did he suspect that James had intended the warning for me? Why else would he have the police drive by our house?

Mom hugged us both. "Try to get some sleep. We'll check in first thing in the morning."

The Professor cleared his throat. "About that. I'd like you to have the officers escort you to the bakeshop in the morning."

"Is that necessary?" Carlos asked. "I can drive Julieta."

"I'd prefer for the officers to do a quick sweep of the bakeshop—again, out of an abundance of caution."

There was something he wasn't telling us. Had they found more incriminating evidence? Was I in more danger than I realized?

Carlos nodded and clutched my shoulder tighter. "Si, this is a good idea. I will drive and come with her. We will make sure that the police inspect Torte. Thank you."

The Professor caught my eye. "All is well. Things are developing and I have faith that we're closing in on a killer. However, the situation calls for the utmost caution if we are to be successful in our quest."

I felt like he was speaking in code. Was he trying to tell me something?

Carlos pulled me toward the door.

My head throbbed. It wasn't from a headache, but rather from trying to piece together the clues. I felt like the solution was dangling right in front of me, but I couldn't reach out and gasp it.

"This is serious, mi querida," Carlos said, his voice husky, as he started the car and steered out of the parking lot. "Doug would not have the police watch the house if he wasn't concerned about your safety."

"I know." I agreed, and yet I couldn't shake the feeling that there was more to the situation. I dropped the subject.

It took less than five minutes to drive home. As the Professor had promised, a squad car was waiting on the street next to our driveway. Carlos approached the vehicle to thank the officers before we headed inside.

Sleep was futile. I tossed and turned all night with strange dreams. Twice I got up to check out the window. The only thing I heard was the rustling of the wind through the trees. The police car was still parked out front. It was pitch-black when I pulled on a pair of capris and a sweatshirt and headed to the kitchen. I made a strong pot of coffee and warmed water to start a batch of my quick-rise cinnamon rolls.

I stirred yeast and a teaspoon of sugar into the warm water. Then melted butter and milk until, it was bubbling. I incorporated the melted butter and milk with the yeast and added in flour and a touch of salt. Once a dough began to form, I rolled up my sleeves and kneaded it by hand. At the bakeshop, we tended to use our industrial mixers with dough hooks when baking on a larger scale. The act of physically kneading the dough was therapeutic. I put all of my weight into punching the dough and letting it rise up. After about five minutes, I had a wonderfully round ball ready for proofing. I covered the dough with a damp dish towel and set it on the stove to rise.

While it was rising, I poured myself a cup of coffee and tried to make sense of the many questions still pounding in my head. James must be the Professor's top suspect, but I couldn't reconcile why he would leave a threatening note for me in his office. There were too many variables. If he really wanted to scare me, there were dozens of other ways he could have succeeded. I kept coming back to a new possibility—James was in danger. Maybe he'd figured out who the killer was and they had threatened him, or worse. Or, could he have gotten suspicious when I asked him about his past with

Sammy? Maybe Carlos was right. Maybe Lance and I had been too obvious in our attempts to help clear Andy's name.

The timer for my dough sounded, making me startle. The dough had doubled in size. I dusted a cutting board with flour and rolled the dough into a large rectangle. Then I lathered it with butter and sprinkled on cinnamon and a touch of brown sugar. I folded the dough, sliced it into two-inch rolls, and arranged them in a buttered baking dish. Then I slid them into the oven to bake for fifteen minutes.

Carlos appeared in the kitchen as I removed the golden rolls from the oven. "What smells so wonderful?" He walked straight to the coffeepot.

"Cinnamon rolls." I drizzled the hot rolls with orange glaze. "I noticed the police car is in the driveway. I wanted to thank them for watching the house last night."

He rubbed sleep from his eyes. "That is nice. Are you ready to go?"

"Yeah, let me put together a breakfast basket for the police and then we can head out." As I went to find paper plates in the pantry, my cell phone buzzed. It was early to be getting a text. I glanced at my phone and was shocked to see that the text was from Sammy.

SORRY TO BUG YOU. ARE YOU AT THE BAKESHOP? NEED TO TALK ASAP! IT'S ABOUT JAMES. I THINK HE'S IN TROUBLE!

Chapter Twenty-Five

I responded to Sammy's text immediately.

ON MY WAY THERE NOW. CAN YOU COME BY IN 30?

Why she wanted to talk to me was a mystery, but I wasn't about to give up the opportunity to hear what she had to say.

I wanted to give the police time to do their sweep. I wasn't worried about meeting with Sammy, even if she had any involvement in Benson's death, because I knew that Andy, Marty, Bethany, and Steph would all be arriving within the next thirty minutes.

Carlos brought a thermos of coffee and I carried plates of hot-from-the-oven cinnamon rolls. The police were grateful for the surprise breakfast and followed us to Torte. They completed a top-to-bottom search of the bakeshop, checking the walk-in fridge, locked closets, and my office before giving me the all-clear.

"What would you like me to do, mi querida? It is too early to go to the vineyard." He caught my eye and held my gaze.

I knew it was his way of letting me know that even if

it wasn't too early, there was no chance he was leaving my side, and I had to admit that the gesture made him that much more attractive.

"You could fire up the pizza oven and start on a lunch special. We had our market delivery yesterday and there are some beautiful veggies in the walk-in. Work your magic. Plus, I know that when Marty and Sterling get here, they'll be eager to go over their ideas for the dinner in the vines with you."

"Okay. It is a plan." He went straight to work, assessing stock in the fridge.

I went upstairs to fire up the espresso machine, start batches of our morning brews, and wait for Sammy. We offer a daily rotation of five house blends, along with a decaf. Our summer coffee line-up included a variety of light and bright roasts with notes of citrus and berries.

I heard Andy and the others arrive downstairs as I finished scooping ground beans into the last pot. Good. Sammy was unlikely to attack me with my staff starting the morning routine in the bakeshop. She arrived at the front door right on time. I went to unlock the door and invite her inside.

Her fingers trembled as I handed her a cup of our blonde roast and pointed her to a window booth.

"Are you okay?" I asked.

She clutched the cup with both hands. "No. I'm pretty freaked out."

"Why did you text me?" I asked. "Is this about Benson's murder?"

Her aloof exterior had disappeared. She shifted from side to side as she spoke. "I think so. I still can't find my meds so I'm already shaky. I'm not sure if I'm fuzzy and not thinking clearly because I haven't taken my medication in two days, or if I should really be freaked out."

"But why me?"

She stared at her shaky fingers as she continued. "The thing is I'm not sure what to do. Sorry for involving you. I know I should go to the police, but James made me promise not to. I couldn't think of what else to do, and you were cool when we chatted earlier, so I came here. I know it's weird but I didn't know what else to do."

Why would he tell her that? To protect himself?

"Maybe you should start from the beginning," I suggested.

She tried to steady her hands to take a sip of coffee, but instead set the mug on the table. "Yeah, okay. I didn't know who to turn to because he made me swear I wouldn't tell the police. You seem like you're pretty connected here, so I figured maybe you can pass this on and then technically speaking I wouldn't be breaking a promise." She formed her lips into a tight circle and blew out air. "I wasn't entirely honest with you the other day. Here's the thing: Benson didn't want anyone to know that he was going to invest in my franchise project. He thought it would be a conflict of interest."

That was for sure.

"He came up with a plan," Sammy continued. Her voice was as wobbly as her hands. "He wanted to stage a fight. He told me he would make sure that I came in third or fourth place in the first couple of rounds. That way no one would suspect that we were teaming up. He didn't want me to blow the entire competition but he didn't want me to be in first place either. He told me we had to be super careful. He thought one of the other judges was watching him. He was kind of paranoid."

"Okay." I wasn't sure where she was going with this.

"He told me to make a scene. He wanted me to blow up at him when I didn't take first place. That way there would be no chance that anyone would think we had a working relationship outside of the Barista Cup. We weren't really fighting—that was an all act. Benson wasn't pulling his funding either. That was just a rumor that started circulating. We met for dinner the night before the first round and he offered me even more money. He wanted the expansion to go bigger. He wanted to roll out a national franchise campaign sooner. I was thrilled. He said he was coming into some money and he wanted to invest it in me." Sammy swallowed. "Now he's dead and I don't have an actual contract. Who's going to believe me? I wouldn't believe me."

I noticed that one of her tattoos was the logo for Fluid. She also had trophies like Andy's inked on her arm to represent her many past wins. Talk about coffee obsessed.

I wasn't sure how to respond.

Sammy paused and wrapped her hands around her coffee cup again. This time she was able to lift it to her quivering lips.

"Am I missing something? I thought you were worried about James?" I asked.

"James found out about the deal. He and Benson have had a long rivalry. He wrote a terrible column about James years ago and James has had it out for him ever since. He threatened to tell Piper and the other judges about our financial partnership."

If James knew about their agreement, how did that put him in danger? I caught Sequoia's eye. She had arrived and began readying the coffee bar for the morning rush.

Sammy answered my question for me. "James pulled me aside yesterday and told me that he had a new proposition for me. He said he learned something very interesting about Benson's personal and financial life that should shed new light on the situation. Those were his exact words." She steadied her hands to take another drink. "Then he went dark. I was supposed to meet him at his office last night, but when I showed up he wasn't there and there was a warning poster on his desk. I haven't heard from him since. I've been texting and calling and he won't answer. I think something might have happened to him."

So Sammy had seen the note on James's desk too.

Her voice sounded weak as she continued. "I'm scared. I don't know how I ended up in the middle of this, but I don't know what to do."

"We have to call the police." There was no question in my mind.

"Yeah, but there's a problem."

"What's that?"

"My fingerprints are all over his office. I picked up the note. I don't know what made me do it. I guess I was curious. If I tell the police, they're going to think I left the note. They've been asking me so many questions. I've had to tell them at least six times my movement from the time the competition started to the time that Benson's body was found. They think I killed him. I know they do. There's no paperwork for our deal. We were planning to finalize everything this weekend. Someone started the rumor that Benson and I had a big blowup and that he was pulling his money. It's not true. He told me to pretend like I was upset at the Barista Cup. That's it. I swear. He had bigger plans for us that he was going to spell out before he was killed. Why would I do it?"

She leaned her elbows on the table, revealing another Barista Cup tattoo near her elbow. "Someone is setting me up. If I go to the police, they'll arrest me."

I understood her hesitation. "Listen, Sammy, I know you're scared, but the Ashland police team is extremely professional. If you explain everything you've told me, you won't have anything to worry about."

She didn't look convinced.

"You don't have any record of your plans with Benson? You must have run financials on the expansions. What about marketing plans? Target cities? Anything?"

"Yeah. I have that, but we hadn't signed a contract yet. The only trail I have is email exchanges between Benson and me. Those are mainly about meeting times. They don't have any details about franchising. Benson was old school that way. He liked to do everything face-to-face."

I studied her. One hand gripped the edge of the table. Her eyes darted around the room as if we were being watched. Was she telling me the truth? Never in my professional life had business transactions as substantial as Sammy's growth plans taken place without a paper trail.

"Now I'm starting to wonder if there was another reason for that." She dug her nails into the wood tabletop.

"How so?"

"I'm starting to think he didn't want any sort of a traceable trail of our communication. I thought he was quirky. He would take notes on a yellow legal pad and record our conversations on an old tape recorder. He said it was a holdover technique from writing his columns. Maybe I'm being paranoid, but I can't help wondering if whoever killed him is trying to frame me."

"Sammy, we need to call the police. Doug, Ashland's lead detective, is my stepfather and I promise he's a very reasonable and brilliant detective. If you want, I can call him now and I can sit in on your conversation."

"Would you do that?" Her cocky exterior had vanished. I was reminded that she wasn't that much older than Steph and Bethany and in an unfamiliar place alone, but I still wasn't entirely convinced about her innocence. She could easily be playing me. The opposite could be true. Maybe Benson decided to back out of the deal. That would explain the lack of any tangible proof that he intended to bankroll her expansion. Either way it was time to involve the police, especially in light of whatever had happened to James. He could be in serious trouble.

"Let me call the Professor now," I said to Sammy before getting up to place the call and refill our coffees. It didn't take long for the Professor to arrive.

As I had explained to Sammy, he listened carefully to her story, taking notes and stopping her every so often for clarification. When she finished, he flipped his Moleskine notebook shut. "Thank you for being forthcoming. This is quite helpful." He looked to the clock. "It's also quite early. I'd like to follow up with you in a few hours. Where might I find you?"

Sammy rubbed her temples. "I guess I'll go back to the hotel."

"Excellent. I'll be in touch." He left without another word. It made me suspect that he believed Sammy's story. Was he concerned about James as well?

"How much do I owe you for the coffee?" Sammy asked.

"Nothing. It's on the house." I picked up our empty cups. "Do you need a ride to The Hills?"

"No. I have my car. I drove here from Spokane. It was cheaper than flying. Plus, I wanted to bring my own gear. It's hard to fly with CO2 canisters and bottles of simple syrup."

"Fair enough." I smiled. "Let me know if there's anything else I can do to help."

"Thanks. I hope James is okay. I don't think I can handle another death right now."

That was a point I completely agreed with her on. The deeper I found myself in this maze, the more I was determined to do anything I could to help find Benson's killer and return my beloved Ashland to normal.

Chapter Twenty-Six

"Who were you talking to?" Carlos asked when I returned to the kitchen.

I told him about my conversation with Sammy and the Professor. "This is a very strange case." He frowned and looked as if he wanted to say more, but stopped himself.

I tried to focus on baking. The team had arrived and the kitchen was alive with chatter and the aromatic smell of bread rising in the ovens. Having Carlos in the kitchen brought a different, livelier energy. He and Marty cracked jokes, while he and Sterling sautéed veggies and seared steaks in perfect rhythm at the stove. Every day that passed made me more grateful that he had been willing to give us a chance. I couldn't believe I had ever doubted that Ashland wasn't right for him. If anything, Ashland had brought out the best qualities in Carlos, and unless I was completely misreading him, he seemed more content and centered. Ashland had that effect on people. I attributed some of that to the healing Lithia waters that flowed through town and the fact that the ancient mountains that surrounded us provided natural grounding, tethering us to the land and those who walked before us.

"Julieta, you must come try this." Carlos called me over to the stove after I had finished two batches of almond-and-chocolate-filled croissants.

Sterling plated the skirt steak they had teamed up on. It was beautifully seared and topped with a brilliant green pesto and a side of herbed butter and sautéed veggies.

Carlos handed me a fork. "Taste this."

The tender steak cut easily with the fork. Before I lifted it to my lips, the intoxicating scent of fresh herbs and garlic hit my nose. "This is heaven," I said to Sterling and Carlos, savoring the buttery steak. "Don't change a thing. This is definitely going to be the star of the show for our dinner in the vines."

"What do you think about the butter?" Sterling asked. "Too much with the pesto?"

"No." I dipped another piece of the tender meat into the ramekin of butter. "Seriously don't change a thing. It's perfect. It melts in your mouth and the flavors are out of this world. I love it."

Carlos beamed at Sterling. "Give our sous chef the credit. This is his creation. I simply took direction from him."

Sterling tried to blow off the compliment, but I saw a spark of appreciation in his crystal blue eyes. "I don't know about that."

"No, no, do not sell yourself short. It is important when you make food as good as this to take in the compliment. It is the cycle. We give a gift of ourselves on the plate and then the customer returns that gift with their thanks. This is the essential way we must cook. We infuse the food with pieces of our soul. That is what we taste in every bite. That is what keeps customers coming back again and again. It is the nourishment of living, of sharing, of coming together around a table and breaking bread."

Sterling took in Carlos's heartfelt words. "Yes, chef." He gave him a two-finger salute.

Carlos clapped him on the back. "Well done. I'm proud to be able to cook next to you."

Bethany came into the kitchen with an empty tray. "Jules, there's a call for you on the main line."

"Okay, thanks." I went to my office to take the call. The line was dead when I picked up our land line. "Hello? Hello?"

No one answered.

That was odd.

I waited for a few minutes to see if the person would call back, to no avail. I decided to take another look at the articles I had found about James and Benson's terrible review. Maybe I had missed something.

I opened my laptop and did another search. I spent the next half hour re-reading the scathing review and the subsequent stories about the collapse of James's coffee shop. Reading the review a second time was as painful and cringeworthy as the first. But what did it mean in terms of Benson's murder?

Had James staged the threatening note? What if he had made his escape? Reading the articles again reminded me that he had the strongest motive for killing Benson. Maybe the note had been a setup. Perhaps James wanted Sammy and me to find the note and assume that someone was targeting him. What if that was just a way to buy himself more time to get out of town?

Surely the Professor was already investigating that possibility.

I did another online search for the Barista Cup. Dozens of links popped up in my search window. I scanned a bunch of them. Most of the articles were about previous competitions and winners. There were pictures of Sammy holding the same trophy that Andy had won, along with a huge check. She posed with Benson and Piper. The photo caption of her first win caught my eye. "Barista Cup organizers and husband-and-wife team Benson and Piper award the champion cup."

Husband-and-wife team?

Benson and Piper were married? Piper had lied. She had said they had a brief fling, which she had called off.

I read the caption three times.

If Benson and Piper were married, that changed everything. But why wouldn't Piper have mentioned it? I thought back to their interactions. They hadn't given off any cues that they were a couple. Sammy had said that they lived together, but if they had been married, that must have meant their finances among other things were connected.

The photo was from four years ago. I wondered how long they'd been divorced.

I copied the link and sent it to the Professor. Then I picked up the phone and called him. He didn't answer, so I left him a message telling him to check his email.

As if he hadn't already discovered that Piper and Benson were married. His police database was undoubtedly a better resource than my Google search. I felt slightly silly for having sent him the link and calling, but then again this was a murder investigation and he always said that you never knew what nugget of information might crack a case.

I closed my laptop and pondered what to do next. I really wanted to get another look in James's office. The question was how?

A solution arrived in the form of Lance's singsong voice in the dining room. I heard him asking about me, and went to the front to greet him.

"Lance, I'm worried about you. This is quickly becoming a habit. It's barely after nine and you're awake and alert."

He waved me off. "Don't give it a thought, darling. Beauty sleep can wait. I've had an ah-ha moment and must share it with you." He looked around the dining room, which was humming with activity. "Not here. Too crowded. Shall we take a stroll?"

Without waiting for my response, he dragged me out the front door.

"What is it?" I asked as we moved away from the bakeshop toward A Rose by Any Other Name. Summer wreaths made from crabapple and grapevines, lush with lemons, bay leaves, and green foliage hung on the windows.

"It's about Piper."

"What a coincidence," I replied. "I just learned something about Piper."

"Oh, well, don't let me hog the spotlight. Ladies first." He clutched his chest.

I knew that Lance loved nothing better than a reveal. "No, I wouldn't dream of it. You go first."

"If you insist." He launched into his news. "Okay, be prepared to be blown away by this. I kept returning to a conversation Piper and I had shortly after Benson's murder. She used the word 'ex' in a strange way. At the time I didn't think much of it, but suddenly at seven this morning I sat straight up in bed with a realization—the 'ex' she was referring to was Benson." He looked to me for my reaction.

"I know! I just found that out too."

He scowled and folded his arms over his chest. "Way to steal the spotlight."

"Sorry. Go on."

"Well, I did some extensive research," Lance continued. "And learned that Benson and Piper were married for five years."

Okay, so he had learned more than me.

"Where did you find that?"

"Darling, I can't divulge a source. What I will tell you is that my theater connections run deep, as in far north to Seattle. Apparently, Piper has a penchant for the arts. She and Benson were quite generous donors to our comrades at Seattle Rep."

"How do you know they were married for five years?"

"Sources. Reliable sources." He paused momentarily as a group of runners passed by. "My sources say that their breakup was ugly, as in bloodshed ugly."

"Bloodshed?"

"Not literally, of course, but the divorce was nasty. Piper comes from money. Old money. She had to pay a large settlement to Benson and they had to split the profits from the Barista Cup fifty-fifty. Apparently, she was not happy about that. Benson had signed a prenup that somehow ended up being tossed out by the judge."

"Wow. You did learn a lot. And, you're sure this is all real, not just rumor?"

"O ye of little faith, Juliet." He pursed his lips in disgust. "Are you suggesting that I would embellish details?"

"Never."

"What are we waiting for then? Let's get ourselves over to The Hills."

"For what?"

"To confront Benson's killer of course."

Chapter Twenty-Seven

Lance drove with a purpose to The Hills, and when we pulled into the parking lot there were three squad cars blocking the front entrance.

"An interesting coincidence, wouldn't you say?" He steered into a parking space.

"Considering there's a murder investigation going on, I would say *no*."

"Don't you dare get sassy with me, Juliet Capshaw." He turned off the car and opened his door. "Shall we?"

"What's our plan?" I pointed to the police officers at either side of the doors. "We can't exactly barge in."

"Of course we can. Don't be daft. Simply follow my lead. It's all about looking like you belong." He strolled toward the entrance with me tagging behind.

"Good morning, to Ashland's team in blue. My friend and I have some important theater business here. I assume it's not a problem for us to proceed." He stepped closer to the automatic doors.

The officers looked at each other and shrugged. "Don't go near any of the areas that are roped off and you'll be fine. The hotel is open."

"Thanks." Lance shot them a dazzling smile and proceeded inside.

Not surprisingly, yellow caution tape stretched across the corridor that led to James's office. Had something happened? Had they found James's body?

Lance marched up to the reception desk. "I have a meeting with Piper. Can you call her room please?"

The clerk asked for her room number, which Lance somehow produced. I looked at him for clarification, he shot me a look to say *Don't ask*.

"I'm sorry, there's no answer. Would you like to leave a message?" the clerk asked.

"No. We'll go check the patio outside. Perhaps she's already waiting for us."

"Feel free." The clerk pointed toward the pool. "You know the way?"

"Yes, many thanks." Lance made a beeline for the hallway opposite James's office.

"What are we doing?" I had to jog to keep up with him. Fortunately, I had opted for tennis shoes for a long day of baking. Comfortable shoes are a must for any professional chef. And, they came in handy when running down a potential killer.

"Trying to find another way into James's office."

"What? You saw that the area is completely closed off."

"That doesn't mean there isn't another way in, does it?"

I gave up arguing and followed him outside, past the pool deck, to the backside of the hotel where the large bays for shipping and receiving were. One of the roll-up doors was open.

"Ah-ha! There's our opportunity." Lance yanked me toward the bay.

"Lance, we can't go in there." I pointed to the many signs plastered on the bays that said EMPLOYEES ONLY.

"That's nothing more than semantics." Lance glanced around. A semitruck had pulled away from the bay. He waited for the driver to maneuver the truck out of sight before climbing up onto the platform and reaching a hand down for me.

"No way. I'm not going up there," I resisted.

"We don't have much time. I can hear the crew unloading the pallets right now. Give me your hand."

Lance aggravated me with his outlandish schemes, and yet I found myself stretching out my arm and letting him drag me up into the loading dock.

"Now what?" I whispered.

"This way." Lance pressed his index finger to his lips and tiptoed away from The Hills staff, who were unloading the cases of craft beer and wine that had been delivered. We snuck out of the bay and found ourselves in a long hallway. Given its lack of décor, I could tell that this section of the hotel was only used by staff. A sign to our left pointed to the laundry. Another sign pointed to the kitchens.

I could hear workers laughing as we scurried past the employee break room. We reached a door marked SUPPLIES. Lance turned the handle then pulled me inside with him. He flipped on the light. "Jackpot."

I looked around. There were a variety of cleaning supplies, towels, and toiletries. Clearly this was a space used for cleaning staff to restock.

Why is this a jackpot? I mouthed.

"Because we just found our in." His eyes drifted to the back of the supply room where at least a dozen uniforms hung in rows. He held up a housekeeping uniform.

"No. No way." I shook my head.

"You're right. My mistake." He returned the house-keeping uniform to its spot on the rack and removed a room-service uniform. "We have to stay on brand. You'll fit right in with this."

He tossed the crisp orange uniform to me. "Hurry." Lance was already slipping on another one.

This was a bad idea. Why did I listen to Lance?

"Let's go. Let's go." Lance waved his hands for me to hurry.

I tugged on the uniform. He handed me a hat. "Wear this. We must stay incognito."

"Lance, if Thomas or Kerry see us in room-service uniforms, hats aren't going to be enough to conceal our identity."

"I know. That's why we're going to keep our heads down and use this." He lifted a domed stainless steel plate cover to shield his face. Then he rolled a cart to the door. He opened it with caution. "The coast is clear. Let's go. Just keep your eyes on your feet."

We shuffled down the hallway. Lance pushed the cart. I pretended to be balancing the plate. We made it the side of the hotel where James's office was located. Surprisingly, no caution tape blocked our entry. The hallway was deserted.

Lance picked up the pace. When we reached James's office, he leaned his head against the door. Then he shot me a thumbs-up.

He opened the door and slipped inside, leaving the cart in the hallway. I did the same.

"Nothing." He sounded disappointed as we surveyed the office.

Everything was exactly as I had found it last night with one exception—the threatening note was gone.

"What did you think? We were going to find a body in here?" I asked, keeping my voice low.

"Perhaps." He tapped his finger to his chin, did a quick sweep of the room. "Well, so much for that. Let's go."

We retraced our steps. I figured we would return the cart and our uniforms to the supply closet, but once we were back in the employee only section Lance headed straight for the freight elevators.

"Where are we going?"

"Third floor. Didn't you hear? Room three hundred twelve is starving. They placed their room-service order forty-five minutes ago. We must get them their food while it's hot. That's our job, after all."

"How are we going to get in?" I asked.

Lance reached into his uniform and removed a key card.

"Where did you get that?"

He pressed the button for the third floor.

"I happened to check my pockets. Good fortune, wouldn't you say?"

I didn't say anything as the elevator chugged up to the third floor. Lance wheeled the cart to Piper's room and knocked on the door. "Room service."

There was no response.

He tried again. "Room service."

Nothing.

He took that as a sign and waved the key card in front

of the door handle. The lock turned green. Lance's face lit up as he turned the handle and went inside.

A wave of fear assaulted my body. This was a bad idea.

I hesitated.

A hand wrapped around my wrist and yanked me inside.

"Lance, don't. This is a bad idea."

The next thing I knew, a hand covered my mouth with a painful slap and the door locked behind me.

Chapter Twenty-Eight

I dropped the domed plate cover and plate. The room was dark, excepting the tiny shaft of light that escaped between the shades that had been pulled shut. I blinked away bright spots scattering in my field of vision and tried to get out of Lance's grasp. His fingers were digging into my top lip.

"Ouch," I murmured. "You're hurting me."

He didn't loosen his grasp.

That's when I realized the person covering my mouth wasn't Lance. Lance was on the floor, facedown.

Terror welled in my throat, making it hard to breath.

Piper, I mouthed.

The hand tightened.

I coughed, trying to get more air.

My head bent backward as the person dragged me toward the bed. I struggled to break free, but I was at a disadvantage.

Lance stirred on the floor. He moaned in pain.

Had he been hurt?

My attacker threw me backward onto the bed. It took

a minute to get my bearings in the dark and musty room.
I blinked rapidly.

Time moved in a strange, slow swirl.

Sweat poured from my forehead. I wasn't sure if it
was from stress or the fact that the heat must have been
set at over ninety degrees. It felt like we could grill our
pizza in the sultry room.

I pushed myself up to standing at the same moment
my attacker lunged for a bedside lamp.

"Piper?" I squinted to try and get a better look.

She stood over Lance with her foot resting on his
head and the lamp in her hand. One move and she could
crush his skull.

"Don't even think about it," she hissed to me. "You
move a muscle and he's dead."

Lance moaned again.

"Look, this is a mistake. Please don't hurt him. I'll
do whatever you want." I tried to appease her.

"I know you will, because by now you must have figured out that I've already killed one person. It's a slip-
pery slope and I'm not afraid to do it again." She kicked
Lance's head to the side as if to prove her point.

He groaned in agony.

"Piper, please. You don't want to do this." I mopped
my brow with the back of my hand.

"How do you know what I want?" she sneered. "You
don't know anything about me."

"I know that you and Benson were married and it
ended badly. Do you want to talk about it?" Maybe if I
could get her talking, I could buy myself time to figure
out how to get out of here.

"You don't know anything," she repeated.

"Piper, really I want to help." I squinted more. My eyes had begun to adjust to the darkness. There was a discarded breakfast tray on the bedside table. I wondered if there was a knife or anything I could use as a weapon.

"Yeah right. I'm not one of your young baristas. I'm a grown woman with plenty of years under my belt. You should have stayed out of it. It didn't need to come to this, but like I said I'm not afraid to see this through."

"The police know about you and Benson," I said, hoping to find any leverage.

"I figured. It's public record."

"I don't understand—how do you think you're going to get away with his murder?" I slowly inched toward the used breakfast dishes.

"I have a plan." She stared at the window.

We were on the third floor. Did she intend to jump?

Different scenarios raced through my brain. Could I stop her? If she made a move toward the window, I could tackle her from behind. The second she moved away from Lance, I could try and take her down.

"I don't understand the threatening note you left for James. Isn't that going to cast even more suspicion on you?"

"They'll never trace that back to me." Her voice had a strange shrill quality.

"What about James?" The slant of light seeping in between the curtains was the only illumination in the room. I had managed to scoot closer to the edge of the bed, but to my disappointment the only items on the breakfast tray were a coffee cup and plate.

"What about him?"

"Did you kill him too?"

"Ha!" She threw her head back. "Like I'm going to tell you."

A loud horn blared outside.

Piper cleared her throat. "Okay, time to do something with you two." She paused as if trying to consider her options. The lamp was still clutched in one hand and her foot remained on the top of Lance's head. *She must be thinking the same thing I was. The minute she moved away from Lance, I could spring into action.*

Unless she threw the lamp at my head.

I wished I had a weapon. Should I try to throw a coffee cup at her head? I also wished I had listened to my intuition and that inner voice that had screamed for me to walk away.

The horn blared again.

Piper started to lift the lamp.

This is your chance, Jules, you have to make your move—now!

As Piper's arm raised higher, I leaped from the bed. I stretched my arms as far as they could reach and ducked to avoid being hit by the lamp. My hands landed on her shoulders. I knocked her off her feet and landed on top of her. The lamp shattered on the floor.

Now I had the advantage. I pinned her down.

She was much stronger than I imagined.

I couldn't hold her off for long.

Lance yelped in pain. He had gotten to his knees. "Help. I'll get help."

He clutched his head and crawled to the door.

I could tell that it took all of his strength to reach

for the handle and open the door. When he did, light flooded into the room and Lance collapsed in the door-frame.

Piper wiggled beneath me.

I wished there was a way I could tie her up. I didn't want to fight her.

Suddenly the sound of heavy footsteps echoed in the hallway.

"Here," Lance waved from the carpet.

Thomas and Kerry along with four other police officers ran into the room. In a flash they freed me from Piper, and had her in handcuffs.

She spewed out obscenities.

Kerry went to check on Lance as two of the officers escorted Piper out of the room. "We need EMS," she said to Thomas. "He has a large contusion on the base of his skull and is showing signs of a concussion."

Thomas called the paramedics, while Kerry helped Lance sit up, careful to support his back.

"Jules, come sit down." Thomas ushered me to the table near the window. He opened the shades and the sliding door, allowing light to pour in. "Do you need some water? It's so hot in here. Can you tell me what happened?"

"No. I'm fine." That wasn't entirely true. I was shaken, but adrenaline pulsed through my body. "It all happened so fast. Lance opened the door. Piper must have hit him with something. He was basically knocked out. Is he going to be okay?"

"He'll be fine. We've got the paramedics on the way." Thomas stood and went to turn down the thermostat. The air-conditioning kicked on right away.

"I know what you're going to say. We shouldn't have interfered." I fanned my face.

"Interfered? I thought you and Lance took jobs. A little extra cash for summer," he teased, referencing my housekeeping uniform.

"It's not my proudest moment," I admitted.

"Jules, you and Lance give us so many laughs. Let's drop it for the moment and fill me on what went down."

That put me at ease. I told him all the embarrassing details from sneaking into the loading dock to breaking into Piper's room.

"How did you find us?" I asked when I finished.

"We were already in route. The Professor found James. He's okay. Piper tried the same trick on him as she had with Benson—spiking his drink. Fortunately, James tasted something off and ingested only a small amount of the sedative. He finished giving the Professor his statement and that gave us the green light to proceed with an arrest. We had no idea you were here."

The paramedics arrived and attended to Lance. They bandaged his head and applied an ice pack. Then they loaded him onto a gurney to take him to the hospital for observation. "He's stable," the paramedic told us. "With head injuries we like to keep patients overnight."

I went to check on him before they took him to the ambulance.

"How are you?" I squeezed his hand.

"Terrible. Absolutely terrible. I've decided that white is no longer my color." He touched the bandage. "I tried to tell them but they wouldn't listen."

A sense of relief came over me. Lance was fine.

"I'll come see you at the hospital. What can I bring you?"

"A martini?" he asked hopefully.

"I think the doctors and nurses might frown on that, but I can probably manage a latte and something sweet."

"It's a deal."

The paramedics started wheeling him down the hall. Lance blew me kisses. "Ta-ta, darling. Another case solved. We're such a team!"

Kerry rolled her eyes.

Thomas chuckled. "You two are *something*, that's for sure." He let out a long exhale and caught Kerry's eye before addressing me. "However, we should arrest both of you for trespassing, and that's just for starters. Am I right, Kerry?"

"Yep. I would tack on interfering with a police investigation and breaking and entering. Should we go on?" Her brows creased. "Do you understand that one tiny mistake can cause a mistrial? Or force the court to completely dismiss the case? We have specific operating procedures for a reason."

"I know. I'm sorry. I guess we got carried away." I felt terrible. She was right. My gut had told me not to get involved. I should have listened to my inner voice rather than getting swept up into the excitement with Lance.

Her face softened. "Look, Ashland might be a small, tight-knit community. I'm learning more about that." She glanced at Thomas. "It's not only our job to apprehend the criminal, but we also have to prove our case."

"You have to admit, they do keep us on our toes," Thomas said with a wink.

Kerry shrugged, but a smile tugged on her cheeks. "That is very true."

I smiled and let out a deep breath. Lance was okay and Piper was in custody. Things hadn't played out exactly as I would have planned, hence the housekeeping uniform that I needed to get out of and put away. But now that Piper had been arrested, I could sleep easy knowing that Andy's name had been cleared and the simple life I knew in Ashland could return to normal once again.

Chapter Twenty-Nine

Later that evening Carlos and I arrived at the hospital with a basket of pastries and an iced latte. I had told Carlos everything. He didn't exactly approve of our antics, but he did thank me for my honesty.

"Julieta, I will not take away your friendship with Lance. I know that you love each other. Friendship like that it is so important, but we cannot have secrets. I do not like that you and Lance have helped the police. It worries me to have you in danger, but I see how your eyes light up and I see the wheels spinning in your head. Promise me, you will be safe, okay? This is all I need."

I had kissed him and lingered in his arms. He was right. Lance and I had formed a strong bond while Carlos and I had been separated, but I wanted him to be part of our friendship. I appreciated that he wasn't asking me to change. He was simply asking to be involved. That was fair.

Lance was sitting up in his hospital bed and in chipper spirits. "Welcome friends. Sit, make yourselves comfortable."

"How are you feeling?" Carlos's voice was heavy with concern. "The bandage looks very big."

"My thoughts exactly, and for nothing more than a little bump." Lance lifted his finger and lightly touched the bandage. "Doctors, always overly cautious." He raised the coffee we had brought for him and winked at me. "Not to worry, they assure me I can break free from this cell soon and be back on the stage where I belong."

"Not so fast, Lance. You have a concussion. I can't imagine the doctor thinks it's a good idea for you to be back at work tomorrow."

Lance looked to Carlos for support. "Your wife is such a mother sometimes. Tell her not to worry. My little gray cells, as everyone's favorite Belgian detective likes to say, are in rare form."

"I agree with Julieta. I think you must rest for a few days. Work, it can wait."

Lance sunk his teeth into a cherry tart. "What can't wait are details about our upcoming fete. I need a happy distraction. Do tell, what's on the final menu and what are we thinking in terms of design?"

Carlos relayed delectable details about every course, and I showed him some of the ideas Steph and Bethany had come up with, including hanging paper lanterns in the trees, using Mason-jar vases for candles to line each row of the vineyard, white linens, and fragrant bouquets of white roses, lilies, and daisies for centerpieces. They wanted to create a photo booth with a white floral backdrop and fun wine props, and Sterling had suggested hiring a local guitar duo to add to the ambiance.

"I love it. I love everything about it," Lance gushed. "There's just one problem."

"What's that?"

"This bandage. I know it's on trend with our color scheme, but I cannot look like a glorified mummy at our first vineyard soirée."

Carlos and I laughed.

"It's five days away. I'm sure you'll be able to tone down the wrap by then."

"You can count on that," Lance insisted. "Fashion comes first."

I could tell Carlos was about to disagree, but a nurse came in to check Lance's vitals, so we made our exit.

"He is kidding, yes?" Carlos asked on our way out.

"Probably." I took it as a good sign that Lance was more concerned about what he was going to wear than his concussion.

After our hospital visit we headed home, where I spent the remainder of the day on the hammock, per Carlos's orders, sipping lemonade and reading a book. "Julieta, you have been through enough. Take the afternoon off. I will go make sure everything is ship shape at Torte."

I must have dozed off. Sometime later Carlos returned to find me still lazing in the hammock. He brought me a fragrant gin and tonic with muddled lime and fresh mint. Then he proceeded to make us a gorgeous dinner of grilled salmon, risotto, and a shaved Brussels sprout salad. We reminisced about our travels and he showed me pictures that Ramiro had sent from Spain. It was a happy distraction from the strange string of events.

Never before I had been so grateful to have the comfort of Carlos's embrace.

I reminded myself not to forget that as I drifted off to sleep.

The next morning I woke feeling refreshed and ready to face the day. I wasn't sure if that was thanks to yesterday's siesta or knowing that Benson's killer would be brought to justice. Carlos still refused to let me walk to Torte alone.

It was business as usual at the bakeshop. Andy was the first to arrive. "Morning, boss. How goes it?"

"Pretty good. How goes it with you?"

"Great. I heard about Piper. That's nuts. I didn't peg her as a killer."

"How did you hear?" News spread quickly in Ashland, that was for sure, but I wondered if the Professor or Thomas had intentionally looped Andy in so that he knew he was off the hook.

"Carlos told us."

"Oh right. I forgot he stopped by."

"Yeah, he filled us in on the whole story. You and Lance brought her down—literally. You're a beast, Jules!" Andy gave me a fist pump.

"I don't know about that, but yes, Lance and I were there."

Andy went to fire up the espresso machine. I replayed yesterday's events for Sterling, Marty, and the rest of the team when they arrived. It felt good to talk about it and get it off my chest. It was almost like every time I told the story, it took away some of the remaining angst in my body.

The person I wanted to talk to the most was the

Professor. My wish was granted shortly after opening. He and Mom came in through the front door.

"Honey, how are you? How's Lance?" Mom hugged me tight. She took off a thin pale blue cardigan and hung it on the rack.

"I'm fine and Lance is consumed with how he's going to coordinate his bandage with his outfit for the dinner in the vines."

Mom chuckled. "In other words, he's fine."

"Exactly."

Mom spotted a group of her friends from Pilates. "I know you two have lots to catch up on, so I'll go say hello to the girls."

The Professor gave me a half bow. "Shall we step outside and compare notes?"

"That would be lovely. I have so many questions."

He opened the door for me. Our outdoor tables were empty. "Is here good?" He moved to the table farthest from the door. Large galvanized tubs that moonlighted as planters divided the tables. The Professor wisely had picked the most private one, shaded by a five-foot Japanese maple tree.

"Sure." My gaze traveled to the Merry Windsor, where one of Richard's bellhops was shouting for people to come try samples of their iced coffee.

I wonder where he got that idea, I thought as I took a seat across from the Professor.

He folded his hands together. "Juliet, I fear I put you in danger by asking for your insight. Please accept my deepest apologies. I assure you it will not happen again."

"No," I placed my hand over his. The Professor had become my second father and someone whose opinion mattered most to me. "I'm embarrassed that Lance and I did something so juvenile. I got carried away in the moment. I should be the one apologizing not you."

"Ah, there's the rub. If it hadn't been for your"—he paused, searching for the right word—"your innovative tactics, we may have missed our window to arrest Piper. She had arranged to steal away in a cargo truck. She may have been across state lines by the time we arrived on the scene if you and Lance hadn't delayed her."

"Wait, does that mean she had an accomplice?" My mind immediately went to her conversation with Diaz and the sound of the beeping horn outside of her hotel room.

"Yes. It appears that way. She became quite cooperative when given the choices in front of her and proceeded to tell us about her escape route with Diaz, amongst other things. She approached Diaz when she learned of Benson's arrangement with Sammy. She decided that if she could ensure a win for Diaz, it would catapult his rise to fame. They had plans to open their own coffee shops in direct competition with Fluid." He paused and greeted a group of tourists who passed by us chatting about the matinee show at OSF.

"Do you think Diaz was in on it?" I asked when the group was out of earshot.

The Professor wavered. "That I can't say for sure. Obviously he confessed to cheating, and he was waiting at the hotel for Piper when she was apprehended. Whether he knew and/or was involved in Benson's death remains to be seen. Piper's claiming that Diaz was her right-hand man, but our interviews with him have painted a different story. He claims that he had no knowledge of Benson's murder, and I'm inclined to believe him."

Piper's hushed conversation at the Hills with Diaz made more sense. They must have been plotting their exit strategy.

"What about James?" I asked the Professor.

"He is well and accounted for."

"I don't get it. Why did she threaten James?"

He strummed his fingers on his tightly shaved beard. "I believe James went too far in his accusation. Rather than coming to us immediately, I suspect that he had other motives. Motives that were . . . shall we say, less than ethical?"

"You mean blackmail?"

"Indeed. They had a common enemy in Benson. He ruined both of their careers. Perhaps that was James's initial pitch, and then the lure of money became too strong."

"Do you think he knew that Piper had killed Benson?"

"He isn't saying as much, but my intuition tells me there is more that will be revealed with time. I don't believe he was successful in his quest."

"What's going to happen to Diaz now?" I felt bad bombarding him with questions, but I knew I wouldn't be able to put Benson's murder behind me until I had more answers.

"His fate will be up to the judicial system. It reminds me of the wise words of King John, 'And oftentimes excusing of a fault doth make the fault worse by the excuse.' It seems that young Diaz found himself in a scene the Bard could have penned himself. His mistake in sabotaging his fellow competitors could mean that the judge or jury—if his case goes to a full trail—will reflect on all of his actions. He could very well be telling the truth about not knowing that Piper killed Benson, but his previous transgressions certainly won't help his case."

My gaze drifted toward the center of the plaza where a trio of little girls in pigtails broke out into a spontaneous dance in front of the Lithia fountains. "How did she do it?"

"You mean slip the sedative into his drink? A slight of hand. The work of street magicians. She offered to hold Benson's coffee while he gathered his things. A fatal error to say the least. Although, I'm quite sure that was her intention. Benson's medical records revealed that he had been suffering from high blood pressure and an arrhythmia for nearly a decade. Given his level of stress, his doctor had him on beta blockers, which interfered with the sedatives. Piper is claiming she didn't know about his other medications. Given their history, I find that highly doubtful."

"Did she steal the medication from Sammy?" I told him how Sammy had been looking for her anti-anxiety prescription.

He confirmed my suspicion with a nod. "We did indeed find an empty prescription bottle with Sammy's name on it in among the pieces of evidence we collected from Piper's room. The lab will have to verify whether the drug in Benson's latte is a match, but I would not be the least bit surprised. Piper believed she had an easy scapegoat in Sammy, so logic implies that using

Sammy's medication as the murder weapon would only serve to heighten our interest."

We were quiet for a moment. The Professor's phone buzzed. "Duty calls. Please excuse me, and please do accept my apology. You must know how dear you are to me. I would be shattered if harm should come to you."

"I feel the same."

He kissed the top of my head and strolled across the street to the police station. I felt satisfied. My questions had been answered. Piper had been arrested, and now I could celebrate Andy's win in earnest.

Chapter Thirty

The rest of the week passed without incident. Andy received well-earned accolades from the community. Not a day went by when a customer didn't ask to pose for a photo with him and the Barista Cup, which we had on display behind the espresso bar. Andy tried to downplay his enthusiasm in an attempt to stay humble, but I caught the look of delight in his eyes as he smiled broadly for each picture. Andy was the last person in any danger of developing an inflated ego. I told him as much on the morning of our dinner in the vines. A customer had asked to take a selfie, and he blushed.

"Soak it in," I said, after he snapped a couple of selfies. "You earned this, and I want you to enjoy every minute."

"Thanks, boss, but it's almost been a week. I can't believe people are still asking for pictures and even my autograph. A woman this morning asked me to sign her coffee mug."

"You are Ashland's coffee celebrity." I grinned.

"It's kind of embarrassing." Andy's cheeks darkened.

"Not at all. Trust me, you should enjoy it. Take in the

love. You spread joy every day through your coffee, now it's your turn to receive."

He considered my words. "Okay. I'll work on that."

It was a good lesson for life—the cycle of giving and receiving. Carlos had been a good role model for me on that. I tended to give freely, but like Andy, allowing other people to return the gesture hadn't come as easily. I remember one night on the *Amour of the Seas*, a guest had asked to meet me. That didn't happen as often in the pastry kitchen as it did in the main kitchen. "What do I say?" I had asked Carlos. He was well versed in having conversations with guests as head chef.

"You smile and take in the compliment. It completes the circle. We give. We receive. We repeat."

His words had struck a chord and I have carried them with me ever since. I hoped that Andy would do the same.

I went downstairs to get started on my dessert. Sterling, Marty, and Carlos would do the bulk of tonight's cooking at Uva. We were fortunate in that the winery had a large house on the property with a full working kitchen. It was a space we could use year-round and offer to wedding parties and special events at no additional cost.

Bethany and Steph were gathering decorations to transform the vineyard. I stopped and watched Steph adorn vanilla macarons in her beautiful cursive handwriting with the Spanish word for cheers, "salud," in chocolate.

"Those are so pretty," I commented.

"We thought they would be a sweet welcome for the

guests," Bethany replied. "We're going to have one on each place setting. Is that cool?"

"It's fabulous."

"Great. We're going to head over to the winery to start decorating in about an hour."

"That works for me. I'm going to make the pavlovas and then pack up everything I need to assemble them. I shouldn't be too far behind you."

Before I began whipping egg whites for the meringue, I heated the ovens to three hundred degrees and lined baking sheets with parchment paper. Then I separated the eggs, reserving the whites for my dessert and saving the yolks for another day. I beat the whites until they were stiff, but not completely firm. The key to a light and airy pavlova is adding the sugar a tablespoon at a time so as not to deflate the whites. I slowly incorporated the sugar and beat the whites until they were silky and glossy. Next, I folded in vanilla beans, fresh lemon juice, and cornstarch. The basic building blocks for the elegant dessert were so simple it almost felt like cheating. However, the real test in creating a pavlova comes in forming it on the parchment. I made a large circle with a Sharpie and filled it in with the fluffy egg white mixture. I worked my way from the center, out to the edges, making sure to build layers as I went so that a depression would form in the middle of the circle.

I slid it into the oven to bake for an hour and turned my attention to the berries. They would steep in red wine, a simple vanilla syrup, and a zest of lemon until we were ready for the dessert course. When it was time to serve the pavlova, I planned to fill the center with the berries and top it with a hearty dollop of hand-whipped cream and a chocolate drizzle.

I couldn't wait to share it with our guests.

Before I knew it, it was time to close up Torte and head to Uva. When I arrived at the winery, Bethany and Steph had already strung up twinkle lights and lined the vineyard with the Mason-jar candles. Rosa folded white napkins, and Sequoia hung signage that would direct guests where to park. Andy helped spread white linens on the tables and Bethany followed behind with plates and silverware. Steph arranged the bouquets of flowers.

"Wow, it's starting to look incredible," I praised the team. "Let me go put everything in the kitchen and then you can task me with a new job."

The smells permeating the kitchen made my knees weak. Salsa music blasted as Sterling, Carlos, and Marty moved in a choreographed rhythm, tossing salad and chopping veggies.

"You guys, I think we need to open the windows or find a way to pipe this smell outside," I said, setting boxes on the counter.

"You like? It smells wonderful, si?" Carlos wore his classic chef's coat. I hadn't seen him in the uniform in a while. His chiseled features and tanned skin against the stark white coat made my heartbeat quicken.

"Yeah." I drank in the scent. "It smells divine."

Carlos dipped his pinkie in Sterling's pesto. "Beautiful. Beautiful. A touch more salt." Then he looked at me. "Julieta, the wine is ready and the first course is plated."

I glanced to my left. On the counter opposite me,

bottles of wine had been placed in neat rows. Each bottle had been uncorked to allow the wine to breathe. Gorgeous platters of meats, cheeses, nuts, dips, and marinated veggies waited next to the wine. They reminded me of works of art with the way colors had been arranged on each tray. "These are too pretty to eat," I commented, popping an olive into my mouth.

"Do not touch, mi querida," Carlos scolded with a grin. "You will ruin Sterling's design, and it is not finished. We still must char the flatbread so it will be warm when we are ready to serve."

Sterling held up a wooden spoon. "That's right, Jules. Hands off."

I held my arms up in a surrender. "Fine, I'll go see if I'm needed outside. I can tell I'm not welcome here."

"That's right, no girls allowed." Marty let out a baritone chuckle. "Ohhh, I'm playing with fire, aren't I, boys?"

Carlos whistled. "This is trouble for you."

I knew Marty was teasing. "That's right. You better watch it, sir. Don't forget which side your bread is buttered on."

Marty bowed down. "I surrender. I surrender."

"That's our cue boys." Sterling winked. The three of them dropped what they were doing and met in the center of the kitchen.

"Gentlemen, let's show Julieta what these legs can do."

They proceeded to do a kick line, while Marty sang, "These legs can-can cook! Oh yes, they can-can."

"That's the worst rendition of the Rockettes I have ever seen." I shook my head in mock disgust.

My words only egged them on. They kicked their legs higher until they collapsed in a fit of laughter.

I left them to their boys' club and went to see if there was anything else that needed to be done. Mom and the Professor had arrived while I was inside. Mom wore an ankle-length flowing cotton sundress that accented her waist. A sheer white shawl covered her shoulders and she had tucked two white rosebuds into the white head-band that pulled back her chestnut hair. She glowed with happiness. The Professor looked equally striking in a pair of white linen slacks, a matching shirt, and sandals.

"You two look amazing." I greeted them with a hug.

"Thanks." Mom organized a stack of menus.

"Helen is a vision in white, if you ask me." The Professor gave her a tender gaze.

"Stop, Doug. You'll make me blush." She handed him the menu. "And, we have work to do. Every place setting needs a menu."

"What can I do?" I asked. The guests were due to arrive in thirty minutes. We were in good shape, but I still needed to change and we needed to bring out the first wine and appetizer course.

Bethany directed me to the macarons. "Can you put those on plates? Steph and I are going to wait until the last minute to light all of the candles."

At that moment, Steph plugged in the twinkle lights, which gave the vineyard a festive glow.

"So pretty," Mom said.

I set out the macarons while Andy placed bottles of our pale pink rosé on the tables. The Professor brought out Sterling's platters and Mom arranged menus and place cards. We stood back to survey our work. The vineyard could have been a movie set. From the fading light hitting the green vines to the cloud-like lanterns waving from the trees to the elegant white tables, I couldn't believe how some simple touches of white had transformed our little grape farm.

Bethany clapped. "It's just what I was picturing." She snapped photos for our social media.

Even Steph couldn't contain the smile that tugged at her lips. "It looks pretty good."

"Pretty good? You have outdone yourselves," I shot back. "I'm calling it now. This is going to be our most popular Sunday Supper."

A car rambled up the long gravel drive. "On that note, let's go change. Our guests are arriving."

Sequoia, who was dressed in Boho style, was positioned near the path that led to the tables nestled in the vines. Her role was to greet guests and give them each a copy of the dinner menu.

Mom and the Professor stayed to welcome the first guests while the rest of us headed inside to change.

I had gone back to London Station and purchased the white dress I had seen in the window. Its fluttering short sleeves and sleek woven knee-length skirt gave it an airy feel. I studied my appearance in the mirror. To accent the romantic dress, I added a pair of daisy earrings and a matching necklace, along with a touch of shimmery opaque eyeshadow, pale pink lip gloss, and a touch of blush. I twisted my hair into a high ponytail and stood back. Not bad for a quick change, Jules.

When I went into the kitchen, Carlos almost dropped

the cast-iron skillet he was using to sear steaks. "Julieta, you take my breath away. You are stunning."

I shot him a flirty grin. "You don't look too shabby in your chef's whites either."

"Hey, we have work to do." Sterling waved a dish towel in front of Carlos's face. "Focus, chef."

"Si, si." Carlos laughed. "Julieta, I will see you later."

"It's a date." I went outside. The guitar duo strummed peaceful background music. Every candle had been lit, casting a soft iridescence on the tables where guests gathered and sipped wine.

I mingled from table to table, stopping to chat with familiar faces and catch up with old friends. The air was scented with vanilla from the candles and the earthy fragrance of the vines. Music floated above us as the wine began to flow.

Rosa waved me over to her table. "Jules, I wanted you to meet my uncle." She introduced me to a distinguished man in his early sixties. "This is my dearest uncle, Javier."

"It's wonderful to meet you." I shook his hand. "You have no idea how lucky we are to have Rosa on the team."

"This must mean you've tried her conchas." Javier gave his niece a proud smile.

She brushed off his compliment. "My uncle is the curator at the art museum at SOU and he has an amazing exhibit coming that he thought we might want to be involved in. That's why I wanted you two to meet."

"Oh, I'm a huge fan of the museum. That was always my favorite field trip as a kid," I said to Javier. "I remember when the ancient Egypt exhibit was on display, we did an entire unit on mummies and hidden tombs. In fact, I still might have my sketches of the pharaohs in the basement." One of the many perks of having a university in town was the culture the students and professors brought in.

Javier smiled at my memory. "Yes, that was a very popular exhibit. What I have coming next is related to Shakespeare. The university has landed a major coup. I can't say more until we send out the official press release, but I would be very interested in having Torte cater the opening-night event. I believe that given the magnitude of what we've curated, there will be press in town not only from the Rogue Valley but from Portland, Seattle, LA, and many other places."

I rubbed my hands together. "How fun. Count us in."

Rosa touched her uncle's arm. "I'll set up a time for you to come into the bakeshop and talk through your vision."

"Wonderful. I'm looking forward to it." I left them and greeted more guests before heading to my table.

Lance had saved a seat for me next to Arlo. "She's breathtaking. Absolutely breathtaking, don't you agree?" He asked Arlo when I sat down.

Arlo kissed my hand. "I most certainly agree."

"This is why she must grace our stage, right Julieta?" He used Carlos's term of endearment.

"No way. We've been over that a thousand times. I'm not getting on any stage, unless it involves delivering pastry."

Lance sucked in a breath. "Oh my God! I've got it. Arlo keeps pestering me to make sure that next season includes a big musical number and seeing you in this moment has given me a stroke of brilliant inspiration. I know exactly what we're going to stage, and you, my dearest Juliet, are going to be a part of it."

"What?" I looked to Arlo for help.

He shrugged.

Lance pressed his finger to his lips. "Ah, not yet. I have some arranging to do behind the scenes. Don't worry, your starring role will be revealed all too soon."

"I can't wait," I said with thick sarcasm.

Lance was undeterred. "This one will be a gem. You won't be able to refuse. Mark my words."

"How's the head?" I changed the subject.

He massaged the back of his skull. "Tender, darling."

"But no bandage."

"Never. Shudder the thought. How could I be seen at the event of the century in a head wrap?"

Arlo raised his wineglass. "I will say salud to this being the event of the century."

We clinked glasses as Thomas and Kerry joined us. Thomas guided her to the table and sat next to Lance. Kerry took the empty seat next to me. Her loose copper waves softened her face and brought out her moss green eyes.

"I love your dress," I said, complimenting her long maxi beach dress with tiny black polka dots.

"Yours is lovely too." She returned the compliment and took the glass of rosé that Lance offered her.

"Do tell, detective. We are absolutely dying to hear news of your upcoming nuptials." He paused momentarily and allowed his gaze to drift off toward Pilot Rock and Mt. A. The craggy peaks had lost their winter snow. Their jagged rocky prominences stood out amongst the swell of green conifers. "Might I suggest this is a wonderfully romantic venue for a wedding. This view alone is swoon worthy."

Thomas grinned. "What do you think, K? A wedding here in the vines, where all of our guests faint, thanks to these views?"

I hadn't heard Thomas use a sweet term of endearment for Kerry before. They shared a brief look that I couldn't quite decipher. Was it concern?

Thomas's cheeks pinched in slightly as Kerry replied, "I'm voting for the courthouse and two witnesses."

Lance gasped. "Oh lord no!"

Arlo titled his head to the side and lifted one eyebrow. "Lance, come on, it's their wedding. If they want to get married at the courthouse, I vote do it."

Kerry raised her glass to him. "Thank you."

Lance stiffened his posture and waved Arlo off. "Not on my watch. A wedding calls for glamour, enchanting beauty, flirty bridesmaids, dashing young groomsmen, and flowing champagne." He made a clicking sound. "Sorry, but a courthouse simply won't do."

Thomas lifted his hands in the air. "Don't look at me, K. I warned you that being friends with the one and only Lance Rousseau would mean that there's no chance of us sneaking off and finding a judge."

"Ha! As if. That is not going to happen on my watch," Lance scoffed.

I patted Kerry's arm. "Don't listen to him. You can do whatever you want—it's your wedding, but I will reiterate that we would love to host the event here and cater it for you, but no pressure, really."

Relief flooded her dewy eyes. "Thanks, I appreciate

it. This would be a pretty spot for a ceremony, though. I can't argue with that."

"Music to my ears. Cue the violins." Lance pretended to play the stringed instrument. "Shall we pull out our calendars and firm up a date?"

Thomas cleared his throat. "Let's just enjoy the evening. Kerry and I need to figure out timing with the Professor before we decide on a final date, right?"

"Right." Their eyes locked. Another brief glimpse of worry clouded Thomas's usually nonchalant face.

I wasn't sure if Arlo picked up on it too. He refreshed everyone's glasses with the rest of the rosé and steered the discussion in a new direction. "Juliet, I have to tell you that I'm not usually a wine guy. Beer is more my speed, but you might have a convert before the night is done."

"That's our mission. One glass at a time," I teased.

The conversation flowed as easily as did the wine. Carlos, Sterling, and Marty brought out the next course to a chorus of cheers. Each dish built on the previous course. The flavors accented with our wines in a balanced harmony.

"This is the stuff of dreams," Lance said as he took a bite of the tender steak. "I'm going to have to call uncle soon. My waistband is beginning to feel like a tourniquet."

"Save room for dessert," I cautioned.

"Dessert?" Lance threw his hand over his forehead. "Help me now. Take away the fork."

I excused myself to go plate the pavlovas. Carlos came to join us for the final course. He wrapped his arm around me as we listened to the music and savored the wine and conversation with dear friends. I was surrounded by my favorite, most beloved friends and family—Lance and Arlo, Thomas and Kerry, Mom and the Professor, Andy, Steph, Sterling, Bethany, Sequoia, Rosa, and Marty. Ashland might be small in number, but my world had expanded infinitely since my return home. Never would I have imagined that I would find these people who were helping to shape and redefine me in this beautiful and remote corner of the globe. Gratitude pulsed through me as I reflected on the hardships and pain that had led me to being here now. What an unexpected gift.

Lance was right. This was the stuff of dreams. I wasn't sure if it was the work of Shakespeare's pen or pure magic, but my dreams had come true. I wanted to bottle up this moment and make it last forever. I knew I couldn't. There were conversations to come. Changes lay ahead. Whether Carlos would be open to the idea of expanding our family. Whether I was ready. Thomas and Kerry's wedding. The Professor's retirement. Andy potentially leaving to start his own endeavors. For now, they could wait. I was content to linger as late as the stars in my beloved Ashland with everyone I loved.

Recipes

Strawberry Cheesecake Bars

Ingredients:
For the crust:
1½ cups finely ground graham crackers
¼ cup brown sugar
6 tablespoons melted butter
½ teaspoon cinnamon

For the filling:
1 8-ounce package cream cheese
1/2 cup sugar
1 teaspoon vanilla bean paste or 2 teaspoons vanilla
   extract
2 eggs

For the topping:
1 quart fresh strawberries (washed and sliced)
2 tablespoons sugar
1 teaspoon vanilla bean paste

Directions:
Preheat oven to 350 degrees. Mix crushed graham crackers, brown sugar, and cinnamon together, then pour in melted butter until combined. Press into an 8 × 8 square pan. Set aside. In a stand mixer or with a hand mixer, whip the cream cheese, sugar, and vanilla together until smooth. Blend in eggs one at a time. Spread mixture evenly over graham cracker crust and bake at 350 degrees for 30 to 35 minutes or until center is done. Remove from oven and allow to chill completely. While the bars are chilling, make a strawberry reduction by combining strawberries, sugar, and vanilla bean paste in a saucepan. Heat over medium low on the stove for 5 minutes, then turn the heat down to low and allow to simmer for an additional 15 to 20 minutes. Spread strawberry reduction over chilled bars, slice into squares, and serve cold.

Panzanella Salad

Ingredients:
1 loaf dry bread
6-8 heirloom tomatoes
2 teaspoons salt
1 bunch of fresh basil
1 red onion
2 cloves garlic
2 tablespoons balsamic vinegar
6 tablespoons olive oil (divided)
1 cup mozzarella (cubed)

Directions:
Preheat oven to 325 degrees. Slice bread into square pieces and spread onto a baking sheet. Drizzle with 2 tablespoons of olive oil and toss until all of the bread is covered. Bake for 15 minutes or until crisp, but not browned. While the bread is toasting, wash tomatoes, slice into cubes, and toss with salt. Finely chop basil, red onion, and garlic. Combine in a large bowl and toss with tomatoes, remaining olive oil, and balsamic vinegar. Add toasted bread. Mix well. Cover with plastic wrap and let rest for 30 minutes. Just before serving, add mozzarella cheese.

Lemon Rosemary Shortbread Cookies

Ingredients:
2 sticks butter (1 cup butter)
1 cup sugar (plus ¼ cup for dusting)
½ teaspoon salt
2 lemons (juice and zest)
1 sprig rosemary (finely chopped)
2 ¼ cups flour (plus ¼ cup for rolling out dough)

Directions:
Preheat oven to 350 degrees. In a mixing bowl, cream butter and 1 cup of sugar together on medium speed until light and fluffy. Add in salt, juice and zest of both lemons, and finely chopped rosemary. Mix together until combined and then slowly add in flour until a batter is formed. Chill in the refrigerator for 30 minutes. Dust a cutting board with flour. Roll out dough into a large rectangle, approximately ¼ inch thick. Cut out shapes

with cookie cutters. Place on a baking sheet lined with parchment paper and sprinkle with sugar. Bake at 350 degrees for 12 minutes or until the cookies are a light golden brown.

Summer Pasta Salad

Ingredients:
For the marinade:
1 cup vinegar
1 cup olive oil
2 cloves of garlic
Bunch of fresh herbs—Jules uses basil, thyme, rosemary, and oregano
1 teaspoon pepper
1 teaspoon lemon rosemary salt
4 chicken breasts

For the salad:
1 box of rotini noodles (boiled and cooled)
1 red onion
2 large carrots
3-4 heirloom tomatoes
4 slices Colby-Jack cheese
4 slices Swiss cheese
1 8oz can olives
Marinade (reserved)

Directions:
To make the marinade, whisk olive oil and vinegar together in a small bowl. Finely chop the garlic and cloves

and add to the mixture. Stir in salt and pepper. Reserve 1 cup of the marinade. Store in an airtight container. Add chicken to remaining marinade and place in the refrigerator until ready to grill. Boil pasta, drain, and allow to cool. Chop onion, carrots, and tomatoes and add to cooled noodles. Cut cheese slices into narrow one-inch strips and add to pasta. Drain olives and add to pasta. Toss the salad with the reserved marinade. Grill chicken for 5 minutes, then flip and grill on the other side for an additional 5 minutes or until cooked through. Slice and serve over cold pasta.

Pavlova with Berries in Red Wine

Ingredients:
For the berries:
2 cups berries (Jules uses raspberries, blackberries, and Oregon marionberries, but you can use whatever is in season)
1 cup red wine
1 vanilla bean
2 teaspoons vanilla
1 lemon (juice and zest)

For the pavlova:
4 egg whites
1 cup sugar
2 teaspoons vanilla
1 teaspoon cream of tarter
1 teaspoon cornstarch

Directions:

Combine berries, wine, vanilla bean seeds, vanilla extract, and lemon juice and zest in a large bowl. Cover with plastic wrap and allow the wine and berries to macerate for at least 2 hours, but up to 10 hours. While the berries are steeping in the wine, line a baking sheet with parchment paper and preheat the oven to 350 degrees. In a stand mixer or with a hand-held mixer whip egg whites until they form soft peaks (usually about 3 to 5 minutes). Then add the sugar and beat until stiff, glossy peaks form. Add the vanilla and beat for another minute. Fold in cream of tartar and cornstarch by hand. Spread mixture into a circle in the center of the lined baking sheet. The circle should be approximately 8 inches in circumference. It doesn't have to be smooth. In fact, Jules uses the back of a spoon to make little peaks along the top.

Place pavlova into the oven and immediately turn the temperature down to 200 degrees. Bake for 1 and ½ hours, rotating the baking sheet every 30 minutes. Turn off oven and allow the pavlova to continue to dry out until the oven is completely cool. Remove and serve immediately with the berries, or store in an air-tight container for two days.

Hot Honey Latte

Andy's hot honey latte won him bragging rights as the best barista on the West Coast. That alone is reason to make this for your morning caffeine hit.

Ingredients:
2 shots of strong espresso
1 tablespoon spicy honey
2 teaspoons simple orange syrup
1 cup milk
½ teaspoon flaked sea salt
½ teaspoon orange zest
½ teaspoon chocolate shavings

Directions:
Add espresso to a warmed coffee mug. Whisk in spicy honey and simple orange syrup. Froth milk, then add to espresso mixture, reserving the foam for the top. Stir milk and espresso. Pour foam over the top and finish with a dusting of flaked sea salt, fresh orange zest, and chocolate shavings.